The Gawain Quest

Jay Margrave has been writing both fiction and non-fiction for many years. It is the author's first published work of fiction.

to Frank

_En_
_C_

Margrave

GW00703318

Other books published by Goldenford Publishers

The Gawain Quest

Jay Margrave

Goldenford Publishers Ltd
Guildford
www.goldenford.co.uk

First published in Great Britain in 2007 by
Goldenford Publishers Limited
The Old Post Office
130 Epsom Road Guildford
Surrey GU1 2PX
Tel: 01483 563307
Fax: 01483 829074
www.goldenford.co.uk

Cover design based on an original ceramic by Iris Davies

Printed and bound by CPI Antony Rowe, Eastbourne

ISBN-13 978-0-9531613-5-5

Contents

Chapter One: The game begins

'...it pleased him not to eat
upon festival so fair, ere he first were apprised
of some strange story or stirring adventure...'

'My Lord Gaunt awaits you, Sir,' crowed the retainer, interrupting Priedeux as he thrust into the girl. Priedeux heaved himself onto one elbow, opened the makeshift curtains around the rope trestle bed and retorted: 'He can wait until I come, then,' and he knew by the way the servant smirked and hastily retreated the chamber that the double entendre was understood.

He turned back to his business. She was trembling now, not with ardour but fear. And he could tell, by the way she held her hands across her breasts, that her interest had waned, she no longer felt lust. The name of Gaunt had been enough. If he had been called by Richard, the King, he knew the girl would not tremble so. As he tried to caress her into willingness, he thought of their King. *He* was known publicly as a pious man and a man of knowledge. Priedeux knew that it was not so. He was privy to the secret whisperings of the King's vices. The girl was softening now, as if she could read his very thoughts. While the King might not condemn such activities in others, Gaunt might, if he thought there was disloyalty in the action.

No one knew where he stood with Gaunt. His power extended everywhere, even, Priedeux suspected as he thrust between the girl's legs, into the bedroom.

As he tarried with the girl his thoughts returned to the bawdy house he'd visited earlier that evening, not to find a whore, but a man.

The wait outside. Then the signal, the gently swinging light from the whorehouse. His nonchalant approach. His disregard for the guards waiting while their master enjoyed the delights of the place. 'No sword, just after a whore.' He brushes past them, spreading his arms wide to display his lack of weaponry. The open entrance. Soft lights. The run up the ladder, a wink from the madame, a sword collected from its hiding place above the beam. The stealthy creep to the door at the end. A pause, the lifting of the sword. With a great bound he crashes in. Good, the whore is not on top. His target looks over his shoulder, his buttocks still grinding. His face fixes in a look of stunned surprise. Priedeux's sword flashes once as he swings it across the man's exposed throat. The veins are standing high, through his sexual exertions, making it easy to aim. The carotid is cut immediately, blood fountains over the horrified woman beneath. She screams as her client topples onto her before she can scrabble out of the way. Priedeux does not stop, jumps over the trestle bed and its gory occupants, to the shuttered window, whistling as he reaches it. There are sounds of running along the corridor. He dives through shutters to land on his horse that has trotted into position, obedient to the whistle. He is away, out of Smithfield, his job completed, cries of 'havoc' and 'murder' behind him fading as he disappears into blackness.

He had come, satiated. The name of Gaunt, the memory of the murder he had carried out for him, had stirred him too.

He rolled off her. She was quiet now, her legs closing quickly. He pushed her off the coverlet, slapping her rump. 'Off with you.'

She quickly gathered her clothes and dressed, not caring whether her stockings were straight. With a couple of strokes through her ruffled hair with a bone comb she was gone.

2

'Didn't even thank me!' he mused ironically, knowing that no-one could hear through the thick walls of this palace, even though it was teeming with servants who might be spies of his master, John of Gaunt. If tales of his amorous activities reached Gaunt he would deal with it. His room was well away from the main quarters, in an out of the way corner of the Bishop's palace. The walls were of strong grey stone and impenetrable. Or else Gaunt would not have accepted the gift, thought Priedeux grimly as he tidied himself. Especially after the riots and flames a few years back.

Priedeux had deliberately chosen this chamber because it was so remote, and made it draught-proof with faded, scorched hangings salvaged from the Savoy. His clothes were hung neatly from pegs driven into the wall. In one corner there was a small chest, covered with parchments. He pushed these onto the floor, as he opened the chest and took out warm hose, under-shirt and jerkin. He dressed quickly now, the warmth and odour of sex fading in the winter chill.

When ready, he scrabbled amongst the parchments that were on the floor. He chose one, a thick paper, but of small size. It was certainly not the usual court charter he was expected to peruse. He tapped it, tucked it into his belt and strode to the door of his chamber, stepped out into a chill that hit him like a body blow.

The old boy waited shivering. 'He wanted you straight away!'

'I know, Wallers, but I can deal with that. It's no concern of yours.'

Wallers shuffled with him, muttering: 'In my day we didn't take hours about it.'

'In your day, you didn't have time. It was ram it in some Norman bint before the husband got home.'

Wallers did not retort but shook his head as he led the way. After a while he broke the silence between them.

'Anyway, where did you find this one?'

Priedeux was not inclined to talk but he knew Wallers. He would persist and they had some way to go. He sighed.

'Weren't you at the fireworks last night?'

'Indeed I was. Very generous, our King, to put on such a great display - those new-fangled fireworks are a wonder, don't you think? Good King Richard can always be relied on to give us great entertainments. Do you remember when we were at Winchester...?'

'Yes, yes, do you want to know or not?'

Wallers stopped his shuffling and looked up at Priedeux.

'I'm only interested, because you always seem to have a different lay, every time I have to summon you.'

Priedeux laughed and slapped the older man on the back, so that he almost fell.

'Ho, Wallers, you're probably too old to learn new tricks now, but if you want, I'll elaborate...'

'And you're not so young yourself, so watch it. A man of your age should be married with a brood of good sons by now.'

'I'll never marry, Wallers. Too much of the same thing. Now,' he put his arm over Wallers' shoulder as they passed through a great hall, decorated with tapestry hangings depicting a hunting scene. 'Firstly you must spot your prey; this one I found in the crowd. You have to assess them, make sure they're the right taste, for want of a better way of putting it. No good wasting time hunting if they're not prepared to play the game.'

'Game, is that how you see it?'

Priedeux shrugged. 'D'you want to know or not?'

'Go on then.'

'I spotted this one because her fair hair and face had an added dimension, a sort of golden-red reflection, and it wasn't just from the flickering lights of the catherine wheels; you remember, there were five all going at once, making a star shape.'

Priedeux paused. He did not tell Wallers that he too had felt excited, not by the fireworks, but by his earlier activities at the whorehouse. He knew he had to have a woman, to calm his beating heart after the thrill of that assassination. One business always followed the other, he found.

Wallers was looking up at him, expectantly.

'She had spark that one, just like the fireworks. Wallers, I can almost smell the ones who are willing! And you know, sometimes they sense someone watching them, just like a nervous doe. This one did, and turned to me. She just gazed and smiled. I kept her gaze as I pushed through the crowd to reach her.'

'Is that all you do?' He sounded wistful.

'Well, Wallers, I suppose I was helped by the display. As I stood by her side, not touching her or saying anything, she was suddenly shocked by a particularly loud bang, accompanied by a shattering of broken white brilliance in the sky. She jumped, and I put my arm round her waist to steady her. She didn't resist, just leant back into me – and that Wallers, is how it happens.'

Wallers quickened his pace, his feet making a shuffling sound on the straw covering the floor's elegant marble. He shook his head. 'You've told me nothing. I'm sure that if I did that, I would have been slapped round the face! Hey ho, you must have something.'

He continued to hurry and Priedeux easily kept up with him. He didn't deny Wallers' comment, he was aware of his own abilities. He turned his thoughts to the impending meeting with his master. He was in no hurry to meet Gaunt, but he knew it was inevitable and he pushed past Wallers to take the lead. Might as well get any unpleasantness over and done with.

They passed through cold narrow corridors, ignoring the men heaped together for warmth, the stragglers left after last night's banquet. They were a sorry bunch, heavy woollen cloaks hiding their humanity. Most of them were still sleeping off the effects of the wine that was served at the King's table at this time of year. Michaelmas was always a time for excess and entertainment. Apart from the fireworks, Priedeux had missed the earlier jugglers and mummers, while he was killing in the whorehouse. They passed other piles heaving in quiet coupling, unashamed and unshaming in this place. Others groaned and snored. Priedeux kept his eyes fixed ahead. He hurried on, wrinkling his nose at the foetid smell of unwashed men and burning tallow.

Wallers was going the long way round, using the old covered cloisters, avoiding the cold damp of the outside courtyard that would have been quicker. It gave Priedeux time to think, for he always needed to be on his mettle when he met his master.

He'd been lucky to find his room, at his lord's present accommodation. While the place was adequate, it was nothing like as large and sumptuous as the burnt out Savoy, even though it was owned by a dissolute cleric who thought he might get the Archbishopric if he fawned to the king's uncle. Priedeux knew though that Gaunt valued him and would always make sure he was nearby for those secret tasks that others might be too lily livered to carry out.

Eventually they reached the great hall, where his lord held court. Wallers shuffled up and opened the door: 'Priedeux, my Lord,' he announced, and stood aside as Priedeux stepped in, leaving Wallers outside to shut the door and disappear.

It was a dull and grey late morning. Great flares, held aloft in the high rafters in sconces, gave an eerie glare and huge candles sent dark wafts of smoke up into the beams. A blazing fire also radiated light and warmth. Its golden glow revealed an imposing room fantastically decorated, with a gold and red motif of repeated flowers, the bishop's choice, continuing round the walls and on the ceiling. It gave a closed-in secret look to the chamber. A large table covered with parchments stood to one side, near the window. Central to the room was a daïs upon which sat John of Gaunt on a high-backed carved, gilded chair, and minions stood to attention below him.

As Priedeux entered, Gaunt stood and slowly stepped down and approached him. The glow from the fire caught the nap of his azure velvet cloak, so that it shone, contrasting with the silvery-white ermine edging. The great gold collar of the House of Lancaster radiated a semicircle of burnished brightness around his chest. Only his face was shadowed, his ducal cap shading his features. The oblique lights made him look thunderous, his brow heavy.

'You grace us with your presence, Priedeux?' The sarcasm made his voice sound more high-pitched than normal.

'My Lord, with many apologies, I had some unfinished business.'

A slight upward curl to his master's lips revealed itself through his beard. Priedeux recognised it as a smile and knew he was forgiven for keeping Gaunt waiting. Gaunt after all was no innocent; he had had mistresses, one of whom he had finally married when his wife had died.

Priedeux changed tack, 'In Smithfield…'

He was interrupted. 'We know, our runners have reported it.' He nodded to a retainer and a bag of coins was handed to Priedeux. Gaunt continued, 'We thank you and trust that you will continue to serve us well.' He paused and Priedeux waited to be dismissed although he thought that something else was on his master's mind. His master had not yet raised the subject of the parchment he had brought with him. Sure enough, Gaunt spoke, his voice now lower, a confidential tone creeping in.

'There is another matter on which I would have words with you now. In private.' A nod from him and the other retainers backed out of the room, silently, as if pulled on strings.

There was a silence. Priedeux had been in John of Gaunt's service now for some years, following him in war and peace, to foreign parts such as Portugal and Spain, and back to cold England, accepting what came his way. He knew his master well enough to respect him but fear him a little too. Priedeux's fear was based on the fact that he was privy to too many of his master's secrets, had carried out too many quiet killings, and might some day prove too dangerous to have around. He was well aware of the saying: *those who preyed on others could also be preyed upon.*

The great man turned to collect something from the table beside him, and Gawain could see how his broad back was bowed with affairs of state. Even so, he was still imposing.

'Drink? After your exercise you may need something?'

His lord was smiling and Priedeux accepted gratefully. When they had both taken a long draught of the wine, Gaunt folded his arms, tucked his hands into the fur trim of the wide sleeves, and started:

'Well, what did you think of it? The poem? Assuming that the night's exertions left you time for study.' He stood still, like a leopard waiting to pounce.

Priedeux pursed his lips and unrolled the parchment in his hands. He'd been handed it only last night at the fireworks by his lord, and ordered to read it. Now he was being called to account. Unfortunately he had not spent the night studying the piece, not in detail anyway, the murder and the girl had seen to that. But he knew he had to give a good rendering if he was to satisfy Gaunt. Once he had satiated his first lust on the girl he had left her sleeping and had slipped out of the bed to read the parchment, returning to her in the early morning.

He began: 'It is a great poem and you tell me written anonymously. It is about a knight called Gawain and his struggle against another noble who is described as 'The Green Knight'. The story starts at King Arthur's Court where Arthur is challenged by this Green Knight who is a stranger to the Court. Gawain takes up the challenge and chops off the knight's head but he miraculously recovers, tucks his head under his arm and challenges Gawain to appear before him in one year's time. Gawain sets out when the year is up, to meet him and on the way stops for the Yuletide festivities at a grand castle which is similar to Arthur's Court. But it is described in such glowing terms that anyone reading this would know immediately that the second court is far better organised than King Arthur's; grander and more sumptuous indeed. The society he meets there is more polite than the court he has just left. There he is entertained by the lady of the house who has the better of him.'

Priedeux broke off from his narrative and exclaimed, 'if I ever meet such a lady she would not better me, I would have my way and forget so-called courtly love.' His voice was harsh and Gaunt grinned at the determination shown, but said nothing. Priedeux, almost embarrassed by revealing such feelings, coughed, and continued in his matter of fact way: 'it then turns out that the castle is owned by the very person who, in disguise, is the Green Knight, and the lady has been asked to seduce him to test his goodness. He fails the test because he keeps one token she has given him, showing that he has fallen under her spell. And, when he returns to Arthur's Court, this token, a green girdle, is adopted by all as their symbol in sympathy with Gawain.'

Silence. Then a slow handclap echoed from a shaded corner of the room. Startled, Priedeux's sword hand was on the hilt and his sword half drawn before his movement was quelled by Gaunt just as quickly, despite his bulk and age, stepping forward to intercept Priedeux's lunge.

'I thought we were alone.' He strained to see who was hiding in the unlit corner. Gaunt stepped back to his chair, and slowly sat down. Priedeux could now dimly make out a heavy armchair set back on the daïs, and sitting in it, leaning forward now as he continued to clap, was a small man in a knee-length cloak, and dark hose, the clothes of a clerk or student. He rose and came forward as he still clapped.

'Well done. Not bad for a man who has only had one night to study the text. But what do you think of the poetry? The words used? What is the meaning?'

Priedeux studied the stranger. Then he realised he was not so. He was a familiar visitor to the Savoy, a relative of some sort of Gaunt's. And then he placed him, although he was not of Priedeux's circle. Chaucer, the Clerk of the King's works, a civil servant. Priedeux had seen him years ago in his master's entourage in Lombardy when there were negotiations between Visconti and the English Court and Hawkwood had been present. He was not of royal blood. He had always been quiet, self-effacing, and usually vanished when Priedeux strode into the presence of his lord. Priedeux also knew he read aloud to the Court works of poetry that he had penned.

Priedeux prevaricated: 'The meaning? You as a poet should have ideas about that.'

Chaucer coughed, as if embarrassed at the comment. Then he answered enthusiastically: 'It is a consummate piece of work! Although not in my style. The words may be strange but it is still excellent. Excellent!'

Gaunt interjected, looking from one to the other, 'Even so, even so, what does it mean? You ask this yourself and I need to know. As a matter of state business. You have been on missions for me before. This is different and I want you to study this piece. I consider it to be written by a rebellious hand.'

He paused and then said quietly, 'Is it a seditious piece of writing, to incite my liege lords from Cheshire and the borders to riot or even raise another king? I need to know.'

Both Priedeux and Chaucer looked surprised, for they knew that Cheshire, while it might be anti-Gaunt, would never rebel against Richard II. Cheshire was the place from where the King's archers came, even from the time of Henry V it had been so.

Priedeux decided to deflect the problem. 'Why do you say

Cheshire, my Lord?'

'The language, man, it derives from the north-west. Many of the words indicate that. We intercepted it in a packet from that area but unfortunately our interceptors were too enthusiastic in their approach and the carriers expired before they could be interrogated.'

Chaucer added: 'It is also in a poetic style now defunct in London social circles but still acceptable amongst the lords of those parts. But the narrative style is interesting, unusual. I would like to know of its creator, whoever he might be.'

Gaunt interrupted, ignoring his kinsman. 'So, we need to know who wrote it. And why. That is your mission.'

Priedeux sighed. At last, he knew what was required of him. He was intrigued. He turned to the court poet: 'Perhaps sir, you could give me a clue, from the words, as to the sort of man I should be looking for?'

Chaucer stroked his small, tidy beard. He thought a while and then picked up a parchment from the table, obviously another copy. He skimmed a few pages, and then began: 'Aye, an educated man, very educated. He knows his Latin and his Greek. A bit of the French of our Norman nobles. A hunting man? Or is that from books? Maybe not a hunting man. A man with many books, undoubtedly. A man who loves materials, the touch of them, the cloth of gold, the silk, the soft wool: all these he describes as if he made the very stuff. A man who knows about good food and appreciates it.

'And finally, a man who knows the courtly rules of love but also enjoys celebrating his Yuletide in style.' Chaucer rubbed his hands together, evidently pleased with his description.

Gaunt interrupted. 'Even so, we don't understand the poem, it doesn't accord to the courtly rules of romance. And consider this.' He skimmed through the manuscript he held, nodded his head as he found a piece and read aloud:

> ' *"Here about on these benches are but beardless children*
> *there is no man here to match me - their might is so feeble."*

11

That's the Green Knight describing Arthur's Court, a visitor to that Court speaking! Is it a direct description of Richard? And *his* Court? Or this, when describing the Green Knight's table:

> *"Gawain and the gay beauty together in mid-table*
> *Sat down in due order, as the dishes were served,*
> *And thereafter throughout the hall, as was held best,"'*

Gaunt looked up then, accentuating the words, but carried on:

' *"Graciously according to his degree, each gallant man was served.*

> *There was meat and merry-making and much delight..."*

'How dare he speak like that, as if our King's table was not well provisioned. Is this a challenge to our Royal Court?' Gaunt was in full swing, and Priedeux knew he was angry. 'These are just two examples, but read it in detail, and you will find many parts where the author points a disparaging finger at the official Court, praising that other place. He even describes the very journey, pin-pointing where the great Court is! As if to encourage rebels and disgruntled knights to find it and join their cause. That's why I suspect it is seditious. What else can it mean? You have read it, Priedeux, you are my most trusted intelligence man, you have seen French and Scots secret papers before. So what does this mean?' He repeated the question, as if he would get an answer.

Priedeux read through the last words of the work, on the basis that the last stanza must sum up the whole. He was struck by the way in which all the knights at King Arthur's court took up the green girdle. Something struck a chord with him. The French words at the end : HONY SOYT QUI MAL Y PENCE. Priedeux recognised it, as the motto of the Order of the Garter. Edward III, the grandfather of the present king, had founded it, as a rallying point. Richard had extended it, as a measure of loyalty to him. Surely not? Was this to be a rallying call to contending parties from strange parts? Should he mention this or keep silent? He didn't know how much Gaunt had read and felt he was already incensed enough. But he was paid for his skills and knowledge, so answered. 'My Lord, are not the last words like those of the Order of the Garter? Could it be a call for a new order? Surely, though, not against our liege Lord.'

'Priedeux, you have not let me down again. I knew I could trust your intellect.' Gaunt turned to his shadowy companion, as much as to say, *I told you so, he's the man for the job*. Then he raised his glass, now nearly drained of wine, and said, 'now you understand the implications, you must undertake this most dangerous mission. I wish you to leave at once for the north-west and find out who wrote this, and why!'

He turned to the table once again and picked up one of the manuscripts with a royal seal prominent on it. 'You go with the King's blessing. But beware, use this pass with great care where you are going, it may not guarantee you free passage. Especially if you find the place and our suppositions are correct.'

'Is this genuine?' asked Priedeux.

Chaucer answered, 'as genuine as it needs to be.'

Gaunt nodded and Chaucer picked up a leather pouch from the table and threw it to Priedeux who caught it. This was followed by another.

Priedeux queried: 'Why the second?'

Again Chaucer answered as Gaunt busied himself with other papers. 'The first covers expenses. With the second you should know what to do when you find our man.'

Priedeux opened the purse and counted the silver inside.

'The price for a kill. Why?'

Chaucer too now turned away and Priedeux knew there would be no answer.

He was dismissed.

Chapter Two: Riding out

'He spurned his steed with the spurs and sprang on his way
so fiercely that the flint-sparks flashed out behind him.'

Priedeux reached his room, closed the door behind him and shut his eyes for a second, trying to picture the future. His head buzzed with plans for the trip. His heart was beating fast. Instead of what he'd suspected, a boring winter reading poetry and trying to decipher it, he was to be sent out on the open road again.

He was becoming tired of court life, of the smell of others and the stuffiness of rushes on the floor and tallow flares and smoke-filled rooms. The fact that it was hard winter, snow and ice abounding this year, did not deter him. The thought of a long ride, in strange territory, pitting his wits against he knew not what, new women, new enemies, strange lands, was what was making his heart race.

Preparation was vital. He knew, without consulting anyone, that the area would be remote and wild. Although he had travelled to the last Crusade and was well acquainted with Mediterranean ports, he had no knowledge of the north-west of his own country. He originally came from Wilcomstou, a tiny hamlet on the edges of the forest of Epping. That was far behind him and he was now a cosmopolitan Londoner, born and bred, or so it seemed to those at Court.

Wilcomstou had been a swampy place, known for its mosquitoes dancing above the still waters around the rivulet Lea. When Sir John Hawkwood fell ill there, on his way south to some campaign, and Priedeux's mother had cured him with her home remedies, he had offered to take the boy to give him a start in life.

'He can be my scribe, as he can read and write. Being a fighting man I cannot decipher the symbols.'

His mother had refused. 'Tom is my only fit and able son, who else would provide for me in my old age?'

When Hawkwood was ready to go, Priedeux had slipped away into the woods and joined him when it was too far to send the boy back. He was a questing youngster of thirteen and had no thoughts for anything other than adventure. He hadn't visited the hamlet of his birth since. He hadn't wanted any more of the monks who taught him Latin and other matters, though this education was to stand him in good stead later. His subsequent training was to be of war and killing. On the way he became a competent linguist, able to converse and write in both Latin and French. His travels with Hawkwood taught him some knowledge of the world outside his own country, but the north-west would be new territory for him.

He studied the pass he had been given.

Looks genuine enough. He pressed the seal. Sometimes an inferior seal was soft, and the indented picture could be worked upon, but this one did not budge. It was of good wax that had hardened well, and the seal certainly looked like that of Richard's, sitting on a throne, holding both sceptre and rod. But what did the words mean: *As genuine as it needs to be.* Priedeux stowed it away in his jerkin, close to his heart. He knew Gaunt had influence over his nephew Richard. If Gaunt had anything to do with it, it would be seen as genuine to most people. Anyway, he had been given a task, and he'd better start on it.

In his room he pushed the remaining papers away from the chest and dug inside. He laid out on the bed hose, linen undershirts, and his woollen padded jupon. From an oiled cloth he extracted his best sword. He dug deep until he found a leather pouch, wrapped in fine cloth. He opened the pouch and unwound the oiled wrappings, extracting a deadly weapon: a tiny crossbow, small enough to fit a child's hand. He handled it carefully, checking the tautness of the bow to make sure it was in working order, then carefully re-wrapped it with subtle knots only a working soldier would know. He checked another, smaller pouch and counted the bolts. After that, in sequence, he collected saddlebags and stowed the pouched weapon away. From the pegs on the wall he pulled down his long riding boots, and thick wool cape, and threw these on the bed.

'To the armoury, now,' he muttered to himself and strode out of the room. The great store-room of weaponry was in an old side hall in one of the wings of the palace, a large cavernous place lit by large windows which showed it had been used as a chapel during the Bishop's time. Great flares added to the comparative lightness of the hall after his dingy quarters and the corridors leading to it. At one end was a forge throwing out welcome heat, while grindstones stood silent. The walls were festooned with hanging harness, steel breastplates, helms for both joust and war, mailshirts, cuisse, and jamb which reflected the glow from the flames of the forge. They reminded Priedeux of parts of bodies on an abandoned battlefield. There were also racks holding swords, axes and other weapons. He turned to the work area and addressed a man who was sitting quietly, rubbing a sword with polishing stone. He was grey, like the armour around him, and an unobservant visitor might not have seen him.

'I need a padded jacket, with arms also padded. And a hand-and-half sword for a job,'

The armourer jumped up and led him to the stores. He followed and, as the man rummaged amongst his wares, Priedeux leant forward and pointed to an old-fashioned jacket.

'I'll try that,'

The armourer handed it down from the peg, but queried,

'we do have newer ones than this, sir.'

But Priedeux was already slipping on the jacket. He moved his arm in a mock punching movement to test the fit. He was satisfied. 'This'll do, for where I'm going. But tell me, your accent's not from these parts?'

His companion nodded. 'Nay, I hail from Quernmore in Lancaster's lands. But I'll not be going back there. So cold and damp that I made sure I came south with Gaunt.'

'Is that by Cheshire then?'

'Aye but it's at least two days' ride further.'

'Are they both on the same road?'

'By Watling Street to Kenilworth and then the road branches left for Chester and straight on for Lancaster. But you'll not be going that way in this weather.'

It was a statement but Priedeux realised it was also a question. He would not be drawn. He knew better than that, all men could be spies. Instead he changed the subject. 'And now for that sword.'

His man walked to the rows of weapons and picked out several hand-and-a-half swords and passed them one at a time to Priedeux, who balanced the weapons in both hands, and then inspected the maker's mark. In the end he chose one with a good stiff narrow blade with the running wolf mark of the Solingen and Passau smiths.

'Thanks for the jacket. And the sword.'

As he left, his voluble companion announced clearly, 'by the way, If you are going up north, by any chance, go wrapped for bad weather.'

Back in his room, Priedeux opened his cape wide. It had no lining, and when he held it up to the dim light from the window for closer inspection, the material was so thin in places that it would soon be shredded. He would have to invest in a new lined cape.

As his preparations were nearly completed, he realised it was getting dark. It was too late to start out that night.

Hunger overtook him and he headed for the great hall. After eating, other needs came to the fore. He felt his manhood rising, the anticipation titillating him. He moved then, towards the common chambers. Where was that wench, what was her name? Joan. As he thought of the earlier coupling with her he knew he must have her again. Fine back, good buttocks, good lay. He came to the apartments where the women could be found taking their post-prandial meanderings, after the meal, catching the last rays of the western sun, which shone through the thin windows on this side of the palace. Some worked delicate embroidery with heads bent, discreetly virginal. Others walked up and down, laughing and talking. He grinned, for Joan was amongst those who walked, following a short way behind her mistress, the Lady Beatrice. Priedeux took a deep breath, watching the taller regal figure of the lady.

Now that was a one. High white forehead, pale face, ermine-edged woollen dress, clinging to the soft waist, the bodice cut just low enough to show the rise of her delicate white breasts but accentuating the soft roundness of her buttocks. Still very young, fifteen at most, he thought. What excited him more was the good dowry that came with her.

Once, at banquet, Gaunt had followed his eyes, as Priedeux was drawn to the girl. The women had been called in with the sweet dishes, displayed for some French diplomatic party. Like displaying the Crown Jewels, Priedeux had thought at the time. Gaunt's wife had headed her retinue and Lady Beatrice had been at her right hand, face lowered, eyelids fluttering, and Priedeux had stared at her and his admiration must have shown. He realised after a while that he, too, was being stared at. He turned from the girl and saw his master glaring at him. The look from Gaunt told Priedeux that he should not even consider it.

Later when they were on their way to bed, Gaunt had slowed and waited for him to catch up with him. Under his breath, the nobleman had explained: 'You're my best man for many things, Priedeux, and I know you need your women. I understand that, for when I was young...' His face softened, but his eyes were like hard flints. 'There are plenty here you can have. But not a lady such as Beatrice. She is a rich heiress, and no male line to worry about. She is valuable to me. Understand?' Priedeux realised his arm hurt, where Gaunt was gripping it so hard. He nodded, looking his lord in the eye. He understood and would not stray from that edict.

He was meandering past the group now, and the women kept their eyes down, for the most part. But as he drew level with Joan he realised she was watching him. Had she seen him staring at her young mistress? He didn't care. She would do for now. He touched her gently on the arm, almost by accident, and she shuddered and fell away from the group of women. He walked on and knew she followed.

He paced through the icy passageways and reached an alcove at a corner of the palace. Here no sun penetrated. He paused, stepped in and stared out of the window at the courtyard below, his hands behind his back. He listened. He heard the slight, agitated swishing of the woollen garment, the slapping of the thin slippers that Joan wore. He turned round, and, as she hurried by, stepped out and grabbed her by the arm, 'come,' he whispered and led her through the corridors to his room.

He piled up the gear he had prepared on the chest as she slipped off her woollen clothing and within a few seconds they slid under the thick bedclothes and he entered her.

With the first glows of dawn Priedeux was noisily moving around the room, ignoring the female still sleeping. The noise eventually penetrated her dreams and she tenderly reached out for her lover. Her arm moved in seeking but when only coldness was found, she slowly roused and looked at him, fully dressed, packing his bags.

'Come back to bed,' she murmured, letting slip the covers, her breasts exposed.

'It's time for you to go. I'm off on a long journey.'

She looked at him, surprised. Then hurt spread across her face. He quickly relented, there was no reason for him to make enemies.

He leant over and kissed her but slipped from her encircling arms.

'Gaunt has called and, this time, I must go, I know not where or for how long.' He handed her the robe she had dropped and continued with his preparations while she dressed. He slipped out of the room before her, heading for the kitchens to gather provisions for the journey.

As he strode along the corridor his way was stopped by two men who stepped out of the gloom of an alcove.

'You come with us, our master will have words.'

Priedeux knew better than to argue. He just nodded and paced himself with them as they led him to an annexe. One of the men entered and muttered to whoever was in the room, 'he came quietly my lord,' and then stepped aside and gestured for Priedeux to enter.

'Thank you for coming, sir.'

The voice was effeminate and although the man was hidden in a shaded corner, Priedeux knew immediately who he was. Should he acknowledge his King by kneeling before him, or should he not? He was obviously here secretly. Priedeux decided. He stood still and bowed, the gesture he would use to a superior.

'At your service, my Lord.'

'Good, it is good you are at *my* service and no other.'

Before Priedeux could respond, Richard II continued: 'You will carry out a small job for me. I understand from my spy that you are going on a long journey, and he believes it is to be near his lands in the north west. I do not ask you to deny or confirm this. All I ask is that you visit Chester and take these with you.'

Curse the armourer.   Priedeux said nothing, as Richard leant forward and he saw the great rings on the fingers of his King, as he handed over a package of letters.

'They are for my Sheriff there, with special instructions. You hand them to no-one else. You understand?'

Priedeux nodded, stowing the package in his tunic.

'You are dismissed.   You have not seen me if my uncle asks.'

Priedeux nodded, bowed again and walked out of the room.   Now he was truly hungry.   He recognised this as a sure sign that he had problems to solve.   To whom did he owe loyalty? His King or Gaunt? Priedeux had lived too long and been on the sidelines of too many great events to know that kings could lose their heads while those who truly pulled the strings, who had the wealth, would carry on.   He also knew whose silver he now felt in his pocket.   He should report his short meeting with the King to his lord, but he knew now he was being watched.   The sooner he left on his mission, the better.

'I need food, first. And after food, I'll choose a good horse,' he thought, as he entered the food hall.

He needed a good solid palfry that would carry him the distance. He knew where to go, where he would have the best choice.   The court of our Lord Gaunt was cramped at the Bishop of Ely's palace and, as far as he was concerned, the choice would be limited.   But he knew royal stables where there was a plentiful supply.

He returned to his room and made his final preparations. He was glad that the woman had been sensible and departed, for he hated unpleasant scenes.   He surveyed his quarters, which he left now without knowing whether he would ever return, without emotion, and strode out.   He left the palace, and strode through the village of rough huts outside the walls, which sheltered the less fortunate of Gaunt's retainers.   Once

21

again Priedeux realised how lucky he'd been to find the room. The Bishop's Palace really was not a fitting seat for a duke. He walked downhill, through the City, and on the way purchased the badly-needed new cape. He chose an expensive thick item, waxed with a coating on the outside that would keep the rain from seeping through. He reached the jetty at the Cut.

Here he hailed a waiting ferryman, to take him out of London, to Walton-on-Thames, where there was a large lodge and stables with paddocks, belonging to the King but administered by his master. He would find what he wanted there.

He looked out over the congested waterway, ferries and fishermen looming out of the mist. It was freezing and those on the water huddled under thick cloaks and other wrappings. With most of his preparations behind him, his quest now preoccupied him; although his ferryman attempted to engage him in conversation, Priedeux stopped his banal flow by simply ignoring him.

When he reached the place, he headed straight for the stables. They were clean, smelling of fresh straw and healthy horse-droppings. Priedeux wandered from stall to stall, stroking the horses' manes, and checking their teeth. No one seemed to be around. It was late afternoon and nobody wanted to take a horse at this time of the day. The household was in the midst of the season's festivities and he guessed that most of the stable-hands were probably sleeping off the effects of ale in some hayloft. Priedeux made a mental note that the place could be a good venue for a tryst if he ever needed one. He heard a slight cough behind him and, turning, saw that the manager had emerged from the cubby-hole at the end of the row of stables which fared as his office. He was a small, round man, with tiny, cunning eyes and a limp. His riding days were over, but he was still good with the horses, and strict with the stable-hands. Priedeux smiled and fetched from his pouch the letter of authority, which he did not at first show:

'Bondon, how are you? The wife? And that little blonde lass of yours, is she breaking hearts yet?'

The man smiled. 'Aah, my little Anne, she's twelve now, sir, soon have to think of her marrying chances. A good mare, with good legs and a fine seat! You wouldn't consider?'

Priedeux laughed, a deep, carefree laugh: 'Bondon, a husband I would not make. My life is not conducive to taking a wife as you well know.'

'Aah, but I would wish her to have a fine man who would mount her well, and you would be such a man.'

'That is because I return your horses without limps, and without sores under the saddle, as we both know.'

The other man nodded sagely and smiled, 'he who looks after his horse will look after his spouse.'

''Tis an old adage that those who look after horses made good philosophers. It must be all the horse-dung you have to study.'

They both laughed then, delighted at each other's wit and fully aware that such pleasantries were a prelude to greater things. Priedeux stopped laughing. He said, in a different tone: 'I have orders from the king to ride out. A long journey in perilous country, I believe. I need a well-shod mount, capable of carrying me and provisions over heavy terrain. Whether stony or sandy, mountainous or swampy, I have no knowledge. So you see what I need.'

The stabler nodded, wiping his rough-bearded chin with his hand. Priedeux could see he was thinking. He knew that Bondon hated any of his horses to be taken from his stables.

''Tis bad weather for a horse to be out, sir,' he prevaricated.

This was true, and Priedeux knew that this man might not even let a rough horse go, let alone a good one, on the basis that he - and the horse - might not return. It was not the value of the creature, but the fact that the man had spent so long with the animals that he loved and cared for them as if they were his own kin. That was why Priedeux had come to him; Bondon was known to have the best horses.

Priedeux said nothing and waited for the thought processes to reach a certain level. Then he too would move into the next stage of the laborious negotiations. He could be patient when the need arose. Next, he would have to persuade this old bore to part with a good reliable mount, for he knew which horse he wanted, and he knew it was going to be difficult to persuade him to let him have the beast.

'There will be silver for you if my venture succeeds. And I promise to take good care of the horse - I vouch for it being returned, one way or another'. Priedeux jangled the coins in his pouch, and waited. The man's face cleared. He nodded and turned away, gesturing for his companion to follow and Priedeux inwardly smiled. The first hurdle was over. He would be allowed a horse. Now for the second hurdle, which might prove more difficult.

They sauntered past each of the stalls, Priedeux occasionally stroking the horses' manes. They reached his chosen animal and Priedeux stopped. The stabler coughed and hurried on. Priedeux grasped the man's arm to stop him.

'This one, I want this one.'

The groom looked down at his arm where it was held, as if in a trap, and shook his head slowly. 'No, I cannot let that one go, it's such a calm beast that I let Anne ride it, and it would break the girl's heart.'

Priedeux continued to hold the man hard while he fumbled to reveal the seals on the letters, the King's seal. He knew the man could not read, but the seal was better than a full letter of instruction.

'As I said, orders from the King. I doubt not, he would sanction the use of this one. I want this one. Come, Bondon, trust me, like you would trust me with your own daughter.'

He released the man's arm then and patted it as if to

comfort him.   Bondon continued to look down, but then shook his head.

'I cannot let this one go.'   He walked away, as if to lead Priedeux out of the stables.   'Come to my home and have something to eat, we can talk further.'

'This one, and only this one, Bondon.'

'I cannot…any other, I will agree.   Not this one.'

'The King's seal, Bondon, I have the King's seal.'

There was a pause as the two men stared at each other.

'How do I know it's genuine?   Usually there is a messenger sent before…'

Priedeux interrupted: 'I've already told you…'

'But you haven't…'

'What?   What can I tell you?   You must know that no-one would set out in the middle of winter by choice.   It is the King's seal, and I must go.'

He tried to put his arm round the man's shoulders but he shrugged the gesture away and walked over to the horse they were discussing, pulled out a carrot and gave it to the horse.

'Bondon, you know me well.   I would not harm…'

'It isn't that.   My girl; she will be saddened.'

'Excuses, Bondon.   You know the King would not like it if he knew one of his best palfreys was being ridden by a stabler's daughter.'

Bondon turned to face him again.   There was surprise in his face.

'Surely, you wouldn't tell?'

Priedeux stared back, his face hard.   Eventually, Bondon looked away.   He took a deep breath and said: 'You always were good at persuasion!   I must let it go, then.   But you must promise...'

Priedeux smiled now, and slapped the man on the shoulder: 'Of course I promise, I've already promised to take good care of it.   It'll be ridden hard but wisely.   Prepare him for the morrow, early.'

He strode off then, patting the waist bag where he had stowed the precious sealed papers.

While he tarried overnight he decided to study the poem again. Where was he to start on his quest for the seditious author? The work was too long for him to read again in the few hours he had to spare so he turned to the description of where Gawain had found the castle in the wild woods of the west.

Priedeux read:

"Now he rides *....through the realm of Logres...*
'til anon he drew *near unto Northern Wales.*
All the isles of Anglesey he held on his left,
and over the *fords he fared by the flats near the sea,*
and then over by the Holy Head to high land again
in the wilderness *of the Wirral...."*

Further description followed and Priedeux muttered: 'North East of Chester, in deep dark woodland, it would seem'.

Priedeux knew that large tracts of land around Cheshire had been cleared, to stop marauders and outlaws from attacking orderly citizens. That had been in old King Edward's time, Edward, the older brother of John of Gaunt. The trees and thickets would be growing again after twenty or more years, but would it have grown enough to hide such a castle as the book described?

Priedeux decided it didn't matter, he would head that way. Gaunt and Chaucer had said the language was a dialect used in the north-west, and the Wirral was that way. Once his provisions were ready he would head west on the great Roman road out of London.

Chapter Three: The hangman

'So many a marvel in the mountains he met
in those lands....with worms he wars, and with wolves also,
at whiles with wood-trolls...'

The next morning dawned with a peach sky in the east and a deep azure cloudless haze overhead.   He looked out on to a land hardened by a glittering frost that whitened the trees, accentuating their skeletal shapes.   The ground would be hard on the horse's hooves and would echo as he rode out.   He could not hope to leave quietly although he did hope that nobody had set spies to make sure he carried out his mission. It was not unknown; he was sure that, on several of his earlier missions for Gaunt he had been shadowed.   Even the last killing had been known to his master before he reported it.

He pulled on several closely-woven woollen under-jerkins before donning the thickly padded tunic he'd acquired from the armoury.   He was pleased he'd purchased the new cloak. Wiping his weapons, the sword and daggers, he replaced them in their scabbards at his waist.

He would be heading away from the wintry early morning sun.   After checking the direction he knew that, if he rode across Hounslow Heath and Hammersmith, missing those hamlets, he would pick up Watling Street, the old Roman road which would lead him straight to Chester.   The journey to that city would take days and when he reached it he had no idea where he would go, except that he would use his instincts and the descriptions in the poem.

He collected his horse from the stables, saddling it himself. He would leave without a farewell to Bondon, which might involve him in more explanations. He rode out of the placid Thames valley countryside of small farms and homesteads, heading for the chalk hills in the distance. He viewed other wayfarers cynically, many on foot, some on wagons with noisy wooden wheels, with pigs snorting in pens and chickens in cages, and babes squawking in their swaddling bands. Thankfully the chill of winter kept the animal stench at bay. Cantering past them, he scattered the brats who held out their hands for small coins, and took no notice of the beggars who called out for alms. He needed his full purse of silver for whatever lay ahead.

Then, leaving behind the heavily populated valleys near the rivers Thames and Cherwell, past small towns such as Aylesbury, he found the terrain changing. There were fewer homesteads; sheep grazed but there were hardly any men and no women or children.

He had been travelling for several hours by the time the winter sun had moved to the southern horizon, slanting its midday rays on one side of him. He knew he would have to stop soon, if only for his horse's sake. He was riding the crest of a hill and, after reaching the summit, he looked down on the long valley below, a thin sliver of silver showing a river running through it. It was almost bare of trees on the plain, but there were patchy green fields of winter weeds and reddish mud ploughed fields, forming a mosaic blanket before him. The gentle rolling hills, where a man could not plough, were covered with sloping copses of trees, like a woolly haircut, the winter bare branches thickly covering the peaks. The valley itself was long and low and flat but, there, at the side of the winding road, was a homestead, with the familiar larger building of a roadside inn, with its outhouses for storage and stabling. He could see groups of people heading for this homestead, most of them carrying heavy loads, or prodding animals before them.   He realised it would be market day at this hamlet.   This did not displease him for he would be less conspicuous in a market-day crowd.   Pressing the horse's flanks, he set off again, and the horse responded going a little faster, as if it recognised a place of rest.

As he reached the rude wattle and daub buildings, the babble of the market reached him, the sounds of squawking chickens, bleating sheep and cackling geese blending with the merchants' sing-song offers of sale.   The smell of matured cheeses, of birds' droppings building up in their cages, and the acrid odour of thick winter sheep wool from the flocks who had been forced to hurry, invaded his nostrils.

Luckily it was too cold for the place to be the usual morass of mud and squelchy animal droppings but his steed picked its way through the hubbub carefully, and they reached the inn without mishap.

An urchin scuttled from the low barns leaning against the main structure and stood at his horse's head.   As Priedeux dismounted, the child caught the reins he tossed to him and started to walk the horse away.

'Wait, child, while I take the panniers.'   Priedeux removed the double bags and threw them over his shoulder and then slapped the horse's flanks to signal that they could now go. He strode into the inn and sat down at a rough bench near the open door.   Experience had taught him to be prepared for flight at any time but he also preferred the fresh air, despite the cold, to the rancid smells of worn-out ale and sour bodies, mixed with the smoke from a fire which couldn't find its way up the chimney.   He also liked to watch the activity in the market.   He looked round, wide-eyed, not only to accustom himself to the interior gloom but to seem naive, to dull any prying eyes.   The smoke from the fire meant that it was hard to see the interior, but, as his eyes became accustomed to the gloom he realised that the place was but a poor inn and knew that not many travellers passed this way.   Behind a rough-hewn bar were a few barrels of beer, but no casks of malmsey. The place was almost empty, the market being still busy, and the locals still involved in their trading.   Not many strangers travelled at this time of the year to give the host custom and Priedeux was surprised the landlord did not hurry over to him to solicit trade.   Travel was mainly reserved for the summer months when pilgrimages were undertaken, or pardoners sought lost souls to forgive - and fleece, at the same time - he thought cynically.   Prioresses might take it into their heads to visit their fellows at other convents for a change of scene during the warm summer months, but not in winter.   It made sense.   The roads might be awash with mire or impassable with fallen trees.   Unless they had good reason, only the innocent, forced to travel by circumstances, a death in the family or some such emergency, would set out during the cold winter months. Priedeux thought what excuse he would give as he waited for service. He knew by experience that it had to be good to convince a landlord.

'Yes?   Ale and food?   A bed for the night?'   Priedeux jumped out of his daydreams, and looked up at the plump maid.   Why were they always plump and red-faced, he wondered, but knew the answer; they ate their master's food as they worked.   The girl was chewing something even now, as she waited for his answer, and she had a glint in her eyes, made small by the podgy child-like face.   At first glance the cherub look made her seem innocent, but a swaying of the hips and a curve of the thick lips belied it.

'Aye, ale will do,' he said shortly, 'and food.   Whatever you have.   Not fussy.   My horse to be tended, carefully.'

'Indeed, the lad'll make sure.   Good with horses, he is. You've a handsome steed there.'

Priedeux merely nodded and looked out.   She knew when to leave her clientele be and waddled off.   Priedeux turned to watch her go, the thick rump only mildly interesting him, and noticed a figure sitting close to the fire who seemed to be leaning forward, as if to catch his eye. He nodded and now rose and approached. Not as tall as Priedeux, he was stocky, with pronounced muscles. The face was twisted, as if permanently grimacing, and a balding head seemed to bulge with hidden sinews giving him a bovine but cunning look. The old leather jerkin, rough-made leggings and leather boots he wore, cracked and stained, emphasised the picture of some wild beast. He stood still, looking down for a full half minute, saying nothing. Priedeux returned the stare. If the man thought he could intimidate, he was wrong. He took a deep breath, as if to expel some unspoken threat, and pulled out the bench on the other side of the table in front of Priedeux. Swinging one leg over it, he sat down heavily, so that the bench creaked. Priedeux said nothing, but continued to eye the man.

They waited. The innkeeper came with a flagon of ale and placed it before Priedeux. He looked from man to man but, receiving no encouragement to deliver another beaker, turned away. Maintaining eye contact, Priedeux poured himself a measure and lifted it to his lips. He assessed his opponent and, deciding he was a foe, weighed up his chances. He shifted his leg in the soft leather of his boot and felt the hard shape of the Spanish-made dagger, the handle at the topmost, easy to reach if needed.

'Can't a man be left alone for a quiet rest?' He asked, deciding that attack was better than defence.

'A man who wants a quiet rest doesn't travel this road, my friend. But let that pass. I *know* you. Your lean face, it was browned by the sun the last time...the English cold has lightened the colouring ...but the features...those cold eyes.'

Priedeux looked down now. A vague unease was flowing through him: *did this man know him or was it bluff?* He did not tremble or twitch; this would have revealed his unease. He had trained himself to be still. Any movement would betray him. The man was rugged, much older than Priedeux,

31

grizzled, but there was something.   It was not his features, Priedeux decided, but his build, his manner, the way he held his head.

'I've travelled widely, my friend, and not necessarily wisely.' he made a joke of it but his opponent continued to stare.   Suddenly, as if satisfied, he nodded and stood up.   He went out, looking over his shoulder as he pulled the door to.

Priedeux peered through the murky gap which stood for a window, covered with thin reeds, and knew, when he saw a shadow flit by, that the man was heading for the stables, to check out the horse.   Let him, he did not care.   Maybe the King's mark, branded into the flanks of the steed underneath the saddle, would satisfy him and prevent him from bothering Priedeux further.   He was not yet in such wild country that it would have no effect, he was sure.

Priedeux sipped his ale.   'Innkeeper, where's the food, man, I'm starving.'

The owner plodded back to him, 'soon, sir, soon.   The serving wench is no cook but she's adding fresh meat to the pot.   It will be good.'

Eventually the food arrived, and, at the same time, as if he could smell it, so did the other customer return, pulling at his filthy breeches, as if he had been to relieve himself.   He sat down in his previous position opposite Priedeux and watched as Priedeux attacked the meat and broth and rough bread that had been placed before him.

'Have some, if you're hungry,' invited Priedeux, always aware that a man who shares food with another is usually reluctant to slit the guts and see the food spilling.   The man shook his head:

'No, I have work to do.   Good reason to be in this district. You can watch, if you like.'

Priedeux was puzzled.   He did not have time to ask anything further.   A commotion outside made his companion grin.   Instead of the normal drone of bartering and animal noises, a jeering crowd could be heard, and it was coming toward them. A wagon arrived, crude and lumbering, with a cortege of people holding onto it. In the wagon were two blindfolded prisoners, one male, one female. They were tied together. Some of those who followed were yelling, taunting the couple. As if by magic the stall-holders packed their wares and hastily retreated. Some of the mob picked up discarded cabbages, soggy potatoes and pelted the prisoners with them. As the group reached the now empty meeting-place outside the inn, a round green of trodden down and blackened icy mud, Priedeux's companion banged his drink down on the table. He stood up, hitched his leathern belt tight across his thick waist and moved lumbrously to the door. Priedeux left his meal and, wrapping his wool cloak around him, followed. He did not join the crowd, but found a vantage point on the steps of a shop to one side, where he was behind everyone and could not be seen, and watched as the prisoners were led his way.

As they approached, the woman stretched her neck from side to side, moving muscles at the back of her head until the tie around her eyes fell down and she gazed around her. She was facing Priedeux and stared fixedly at him, as if to accuse. As the cart rumbled past him she stumbled and he jumped from his vantage point and grabbed at her, to prevent her from falling out of the cart into the muck, and pushed her back into a standing position. It was a reflex action.

'Thank you, but make it quick,' she whispered.

'No, not me, I'm not your executioner.' he said it quickly, shocked. He realised now the job of his drinking companion. It still didn't explain the man's interest in him, but it did explain his presence in this quiet hamlet. He stood aside as the cart moved on. As they reached the centre of the area, the crowd bayed ever louder and their leaders grabbed at the couple and dragged them roughly off the cart. She and her companion were led to a bare oak tree at the edge of the tiny hamlet. They were forced forward by their captors pulling on long ropes tied around their necks. A ladder was propped against the tree, which, with its heavy branches resembled a makeshift gallows. The crowd's murmurings rose to an audible shout.

'The woman first, the woman first, take her first.'

The shouting became a unified roar and the crowd surged forward, so that all Priedeux could see was the ladder and the rope that was now being strung over the branches. He turned away. He preferred the quick sure slice of a sword to a long drawn out hanging from a tree and the girl's plea to him had heightened his horror at the scene. Suddenly there was a gap in the crowd and he saw his companion, at the edge of the people, grinning, and pulling a sack-like cloth from out of the bulky bundle attached to his thick leather belt.

Priedeux pushed through the crowd, which fell back, recognising his authority as a stranger and stopped the hangman, whispering. 'Make it quick, for the girl.' He moved back quickly knowing the hangman had heard, to his vantage point. He could smell the sweat on the crowd as he moved between them. Even though he could taste the bile in his mouth, he still turned to view the spectacle. *I just want to make sure he doesn't prolong her agony*, he excused himself. He watched as the hangman pulled on his mask, so that only his eyes showed through slits. Priedeux continued to watch from the edge as the man approached his victims, striding through the quiescent crowd, who stepped back from him, like they had for Priedeux but it was a different motion; this time it was as if the hangman was infected with the plague. Priedeux blinked but still watched as he reached the two prisoners, and put his hand on the woman's shoulder first, asking, 'is this the guilty person?'

The crowd sighed in unison, nobody taking sole responsibility:

'Aye.'

He took the rope hanging from the girl's neck, and slung it over the horizontal branch of the tree, more than two men's height high. He re-tied the blindfold around her eyes, so tightly that it pressed into her skull at each side. He pushed her up the ladder, his heavy hands at her waist, until her head was nearly touching the branch. He stood a moment, but then wound the other end of the rope round a piece of wood he took out of the wagon. All the while the prisoner stood quiescent, her head moving from side to side, as if listening to her fate. He wound the rope around the wood and then tied the end to a further tree, so that it was taut. He tested the rope, checking it. All who watched knew it would not do if it broke. Then he nodded and kicked the ladder away. She swung in the air, her legs jerking trying to find the steps and safety again. It was so suddenly done that the crowd gave a surprised "Aah" and fell back. The woman swung, her legs moving in her last macabre dance.

The hangman started the same process again on the adjoining tree, fetching the man this time. Once he was swinging as well, the hangman stood back and surveyed his handiwork. He walked away, towards Priedeux, removing the hood when he was no longer near the crowd. He watched Priedeux. Priedeux stared him out as he had done in the inn. The man shrugged, and turned back to the woman who was still jerking, still alive. He pulled on her swinging legs, hard and quick, to end her life.

Priedeux watched dispassionately and, once he saw this, walked back into the inn, returned to his broth and systematically ate, spoonful after spoonful. When he finished he wiped his face on the sleeve of his jerkin.

'Innkeeper, the bill, I must be on my way,' he called. The hangman was talking to some of the crowd and looked like he was haggling for his fee. Priedeux wanted none of his companion now.

He settled up, and, ignoring the crowd outside, who were

now becoming boisterous, he wandered to the back of the inn, past the fire, and through the private quarters, where the maid looked up, startled, to the barn where his horse had been led. It was time he was on his way.

As he felt through the gloom of the narrow unlit passage from the cooking area, he suddenly sensed a presence. The hair on the back of his neck tingled and he tensed himself, half crouched, ready to pull the knife from his boot.

'Shh, this way, come....'

It was a soft, beguiling voice and he relaxed. The serving-wench. She held out a grubby arm, faintly visible in the gloom and pulled him to her. He followed and she led him through a porch-way and into the stables where the hot rancid straw and horse smell assailed him. When they reached the rear of the stalls she turned to him, eagerly, red-faced, panting, and pulled at his hose, beneath his tunic sliding her cool hands on to his member.

'Please, take me, I need you,' she panted, kissing his face, his eyes, the tip of his nose, his mouth. She knew exactly what she was doing and he realised that he had need of her, despite the coarseness of her face, the thickness of her body. He rose under her expert touch, and he realised dimly that this lust was not born out of either of them, but that they were both aroused by the sight of the drama outside. Death. Life. Lust. He dimly thought of the words as he rolled on to her, pulling up her damp beer-smelling skirts, feeling for the warmth of her sex between her willingly open legs. Yes. She was ready for him and he thrust home, she gasping and closing her eyes. There was no resistance. He cruelly pierced to the very heart of her, she writhing beneath him, as they rode together into a lustful orgasm. It did not last long. Spent, they stopped. But he did not rest. He jumped up from her, wiping himself on her grubby skirts and felt in his purse at his waist.

'A groat, sir, for services rendered,' she taunted. He was prepared and tossed it back at her, without a glance. She was too chubby, with a coarseness about her that he did not want to acknowledge he had just used.

He sauntered to his horse, checked the tightness of the saddle, which he adjusted and, without acknowledging the girl as she sloped back to her work, adjusting her skirts, he led the horse out of the stable, mounted and rode away.

He did not look back until he reached a vantage point, where he stopped to give the horse a rest after it had laboured up the slope. 'All right, my Gringolay, for I shall name you after that man Gawain's steed, as it was trusty and strong for him, so you shall be for me. We'll tarry here a moment.'

Now he looked back the way he had come, as if to say farewell to a loved place, and surveyed the village. The way in which the hangman appeared to recognise him disturbed him and he expected to be followed, even if it was for that man to satisfy his curiosity. He could see no-one. It was as if, after the hanging the whole village had quietly dispersed to their homes. It was now well after the time that a market ended. Priedeux reined the horse round and spurred him over the hill. As he rode on, he laughed to himself. *It was just a way to worry me. To see if I would justify myself. Come on, Tom, keep calm.*

He noticed that, as he climbed, he was heading towards one of the woods which covered the higher peaks. He could see no end to it and realised he would soon be tracing a way through dense trees, some having been pollarded so that their branches were low. He had heard tales of marauding bands who attacked strangers in such woods but, from the villagers and the market, he reckoned that this was quiet farming country, where there should be no raiders, so he was not too concerned. Beyond, how far he did not know, lay Kenilworth, his lord Gaunt's summer quarters and then...then the wild country where he had to begin his search for the seditious author. It was now afternoon and he hoped to be through these woods before nightfall, but he would have to hurry for night came early at this time of year.   He spurred Gringolay forward.

Soon he was in the thickest of woods of rowan and ash and holly, with dead undergrowth, which crackled loudly as the horse stepped slowly forward.   Priedeux guessed that underfoot was the winter residue of nettles and ferns, which would blossom again bright green in the spring but were now flattened to create a thick crackly mat for the floor of the forest. Any dampness did not penetrate here, through the thickness of the trees.   As he guided the horse, there was a four-beat crunching noise, and a steamy herby smell emanated from below, as if the dead foliage held an echo of its summer odours.   The gloom meant he had to keep his eyes peeled for lowering branches and a way through dark holly bushes.   The horse too was hesitant.   Gringolay had to be constantly encouraged, and Priedeux himself had to bend and duck to avoid low branches.   There was no real path that he could discern and he merely followed a track, perhaps of one horse width, which he guessed, from his sense of direction that over the years had become innate, took him north westward.   There was no sound of birds in the woods and he began to feel lulled by the regular crackling coming from below, like the noise of a welcoming fire.

He thought he was imagining the extra sounds at first, his imagination heightened by the intense concentration needed to work his way slowly through the gloom.   He stopped and listened.   Sure enough, there was the crack again, of horse's hoof on crunchy undergrowth, a ca-lack, ca-lack; an extra four beat echoing his movements.   He did not turn, but moved on, hoping the follower had not noticed him stopping.

As he plodded on he slowly reached into the inner lining of his pannier, tearing open the leather pouch to reach the crossbow.   He extracted the bolts, and fitted one to the bow. He tried the tension.   It was so taut it ricocheted back onto his bare wrist leaving a sharp weal that slowly filled with his own blood. Priedeux licked away the liquid quickly, pressing the edges of the wound together. Not a good way to make sure of his tools but he was satisfied that the weapon was ready.

All the time he guided the horse at the same gentle pace. He thought with relief and a certain elation that the horse was good, as he thought it would be, obedient and with an easy gait, making the ride a smooth one. As Priedeux fiddled with the crossbow and momentarily relaxed his control of the horse, it slowed down but a quick dig of his heels made him move again, at the same pace as before.

He looked ahead, his eyes screwed up, working hard to see through the gathering gloom. He was trying to find a spot where the trees cleared. There were many such fairy rings in woods, where perhaps a tree had crashed down in some storm, or, as ignorant folk believed, goblins and dragons gambolled together. Priedeux of course did not believe such tales and the only reason he wanted to find such a glade now was to gain a vantage point to deal with his follower. Still his horse's ca-clack, ca-clack was being echoed, the rider keeping a steady distance. Priedeux did not turn round for he knew that the man following him must be able to see Priedeux and in this gloom, he must only be a few feet away.

I swear *I can smell the sweat of the man, he's so close*, thought Priedeux calmly.

Then he saw what he wanted ahead; a brighter place, a clearing where the winter sun shone almost horizontally, shafts of light from the west. He would not have long before those rays would disappear as night drew on.

He rode into the clearing, a shiver fizzling down his spine even though he was now out into a slightly warmer area. He knew he was the exposed one and a dagger or sword might easily reach him and he felt the chest of his padded jacket, the thickness comforting him. He forced the steed to walk gently, at the same steady pace, across the clearing that was perhaps some five horses' length across. Then he was through and for a moment he was blinded, his eyes taking time to adjust to the gloom.   Even so he quickly steered his horse to one side and around, with a sharp pull of the reins, so that he was now facing the clearing. As he turned, his foe came into sight.

Of course. It was the hangman. He held a drawn sword and his face was hard. Not only did he take the King's silver for the job he did but he obviously took pickings on the side by waylaying lone travellers.   Or that was what Priedeux assumed.   His whole demeanour was one of plunder and killing.

Priedeux lifted the bow to his shoulder, pressed it against the collar-bone where it sat well, fitted the small bolt, and aimed with one eye screwed tight. He waited, a vital second, knew the aim was straight, with the hangman's heart at the centre, tautened the bow and fired.

Chapter Four : Conversation

'At every wading of water on the way that he passed
he found a foe before him',

His aim was true and the man jerked, his face twisted into shock and astonishment as the arrow pierced his chest. He dropped to one side of his steed, a puny beast which stopped, as shocked as his master at the unexpected jerking blow. The hangman's foot stayed in its stirrup but the heaviness of the body meant that the horse was being dragged down and it started to tread air, and whinny in fear of the unknown.

Priedeux dispassionately watched the scene for a while. He believed the hangman to be travelling alone but he didn't know. He didn't know either if the arrow had indeed killed, piercing the heart at which it was aimed, or whether the hangman was just stunned. The horse's fear increased, white foam appearing at its mouth, and it stamped in a circling movement around the unusual burden. The body flopped about against its flanks, one arm dragging on the earth of the clearing as if the man were still living and he were trying to get a handhold and stop the bizarre mumming act. Priedeux could see blood dripping from the wound and he reached for his dagger where it lay snug in his boot. He dismounted and quickly approached the horse and ghastly non-rider.

'Steady now, steady,' he whispered to the trembling horse as he approached slowly. 'Come, slow, stop, steady.' He reached the horse and caught the reins pulling hard to make the animal stop, but keeping away from the swinging body.

When the horse was calmed, he walked round and quickly slashed his dagger along the line of the man's neck, stabbing at the point where the jugular was already protruding as a purple line.   The blood seeped slowly but Priedeux had already jumped out of the way.   He knew for sure the man was dead now.   He kicked the foot from the stirrup and led the horse out of the clearing.   In the safety of the brush, he quickly inspected the man's panniers.   He found the royal warrant confirming his appointment as hangman and the right to hang one Walter of Scobey and a maid Sarah of the same hamlet, for murdering Sarah's father and stealing his goods and chattels, and thereafter moving into the father's cottage as man and wife.   He found the purse of gold the hangman carried to pay his way, but Priedeux left it where he found it.   He had already committed a crime against his monarch,   he didn't want evidence of the crime to be found on his person later. There was nothing else of interest in the bags so he threw them away, slapped the beast on its rump to encourage it to gallop to safety, before mounting his own horse and going on his way, he knew not where.   The incident had unsettled him and, after calming the horse's wild circlings, he had lost his bearings.

All he knew was that he should follow the now disappearing sun and ride westwards.   He kept riding for some days, sleeping where he could find shelter, and if none was found, bedding down in the dead bracken.   The days blended into a blurred period and he could not work out how long he had been on the road.   Or where he was.   He was sure he should have reached Chester by now but the locals denied all knowledge of such a town.   He realised he had lost his way. The dialect of the serfs he had spoken to recently was sing-song and strange and he guessed he was in north Wales, well out of his King's controlled territory.   The hamlets were few and far between and there were not many large houses or farms.   He had passed through sparse and rocky areas where

42

scrawny sheep ran from him, and the air smelt damp and rancid. Then, one clear and sunny day he realised the smell had changed. Here the air was salty-clear and fresh. He recognised the tang. The sea was not far away. Somehow he had skirted the way to Chester. He guessed that he was close to the western ocean where, if men travelled ever onwards, they would fall off the edge of the world. There were dark blue shadows on the horizon to the south, that hinted of high mountains and he decided to turn aside from them, and find the coast which he would follow. As he climbed, the air continued to freshen and, as he reached the top of a long promontory, he looked down and before him was a marshy coast with what looked like another land on the other side of a wide estuary.

Here it was warmer and the snow was sparse, with tufts of yellowed grass showing through. It was still early morning and all the gnarled trees, bending landwards, were hoared with frost.

He remembered his directions from the servant at court who had hailed from these parts. The landscape mirrored the descriptions in the poem, and Priedeux made his decision. He guessed that, across the water, was the south coast of that part of the land called the Wirral and he must find a way to get there. There were no boatmen along this part of the coast, where the marshes prevented a good landing, so he continued riding, keeping the estuary to his left.

Soon the lie of the land changed, and he approached sandy flatlands. He spurred Gringolay into a gallop along the soft wetness of the coast, feeling secure that there were no sharp stones or boulders to lame him. Gringolay whinnied with delight as they sped along. But Priedeux knew horses and soon, as they came to a wooded hill hiding their way, he reined in and walked the horse. Priedeux knew he could not gallop forever. As they reached the hill he spurred his steed to the peak, so he could survey the land before him.

The sandy earth turned brown beneath the thickness of the trees, and here and there was covered by banks of dried up leaves with tussocks of thick grass peering through. As he climbed, the trees thinned and he found himself on a bare high promontory of seamed brown and yellow earth, with grey heathers and dull gorse, bereft of its summer yellow, blowing in a sea-wind and topped with hats of snow. He circled the horse and surveyed the land from this high vantage point; to the south, the blue hills of mid Wales and to the north, the land of the Wirral. Immediately on the opposite shore he could see a tiny turretted church and before it a hut and jetty. There was no boat moored there. He would have to cross that expanse if he were not to detour too much to reach his goal. He looked down on the beach beneath him.

Suddenly he pulled Gringolay up short and froze. The horse obeyed for he too became rooted to the spot. What had caught Priedeux's attention was a tableau of people on the beach. It appeared that some sort of argument was going on between two groups. Arms were being waved; women held children to their bodies as if to protect them. Priedeux was glad to see they were all too preoccupied to notice him.

Floating just off shore, behind the group, was the ferry boat, gently rocking on the tidal waters. One cowled man stood on the prow, arms akimbo. On the beach, milling around the gang plank leading to the ferry, Priedeux saw a number of serfs with pigs and sheep, huddled together in a protecting group. One man with a stave, his back to Priedeux, stood in a stance that showed he was arguing with what looked like a group of monks who barred the way to the boat. Priedeux appraised the scene and guessed what was going on, having heard of such things and knew that in a remote area like this sometimes anarchy ruled. He recognised what was happening here; monks who had acquired the right to extract fording fees; and they had become greedy. Priedeux watched and after a while, realised the monks were refusing the serfs a

44

crossing. He needed to cross; he had to do something about it.

He counted their number. Seven monks. *Seven.* Priedeux thought it would be foolish to take on all seven at once. They might be monks but that did not mean they did not know how to fight. In these remote corners, even the celibate had to look to their own and often hid swords and staves under their copious habits in case of marauding bands. Facing the monks Priedeux counted twelve men, two boys and possibly a few women waiting to cross. His first idea was to try to persuade the monks to allow him and the party a crossing. If that failed, he would force them to do so. Only with help from the serfs, though. He hoped that they would follow his lead, if he took the first step.

He surveyed the rest of the countryside. All he could see was marshy swampland, with rushes bending gently in the wind. This inhospitable terrain spread inland, a tidal inlet preventing further movement eastwards. If he were to continue on this side of the coast, he would have a lengthy detour, going back south into Wales, towards the mountains, before he could go east and round the inlet. It was no good, he would have to use the ferry. He decided to go down.

He guided Gringolay, zig-zagging down the slope, passing back through woodland and around the headland so that Priedeux arrived at the scene behind the serfs. The rough smell of farm animals came to him as he soundlessly rode nearer across the sand. As he approached, he could hear wailing protests from the peasants, sharp retorts from the holy men. A monk saw him first and shouted to a colleague, pointing over the crowd. They too turned until the whole group watched as Priedeux approached.

He said nothing until he was among the people, and then he reined in and said: 'So what goes here?'

The people watched him sullenly, unsure, but stood aside, recognising his superiority, his right to deal with the situation. His demeanour and the steed would show he was not a working man, a serf like they appeared to be. Priedeux rode slowly up and stopped at the side of the man who was their negotiator.

One monk, standing with water lapping at his feet, whose brown cowl hid his head, looked up at the horseman. His eyes were deep-set and all Priedeux could make out was a rough stubbled chin. He spoke directly to Priedeux:

'I have explained to this scum that it is a penny per person and a farthing per animal to cross but they argue they do not have such funds. I have told them they must move on, then, around the inlet and travel by land but they say they need to get to market.' His voice was whining, effeminate.

The man next to Priedeux looked up at him and interrupted: 'It would take us at least three days to go by the marshes and we do not have enough fodder for our animals. We must get them to Chester by this route. I have kin in Shotwick just across there, who would provide more fodder and allow us to go on our way.'

Priedeux nodded to him, turned to the monk and asked: 'And by what right do you extract such tallies?'

'What right do you have to ask?'

Priedeux thought but a moment and decided to take the risk. What did he have to lose? If he wanted to continue with his quest, he should be heading for the Wirral, and the easiest way to get there was this ferry.

'By the King's seal, I ask. I travel under the King's seal and would show it if you wish.'

The monk's face changed, his mouth dropping slightly and Priedeux noticed his brothers moving closer together. Their very air of defensiveness told him that these were not genuine monks or if they were, they were renegades. They were certainly not carrying out the King's orders. He steeled himself for something unexpected but the leader decided to try once more.

'We do wish, for our orders come from the Bishop and we

are not easily swayed from our purpose of gathering groats for the poor in such a way as this. We maintain the ferry and would expect to be paid for it.'

Priedeux laughed. 'True Christian charity! Robbing the poor to pay to the poor. What a wonderful system.'

The crowd behind him laughed uncertainly, still unsure that this one person, even with the King's seal, could fight their cause. But Priedeux had seen a quick movement in the gathering of monks and he shouted: 'Look, I will show you the King's seal!' At the same time he reached behind and pulled out a roped collection of three balls which he swung in the air and threw before the staves that the monks had hidden had been pulled from the back of their habits. Three of them were entangled in Priedeux's contraption and fell into the water. The ferry bobbed in the water and their companions were so surprised that two of them splashed over to join them. Priedeux then spurred Gringolay and rode full tilt at their leader and his remaining crony who was now trying to punt the ferry out to sea. Pulling his sword from its scabbard as he rode, dagger in his other hand, he splashed into the water and reached the boat. He slashed at the leader as he passed him and did not wait to see the result. With a circular, continuous movement, he swung the sword and caught the boat man, slashing his habit to reveal a padded green jerkin beneath. As the renegades fell into the sea and red flowed from them to colour the surrounding area, the peasants cheered and Priedeux heard them splashing and crashing into the waves behind him. He turned the horse and rode back and slashed at the so-called monks who were entangled in his tricks of balls and, as they fell back, he untangled his weapon and pulled it free from them. Before Gringolay was neck-high wet, he turned again, and saw the serfs slashing with small meat-knives at the bodies of their tormentors.

It was all over in a few minutes and Priedeux urged his steed out of the murky water that was now dark with disturbed sand and debris and spreading blood and guts from the dead men.

He dismounted and found the rags and hard brush, which he had packed to clean down his horse and set to, as if he had reached home and all was at rest. As he worked, the leader of the group came and stood next to him. Priedeux stopped working and stood up.

The man was dark-tanned and grizzled and his clothes were ragged but of strong leather and good padding, as if he had been wealthy once. As he held out his hand, Priedeux noticed that although this was now darkened by the sun, it was smooth and the cuticles were clean and well-cut.

'My Lord, I thank you, we all thank you.'

'I am no lord, just a wanderer, like yourself, I would guess. I only despatched them so I could cross the water and they were in my way.'

The man looked at him keenly, his dark eyes assessing. Priedeux realised he too might not be what he purported to be, but would not worry about it. He returned the gaze squarely without flinching.

'You may not know it but you are a good man, even so.'

Priedeux laughed, 'I am not, for my self interest only is being served. I would travel across and therefore had to get them despatched. If that is good for you so be it.'

'Indeed. So be it, we will cross together. Which way go you?'

'I head for Chester on the King's business. I fear I am a little lost.'

'If you come from the Court in England indeed you are lost, but the easiest way is the ferry; the land on this side of the estuary is marshy and dangerous. If you cross here, there is a good road leading to Chester.'

'I thank you. Shall we start?'

'Indeed, we head for Chester too for the market. Once we have sold our wares and raised some coin, we will move on, for there is little for us here. The land has been laid waste by these plunderers.'

He held out his hand and Priedeux took it. He felt something passing from the palm of this dignified leader into his.

'But if we meet again, I know I am indebted to you and it will not be forgotten.'

They shook hands solemnly, the others looking on. Priedeux guessed this was a dispossessed manor lord and his companions were his serfs who owed him fealty, but he did not really want to know. Such people he had met all over Europe and if they were of no use for his purposes, he would not dally with them.

They spoke no more but set to the ferry and rowed across, nobody saying anything until they reached the opposite shore. Everyone waited for Priedeux to disembark first, and he led Gringolay up the beach.

As he moved away the man called, 'Wait, have you provisions? Here, take this, a chicken is as good a feast as any if there is nothing.'

Priedeux thanked him and accepted the gift, before riding away. When he reached woodland that gave him some cover, he inspected the item the man had palmed to him. It was of reddish hard stone, and engraved on it was the mark of a seal but the pattern was not easy to decipher in its reverse position. Priedeux, if he wanted to see the pattern, would have to wait until he had some wax to imprint the mark on vellum. He stowed the item away in a slit in his sleeve. He realised such an object might be dangerous if it was from the wrong lord.

As soon as could he would throw the token away, not bothering to find out the pattern of the seal. For the moment, he stowed it away in his inner garments, puzzled. Why should a man give away his seal?

Chapter Five: The calm of Chester

'He struck his steed with his spurs and sprang on his way
so forcefully that the fire flew up from the flinty stones....'

Priedeux surveyed the city of Chester from some distance,
looking down from surrounding hills.   He saw tall buildings,
clustered close together, which formed the centre of the town,
behind the warehouses and wharves on the banks of the river
Dee, which snaked its way around the walls in front of him.
In the river were ships of all kinds, impressing Priedeux and
he realised that large numbers of traders must travel to the
port to trade from all over the known world.   Indeed, Chester
must be an important port and centre of trade for this area.   A
wealthy town indeed.   Not anything like London of course,
but a place with plenty of different goods from all over the
known world, he guessed.

Outside the eastern boundary, there was a cluster of shanty
suburbs which edged the straight roads heading north-east.
He'd avoided the smaller port of Shotwick, not wanting to
involve himself again with the wandering lord and his band
and had pushed on, hoping to be out of Chester before they
arrived.   He cheered up at the thought of the large town
before him.   He was bored with bare country and no
excitement.   He could do with good brewed ale and a willing
wench.   He knew the townsmen to be loyal to Richard, if not
Gaunt as well.   And he had letters from his King which he had
to deliver.

Of course he'd heard something else about Chester; it was one of the first places where the Black Death had appeared which Priedeux had heard so much about in his childhood. Priedeux had been frightened with such stories his mother told, but his life long wanderings had taught him one thing; the plague did not strike when it was winter-cold.

He felt he could relax and check his weapons, rest his steed and re-provision properly, for the chicken had been a scrawny bird, before heading back northwest to continue his quest for Gaunt's enemies.

Priedeux spurred his horse to cross the wooden bridge over the River Dee to enter the City by way of Shipgate.

He joined a mixed crowd making for the town. He had to walk his horse through the throng, it was so busy. On horseback he felt conspicuous amongst the peasants and farmers flocking in with their country wares. They were either walking, heavily laden with winter greens or clucking chickens, or trundling in with piled high wagons, which creaked on the cobbled streets with a noise which set Priedeux's teeth on edge. There was a babble of common talk in the local sing-song dialect, as country peasant met town-cousin with greetings, their animals making so much noise that the 'hellos' had to be yelled into cupped ears. Children ran in between the wagons, chasing each other and screaming with joy while their mothers, holding babes, tried to bring them back to their sides.

He noticed that, on the walls of the town, above the great gate where he was about to pass, soldiers stood looking down on the crowds. He deliberately relaxed, but could feel that they watched him; a man well robed, riding alone, on a good steed, with well-stocked panniers either side of that steed's haunches, riding in winter, all of these made him conspicuous. He comforted himself with the thought that this was the King's town and, if he were asked to give account of himself, he had the King's seal about him, so he rode confidently on.

The guards on the city gates gave no indication of taking particular notice of him. Soon he found himself swept along with the crowd past the quays and the Franciscan friary into the main centre streets. As he rode slowly through The Rows he appreciated the fine colonnaded walkways which he could well see on horseback. There was a smell of fresh wood. Some of the buildings were new, the shopkeepers standing outside, preening themselves, proud of their modish premises.

Priedeux was seeking a particular shop and scanned each walkway. They could be reached by a set of stairs at the corners of each row and there were banners hanging from the railings, indicating the trades or their wares. The lower shops, which were reached by stepping down into them, also had banners outside, advertising their particular speciality. He had seen similar malls in Italy, Padua, he thought it was, but this was the first he had seen in his own country. He wondered if Italians had arrived here and influenced the lay-out of the shopping mall.

The crowd became thicker and forced him to turn along Eastgate. Merchants shook hands, papers were exchanged, rich silks were held up to the sunlight at shop doorways. Housewives argued over prices. Butchers chopped new meat, the blood spattering onto their wooden blocks. Priedeux rode past holding his nose against the acrid smell of the blood and innards. He had forgotten how a town smelt.

For the moment he was content to observe, assessing the place, working out the possibilities for new supplies, a bed for the night, some food. And how to deliver the King's letters to the sheriff without being too conspicuous. Could he just ride up to the mansion house and demand an audience? He instinctively knew this would be a bad move. Chester was close, he was sure, to the place where the poem had been written. He had a strong feeling of being watched but did not know by whom. He would bide his time.

He was even more impressed with the town as he reached

its centre. It appeared to have all the crafts that could be found in London. There were leather works, metal works, jewellers, clothiers and shoe smiths. A hum of conversation echoed from the wooden ways, and cries and shouts from the hawkers in the streets. He became aware of a strong smell of cooking beef, onions, and offal and knew he was hungry. How many days had he travelled with rough food just to keep alive he could not recall. The chicken he had cooked and eaten some hours ago, but it had only whetted his appetite for more. Today he would spend a king's groat for a good meal with strong bread and fresh brewed ale served by clean wenches, a well-stuffed, flea-free mattress under cover, with a hot bath.

He was looking out for an apothecary, for the weal on his wrist had risen, and he knew he needed something to rub into the wound to sting the infection away. In summer he could obtain such herbs from the hedgerows or meadows, but in the middle of winter he had to turn to those who could preserve the astringents for such as needed it. He cursed himself for being so thoughtless as to pull the bow without the protective gauntlet but knew the reason - the tension of knowing he had to kill a man.

Suddenly he saw what he was looking for; the apothecary's sign, and reined in Gringolay, dismounted, and tied the horse to the lower railings of the shop frontage - the apothecary he wanted was on the upper floor. As he walked away he noticed a group of three men, also on horseback, who had been pacing themselves with him, weaving amongst the walking crowd at the same steady step as he had gone. He'd thought nothing of it, for it had been difficult enough to move at any other speed, but now they also reined in and tethered their horses a few yards from him and dismounted. He realised that he had heard their horses' hooves, without thinking about it, since he had entered the walled city.

So, he was being spied on here, in one of the King's towns. He'd assumed that the King's peace would mean that strangers would be safe. He was sure he did not stand out for special notice to be taken of him by the King's officers. Then he recalled his tension as he rode into the town; he *was* conspicuous and if the sheriff was overzealous, he might give the order to check up on such a stranger. Maybe that would solve his problem of approaching the sheriff.

Best to go about his business in as calm a manner as possible. He sauntered up the wooden steps to the upper floor and walked the short distance to the shop he wanted. There were not many shoppers in this parade, with its medicinal quarters and a leather hose warehouse. His shop was nearly at the end, before the wooden structure curved round a corner. He stopped short and leaned down, casually, as if to enjoy the view from the upper storey. He could hear his footsteps being repeated on the wooden boards of the steps and knew they had followed him. Out of the corner of his eye he saw the three men, walking together, arms locked, as if to prevent another from passing between them, creeping along the path he had trod, their very gait making them seem suspicious.

Priedeux sauntered on, knowing he had his sword and daggers at the ready.

He entered the shop. It was gloomy at first but he could see through an opening at the back where there was a workshop, lit by soft tallow lights, from which came a smell of acrid brewing. Dried leaves hung from rafters and there were rows of dark pottery jars. As he entered, the apothecary bustled into the shop, wiping his hands on a cloth. At the back were shelves filled with small packets, clay jars and bundles of desiccated materials. The shopkeeper looked enquiringly at him and Priedeux showed his wound, and suggested as if tentatively, 'I believe ramsons would be a good antidote for the poison.'

The shopkeeper nodded, saying, 'I agree your prognosis. One clove would soon clean out that wound.'

He opened one of the many drawers behind him and handed over a desiccated garlic plant. 'Break the seal of papery outer-covering of this and cut into the centre until the juices run, rub the soft interior into the wound. It will sting but it will clean.'

Priedeux nodded, saying, 'aye, 'tis well known by me.'

The man said, curiously: 'Where did you learn such ways?'

Priedeux eyed him keenly, wondering if he too had an ulterior motive in the question, but he decided the man was merely interested. As he picked up the clove, there was a sudden dimming of the daylight in the already gloomy interior, and he realised the entrance, being the main source of light, was blocked. He turned and saw, as he had already guessed, the three men. Two of them were leaning nonchalantly on either side of the door as if waiting for the area to be free. The other leant against the low wooden balcony outside. They could obviously hear the conversation, but he turned back to the apothecary and answered: 'At my mother's knee, kind sir, my mother was a wise woman.' He wasn't going to admit that it was a good French cure, picked up on his travels on the Continent after he had left home. No, he would act the innocent traveller.

Priedeux quickly stowed the garlic away. It would not do to let these men know he was wounded.

'Many thanks for the advice and the wares - I'll be on my way now.' The last he said loudly as he smiled at the shopkeeper, who seemed oblivious of the men, and placed a groat on the counter before him. Then he turned on his heel and walked swiftly to the door, as if he hadn't realised the way was barred.

The shop was not large and with a few strides he was there. Almost nose to nose with them. Priedeux assessed the group coolly, surveying them as if they were possible purchases, animals to be bought. The middle one, waiting outside, was the leader; the other two leaning slightly towards him as if they would hear his hidden intentions, waiting on his cue. They were all dressed in thick leather, with high boots and jerkins, huntsmen's outfits. No exotic liripipes or soft felt hats for them, but helmets of tight-fitting leather, with raised ear-pieces, functional and protective. They had weapons, swords at their waists, and, he was sure, daggers, hidden in the armlets perhaps. All this he calculated in a second. But he also saw a hint in their eyes of wariness of him.

He smiled, pausing a moment. This seemed to off-guard them and they relaxed.

'Well, kind sirs, you have come to the right apothecary for a cure. He has served me well, Perhaps a cure for piles, the way you are all standing?'

They all three gaped at him as he pushed past, breaking through their ranks. At first they did nothing. He could smell the rank sweat of fear as he passed them. The open gangway was before him, and he was swiftly on his way before they moved. Not practised assassins, then. No swift-bladed movement to stab him in the back. As he hurried away he heard the leather of their clothes creak and knew they were after him. What did they want? As he moved he looked down and saw another man, dressed in similar garb to the others, peeping under the saddle of Gringolay, inspecting the horse, stroking its haunch as he did so. The royal mark would be clearly seen. So, thought Priedeux, they *are* checking me out. No doubt, if they were official Chester men the royal sign on the horse would placate their suspicions. He remembered what Gaunt had said: Chester was always loyal to the King. The man below, sensing he was being watched, looked up and met Priedeux's gaze and then looked away towards the men following. Priedeux swore that there was a slight nod, to those behind Priedeux.

He began to walk faster, as if his business of the day suddenly became pressing but the steps behind mirrored his, tapping at the same speed. He decided to escape as quickly as possible. To deal with a lone hangman was one thing, but to encounter a host such as this, four against one, would be tough going. Without warning, he leapt across the parapet of the upstairs walkway and landed just in front of Gringolay in a crouching movement, pulling his sword at the same time. He had moved so suddenly that the man who stood by his horse did not have time to properly pull his sword. Priedeux jumped, weaving his sword rapidly so that it swiped the man viciously. The man fell, clutching his chest and Priedeux quickly despatched him with a rapid swipe to his throat. Turning immediately, he confronted the others who came clattering towards him.

It would be no good trying to swing himself onto Gringolay, his sword made him clumsy, so he backed around the horse, and positioned himself against the wall of the shop, then turned to meet his foes.

They edged towards him. He could smell their fear. Fear did not figure for him, he was too preoccupied in cold assessment of the situation, which quickly turned into the usual blood rush he felt at the task in hand. It was the excitement of an experienced man knowing exactly what he had to do and knowing he could manage it, that his opponents did not have the same skills. They might be fighting men, but they were inexperienced: that was his rapid judgement of them. Otherwise it would have been a midnight silent attack in an inn, such as Priedeux himself had used, with no margin for error. Leaning back, firm plaster pressed into his shoulders, he would not be attacked from behind. The men came on, grinning, believing he was caught. Priedeux, using the wall as a lever, kicked out at the same time as lashing with his sword. With three of them he knew he had to dispense with polite swordsmanship, and that his only chance was guile. The kick reached home, and one of the men reeled away in pained surprise, gripping between his legs. As he stumbled away, Priedeux continued to parry and twist and kick in almost a circular movement, forcing the remaining two assailants backwards, in their efforts to find an opening for their swords. Suddenly there was a flash of gleaming metal before his chest and he stepped back.

He felt a coldness in the crook of his arm between the thickness of his breast plate of leather and the padded arm. Stabbed, he could not tell by whom, he knew he had to finish this debacle quickly. Dropping his sword which clattered to the ground, he paused for only a second. The other two stood back, preparing themselves for a final lunge. They relaxed, sure now they had him caught, to their downfall. Bending, as if to retrieve the dropped sword, he pulled out his knives from his boots and with a double flash of silver, he caught the thighs of both men, so that blood, almost identical spurts, was drawn from them. His lunge had parried a sudden thrust from one of them, which would have certainly found his jugular. They staggered and fell away, blood spurting.

'Want more? Come on, my sons, let's see what you're made of.'

The men grunted but watched him from a sword's distance, not sure of their next move.

Priedeux turned to Gringolay. If he could reach the horse he could escape, but the palfrey was pawing the ground, confused by all the movement and the smell of blood. Out of the corner of his eye he could see his third foe, the one he had kicked, scrambling back into a standing position and Priedeux knew he would be the worst to conquer, with pride wounded, anger would make him blind to danger. Priedeux clenched all his muscles, breathing hard, knowing his strength was ebbing.

He looked around for a way to escape, and realised that a crowd had gathered, making a large circle around them and the faces of the onlookers were twisted with hunger for more spectacle. They would not help him, too eager to see more blood. As he gazed around, there came a thundering that he recognised as a company of horsemen. Suddenly, from afar, came a cry: 'Hey, hey there, what's a-miss?'

He and his assailants turned and looked across the corner towards Bridge Street and the grouping at that point suddenly separated, to create a channel for the newcomers. Galloping towards them was a band of horsemen, all wearing the same coat of arms showing they could only be officials of the town. They yelled:

'Stop, in the name of the King, stop!' They were waving swords and banners, and came on riding a-pace, mowing down a slow woman and her child who fell to one side as they came. The assassins scuttled to their horses, blood dripping from the two that Priedeux had injured. They quickly untied them and the horses were moving before the men were in their saddles as they whipped them into a gallop to escape.

Priedeux tried to reach his horse, which had moved to one side, and, after its scare, stood there shivering, awaiting further events. Priedeux knew he was weak and would not get far so he watched, leaning against Gringolay, who stamped the earth, disturbed by the violence. The new contingent gave chase but suddenly Priedeux saw them rein in, wheel round and ride back to him.

When they reached him, they circled around, and one of them, dressed in good chainmail and helmet, reached for Gringolay's dangling reins. He said in the rough local accent: 'In the name of the King and the Sheriff, you come with us. Causing an affray is a civil offence!'

Priedeux tried to see the man's eyes, to assess him, but he was holding Gringolay tight and controlling his own horse and moving in semi-circles. Even if Priedeux could have talked his way out of the situation with the leader, he realised that with his regiment behind him he was unlikely to release his prisoner. It was no good, he was cornered. He climbed onto the horse and they led him towards the forbidding castle, which stood on the riverbank a short distance away.

He was taken into the keep and made to dismount. They

marched him into a hall, all grey stone with plain whitewashed walls. The leader walked the length of the room until he reached a refectory table. Behind it was a magistrate, red cloak of office draped around his shoulders. A brazier of coals was blazing to one side of him but apart from this there was no heating, or lighting in the hall.

'Sir, I bring before you the man...'

The magistrate looked up quickly and raised his arm, as if in warning. He stared at Priedeux. 'Explain yourself, sir, for causing an affray during market. It is an offence in this City.'

'But I am a harmless traveller who was attacked by other wayfarers sir, 'tis not my fault.' protested Priedeux.

'But there are no other people here - so I must interrogate you.'

'But, sir,' Priedeux began and then stopped. He decided to await events.

'Name?'

'Priedeux'

'Why are you travelling?'

'I am a soldier on my way home, and I seem to have missed my way,' he decided it was the best story to tell.

'From where do you come?'

'London.'

'And where do you go?'

Priedeux hesitated.

'Where do you go?' It was said insistently, and the soldier behind him prodded him: 'Answer!'

'It is a small place in the Shire of Richmond, beyond Lancaster - you would not know of it.'

'Tell me...'

'My Lord, why should I be questioned in such a manner, when I am going about my lawful business? As I said, 'twas I that was attacked.'

'And I say again, you are the only one here...so you must explain yourself. Otherwise, you will see the walls of our cells here, and taste only water for we do not have civic funds to pay for food for prisoners.'

His voice was sibilant, the words whispering off his tongue and floating in the air as if they would be lost. But the insidiousness of his threats was not lost on him whom he interrogated. Priedeux decided to use his trump card.

'I need to speak with you in private.'

'I need the guards to stay with me,' the magistrate almost sneered his corresponding answer.

'I have something I can only impart to you.'

The magistrate looked at him, and Priedeux realised from the sharp look he was being given that this man was no fool. The brows were arched, the eyes clear and wide. The jaw was square and the thin mouth was set tightly. His whole demeanour was one of intelligent inquisition, of assessment. Priedeux stood straight, his arms by his sides, and returned the gaze steadily, almost holding his breath.

The red-robed town official leant back in his chair, looking around the room as if this would give him inspiration. Then he waved a hand in dismissal. The soldiers clicked their heels in acknowledgement and marched sharply out and he and Priedeux were left alone.

'Speak - but do not move.'

As he said this, the magistrate stood and shrugged off the red cloak, so that it fell over the arms of his chair, and revealed soldierly gear, and a sword in its scabbard. He stood behind the table, his palms resting on the parchments before him.

Priedeux took a deep breath. 'I am surprised at the reception I have received in the King's town. I am on the King's business. And I have letters to prove it. But such business as I am on is not to be acknowledged or known in these parts. I need to hand my letters to the sheriff and only the sheriff. I can show the King's seal if needed.'

He did not move to extract his papers from where they were hidden on his person. He waited. The man before him came closer, leaving the refuge of the table. There was a silence in the room but Priedeux could hear sounds from outside, the clanging and shouting of the business of a castle such as this. The normal sounds accentuated the tension between the two men.

The man was so close now that Priedeux could feel his pungent breath on his face.

'Show me,' he whispered. 'Show me your letters with their seals.'

It was said with so much cynicism that Priedeux almost took a step back. He was trapped. He had to give up his trump card or kill this man. He didn't think killing was an option, there were too many soldiers outside, he would never escape. He reached inside his shirt, inside his padded outer jacket. The magistrate's hand went to the hilt of his sword. Priedeux pulled out the safe warrant, with the obvious red seal dangling from it. The man's hand lifted off his sword. He took the parchment.

Unravelling it, he read the missive. He took it back to the table, where the dim glow from the brazier afforded him a little more light, and read it again. Then he walked over to a chain and pulled it. Shortly afterwards a clerk entered, dressed in the dark short cloak of his kind. He stood respectfully, not speaking.

'Take this to the reader and ask him to report. Send in the guards.'

'Sir! Immediately.' The clerk took the offered parchment and scuttled out. The guards entered as soon as he had gone and the magistrate ordered:

'Take our prisoner to the cells, while I await the results of investigations.'

'But sir, please.'

The man waved his hand and Priedeux was manhandled away, and along corridors which went downhill, ending in a row of thick doors, where the guards almost threw him on to the straw-covered stone flags of a windowless cell. It was lit dimly by a flare from the corridor outside. Muted laughter came from them as they clanged the door shut and strode away.

Priedeux did not have long to wait. Before the night was out, he was disturbed from a fitful slumber, and taken back into the presence of the same magistrate.

'I return your letter,' said he, with the same cynical tone, throwing the packet, with its seal broken, across the table. 'Take it, and go,' He turned away, as if bored by the proceedings. Priedeux moved forward and collected the letter, but remained standing

'Sir, I need to see the sheriff. It is important. Alone.'

The magistrate stopped what he was doing and approached Priedeux.

'You see him before you. What more do you want?'

He said it with such venom that Priedeux wondered whether he had been right to reveal the letters.

'Alone.' Priedeux repeated.

Again the official waved his hand and the attendants marched out of the room. Priedeux waited and moved from foot to foot.

'Well, what is it? I am a busy man.'

Priedeux pulled out the letters King Richard had handed to him.

'These were handed to me by the King himself. I was to pass them over to the Sheriff and no-one else.'

As he began to hand them over, the Sheriff strode towards him and grabbed the package, took it back to his table and hastily slit the seals and held them up to the light from the flares. He nodded.

'Good, good,' he muttered to himself. 'You may go. Leave Chester soon; that is my advice.'

He rang a bell as he spoke and attendants came running.

'Take this man – give him back his horse and release him.'

Priedeux noticed that the letters had been hastily concealed in the man's robes before anyone returned. He bowed to the Sheriff and followed his guard of the night before through the hall and into the courtyard, where the pale light of morning was giving shape to the first activities of the day. His horse was led out, freshly rubbed down.

Priedeux did not wait, he pulled himself onto the saddle, and slapped Gringolay's sides. Immediately the horse started to trot, as if eager to be on the road, but Priedeux reined him in until they were away from the castle grounds.

When they were well in the suburbs of the City, Priedeux urged the horse faster, for the narrow town roads were virtually empty at this time of the morning, with only early tradesmen such as the baker about. Priedeux sniffed the air as he passed the glowing oven, the smell of the baking bread whetting his appetite.

The buildings in these outskirts were of rough wattle and daub, the ornate crosshatchings of beamwork on the outside of the shops giving way to mud plastered shapes and thatch.

So much for rest *and good food in a peaceful town*, thought Priedeux, his stomach rumbling and the need for sustenance becoming urgent. He assessed the situation. He was certain now that the first group were not king's men checking on him. Who were they then? And why his arrest by the city authorities? More importantly, why had they let him go? This, he assumed, was because his letters stood up to their scrutiny and they had accepted he was who he said he was. Why had he been dismissed so summarily? Normally, he would have expected to be given some hospitality, even if was kitchen food. And they had not changed his horse, although Gringolay had been groomed. In one way that pleased him, he had become attached to this beast.

And whose henchmen were his original attackers? There had been no sign, no knightly emblazon - so he guessed they could be the henchmen of an outlaw baron or one who would not want his foe to know who he was. But why attack him? Priedeux knew royalty could act anonymously as well. It was never far from his mind that he knew many of Gaunt's secrets and could be expendable. Apart from being famished, he felt uneasy and out of sorts, not being able to unravel all the threads of the attach, his arrest and release.

He hadn't felt comfortable since meeting the hangman. Could he have been connected with Priedeux's quest, or had it been just a chance encounter? Priedeux was too worldly-wise to assume a chance meeting, and, if it was, why had the hangman followed him? He had dismissed it as a piece of personal enterprise, the hangman thinking Priedeux might not be missed if he were killed in a strange wood far from home. But was that too easy an answer? In any case, thought Priedeux, the hangman had been despatched so he could not cause further trouble. Could it be though, that a relay of messages had been sent ahead to watch him, or kill him?

As he rode, Priedeux felt light-headed, and unable to think further of the various incidents. And his shoulder ached. The bleeding had stopped and he was sure it was not serious but he needed to rest. He inspected the dried blood, which had seeped from his armpit and had stained his leathern garment. The cold night in the cells had numbed the wound but now it started throbbing with pain. He had to find a safe haven where he could rest, use the garlic clove, or ramsons as he called it, if not on the weal on his wrist, which he had forgotten about, at least now on the new wound. It was imperative he found somewhere to shelter and tend his wounds.

He looked around him. Even in this suburb, there would be an inn and he soon saw the sign of a leather bottle and a little further on, hanging from the same building a crude wooden sign with a dancing bear cleverly painted, gold chain as well. The Bear, he thought, and remembered the lines from the poem he had been forced to read before he left the safety of London and civilisation: '*Gawain fought with bears, along with other strange creatures.'* Well, that was turning out to be true. He swung the horse's head into the narrow lane and headed for the sign.

As he approached, there was a bustle as if his arrival was noticed and signs given.

The boy who came from the stables was handed the reins: 'Place him well back in the stables, boy, for warmth, mind, and feed him well. After you've brushed him down, loosen his girth, but ensure he is ready to ride again shortly.' He handed the boy a small silver coin.

'And if anyone asks after such a steed, you know of none, understand?' Priedeux could see the appreciation and understanding in the streetwise boy's eyes. He was dressed in rags, with bare, dirty feet, but his clothes were of leather and good quality although old. He knew what he was about. In him, Priedeux, the hardened traveller, recognised himself of years ago; hungry for excitement, for a change of scene, for new experiences. In him, Priedeux saw intelligence, quick-thinking, and self-interest. The boy caught on fast and Priedeux knew he would look after the horse, expecting another silver coin when the guest left.

As he spoke, he swung the panniers off the horse and awkwardly slung them over his shoulder, trying to avoid wincing from the pain of his injury, which had now started to throb, and then strode into the inn where he ordered a private room and asked for a flagon of ale and food to be brought to him there. He strode towards the stairs in an assumption of service and the man of the house scurried forward and hedged round him and led him, bowing obsequiously, up rough narrow steps to the upper chambers. He kicked a wooden door that resisted at first and then gave, so that the innkeeper almost fell into the room. With surprising agility he straightened up and stepped aside to allow Priedeux to enter. Priedeux look around and noticed that there was no bolt or lock, just the levered wooden handle of such a dwelling. He nodded to the man without speaking and was left alone.

It was not long before there was a rap at the door and another man, the alemaster, entered. Priedeux eyed him. He was probably the father of the boy, with the same wise air about him. Priedeux understood. By sheer luck he had found the inn where the local burghers came with their mistresses; where the king's spies met their local informers, and, even, where stolen goods were traded. He was trained to recognise such places. It was the air of all-knowingness, almost arrogance, of the specimen who stood in front of him.

Priedeux jangled a leather money pouch and said nonchalantly, as he swigged the drink: 'I'll not be known to be here if anyone asks?'

The man looked at his guest, eyed away from the dark bloody stain beneath his arm, that Priedeux was now revealing, as he peeled off the stiffened clothes, and nodded. 'I'll bring some hot water and rags, sir, for you to clean up.'

Priedeux nodded and waved his thanks, as he stepped to the small window showing a view down the street. It would be hardly noticeable from outside, hidden as it was by eaves, but it commanded a good long sighting of anyone who might come down that way

He turned back into the room. No brightly coloured tapestries here, all was gloomy, the predominant colour of the hangings a dark brown, gleaned from some local vegetable dye, no doubt. Priedeux established there were no other doors to the room, even hidden behind the hangings as he swished them aside to be shown more bare wall; the only way was through the small window, on to the eaves and across the roof. *Either a safe haven or a cage, from which there is no escape,* he thought uneasily.

When the water was brought, and Priedeux inspected the street again, he gingerly undressed, dabbing at the now dried blood, which stuck his inner garment to his flesh. He bathed the wound, through the undershirt, dampening it until it loosened. He pulled at it to open it up, revealing the bloody mess inside, even though it stung. The knife had torn at the outer flesh but had not punctured the muscle tissue. Firstly, Priedeux rubbed hot water onto his own knife and wiped it clean, leaving the blade shiny silver. He knew this was not ideal, but would have to serve for the time being. Then he picked up the garlic clove again and with his dagger cut into it, tearing the outer papery covering away, as the apothecary had instructed. He cut the clove longwise so that the oily inner flesh was exposed and then rubbed it hard into the wound, gritting his teeth as the clove's juices ran into the opening. He did likewise with the weal on his wrist, which was by now, a suppurating yellow raised line. He opened up the line, pressed out the obvious pus and rubbed another of the garlic's cloves into it, almost crying out as the astringency caught at the inner tender parts under his skin. He knew that the greater pain was for the better cure and clenched his teeth and allowed the agony to waft over him until he fell back on the pallet bed, almost in a faint.

As he did so he heard the patter of soft shoes on the wooden stairs and a creak. Immediately he was alert, the knife in his hand turned so quickly outwards, the darkness of bodily aches dismissed, as if the adrenalin flowed so fast through his veins that it killed any sensation except the alertness of a wild animal. He pulled on the jerkin he had discarded and reached for his bags, wheeling them across his shoulder.

The door burst open and again he was ready.

There stood his three assailants of yesterday. The tallest came through first, his leg still extended as he kicked the door open, but his two companions jumped into the room either side of him in a dramatic side dance which made Priedeux smile grimly.

'Not again, I thought you scum had been routed.' He said ironically, at the same time recognising their manoeuvre and knew he could do nothing about it. He was caught, like a deer in a gully, like a boar in a copse, like a fox in a hole. Unless he could back away and flee through the window. There was no time for that. He leant back and waited, therefore, to see what would happen next. He might, if he looked relaxed enough, make a straight run through the open door. He retracted the knife, so that the blade was hidden in the sleeve of his undershirt and posed his face into one of astonished surprise.

'Oh, no, wily traveller, you fool us not! You *will* await our liege's call, and come with us NOW,' and with that they all three lunged forward. Priedeux leant forward as if to counter attack but then fell back, double somersaulted and jumped through the window in a crouching movement which was so fast anyone who saw it would have been reminded of wandering mountebanks, jugglers, double-jointed gymnasts. He landed on the eaves and nearly dropped the saddlebags before righting himself and then ran over the roofs until he came to the overhang of the courtyard. He jumped, landing squarely on his feet and ran towards the stable. Gringolay had not yet been unsaddled and with an apologetic : 'Sorry, my steed, you must ride again,' Priedeux led him out of the stables, mounted and they were off.

He galloped out of the place, and kept galloping until he found himself in the coppiced wood which overlooked the City. It was only when he was among the thin bare branches which forced him to slow down that he wheeled about and looked back.

Nobody.

He could see the rough path he had taken sloping away and Chester behind him, in the valley, nestling along the estuary, toy ships in the harbour. It seemed so peaceful, he stared for a while, realising he needed to let Gringolay cool from the hard ride.

Eventually he turned his horse's head and rode forward into the unknown, galloping away from the scene. He sensed that, even though he had left the town, this would not be an end to his brushes with attackers. He was riding upward now, on a steep hill away from the lowlands and he was even more pleased with the creature he had acquired whom he urged forward. The horse did not flinch or lose his footing, despite the unevenness of the ground, the jutting hard stones and flints.

Soon he was over the brow of the spur and saw before and slightly below him another, thicker, pollarded wood where thin new branches shot from ground. This provided some cover but not enough to hide a man and horse.

He reined in and surveyed the area but it seemed dead in the gathering gloom of the winter afternoon. The young stems shone coppery brown in the lengthening light and a shimmer arose from the wood, the damp drifting upward awaiting a frost to beat it down again. No sign of life broke the scene, not even a startled rabbit or gliding bird of prey.

A strange silence seemed to hang over the place as if a Persian carpet had been draped over it, dulling all noise.

He reached the thin woodland. As Gringolay stepped forward on the deep brushwood of broken twigs, greying, rotting leaves and flattened bracken, he remembered how these wild lands had been deforested by Edward III to repel bandits.

He moved on to where the trees thickened not with old tree trunks but with lopped branches, the work of wood gatherers who always kept to the edge of the forest. He realised he was following a path, narrow as it might be, for the way was dipped with a slight bank each side and where he trod there was deep shadow. He slowed Gringolay so they were barely moving.

Suddenly ahead of him he saw light - a clearing. He rode downwards into the dip of a natural valley and Priedeux guessed there might be a stream there. If he were right, he would stop and rest. He reached the edge of the clearing where he saw moss-covered ground and small hillocks of grass, all bathed in slanting winter light.

As he did so, a gloom came over the area and all round him, as if risen from the very ground itself, longbow men appeared, all standing, weapons stretched taut, all aimed at him.

'Whoa, Gringolay my friend, we are fenced in here,' he said aloud.

'Halt, in the King's name!' called one of the men at the side, and Priedeux obeyed. He recognised the mass as crack Cheshire bowmen, with their heavy over-developed shoulders and thin legs. He was sure now he was in the thick of some royalist plot.

'What will you have of me?'

The leader hesitated before he answered. Priedeux wheeled his horse in a jerking semi-circle to make it difficult for the bowmen to aim.

'To kill you and dispose of your body, well away from where it will be found.'

'But I have the King's seal here, and you mention the King's name.' He continued to wheel the horse around, jerking and jumping, so as to confuse the bowmen.

Their leader laughed then, a coarse derisive sound. Think again, oh knight. For we have heard differently. The seal is not genuine, we have been informed. You are a spy, but for whom, our leader cannot tell, so this is the way you will disappear.' He lifted his arm, but before he could lower it in the usual sign for firing, there was a loud hubbub of calls and thunderous hooves. Suddenly, from behind the bowmen rode Priedeux's first assailants, the men he had twice escaped from in Chester, slashing and wielding their swords and charging into the troop.

'Go, ride, that way,' said their leader, and Priedeux did nothing more but spur Gringolay and gallop across the startled bowmen, crashing through the underbrush, thin branches of trees whipping his legs and face as he rode.

71

One of the men did not stay and fight but caught up with him and rode alongside him. Priedeux spurred his horse onwards but his co-rider stayed with him until the wood became a thicket and he could no longer gallop. Indeed, at one point he was almost thrown as a thicker branch caught him on the chest. He knew he had to stop if he was not to be killed. The evening was fast approaching now. Priedeux reined in and stopped. He faced his companion.

It was the leader of the men. He leant over and gripped the reins of Gringolay.

'No more escaping, stranger. You are mine now.'

Fallen from the spit into the fire, Priedeux thought.

Chapter Six: Meeting with a lady

'That loveliest lady there
on them glanced with eyes of grey;
that he found ever one more fair
in sooth might no man say'.

Priedeux said nothing, waited.

'Our mistress wishes to see you.' The man was breathless and gasped as he spoke. 'You have wounded two of her men, and my mistress will not be pleased. She wishes speech with you and you will come with us.'

Priedeux assessed the man. He was one of the men that Priedeux had stabbed in the thigh, and dried blood could be seen on the leather of his hose. He hadn't had time to clean up, thought Priedeux. He now acted as the leader of the trio. Priedeux did not reply, assessing his chances of further escape, but gave up any such thoughts as the sound of hooves could be heard. Soon they were joined by other men who circled around Priedeux, grinning, confident they at last had him. The fourth assailant, who had been looking at the horse when it was tethered before the apothecary, was nowhere to be seen. Priedeux suspected that his slash had severed an artery and the man was dead. For this, he thought, the cavalcade he now faced, were additionally angry, afeared and therefore dangerous.

Priedeux recognised their leader as a fighting man, a man who served, like himself. Like Priedeux, his whole life had been one of assessing danger, taking risks, but not to the point of inviting his own death. Life was but once, he knew, so prolong it as far as possible. Priedeux recognised a kindred spirit. He grinned and relaxed.

'A mistress, hey? Dangerous wily creatures, females. I will do nothing but obey you. But I demand to know the nature and name of such a mistress who forces strangers to her presence.'

'Her name you will know soon enough! It is but a day's ride from here - you will come willingly?'

The man who spoke looked surprised and gratified at Priedeux's change of stance. He served his mistress, Priedeux guessed, with a mixture of fear and greed. He was pleased he did not have to take further risks with his life at present for her.

'Willingly I come - but for you, a comrade in arms, a man experienced in war, not for some mistress whose name I know not. Your name?'

'My name is Bodres , let that suffice for now, and we shall treat each other with the respect due to men of arms and who serve, yes?'

Priedeux held out his right hand in token and they shook hands solemnly, the two others who had attacked him doing likewise. After all had shaken hands with Priedeux, he spoke again:

'I shall come with you but first, let me treat that wound, sir. Don't be troubled, it is a good - *English* - cure.'

They dismounted. Bodres visibly relaxed at the word 'English' and lifted his leg with his foot resting on the stirrup of his horse so that his thigh was open to Priedeux's inspection.

'Like all good mothers' cures, this will sting.'

Priedeux held the garlic in the palm of his hand so that Bodres could see that the clove was the source of the magic cure, and rubbed the wound hard and violently to release the juices quickly. The wounded man winced; he could surely feel the astringent juices penetrating the wounded skin, but his face also grimaced into an approving smile, if that was possible, to show he understood Priedeux's actions.

Priedeux knew he was gaining a friend for the future.

He nodded and threw the clove into the brush, its usefulness gone now it was a dry husk.

'Come, you are ready now to ride, and I am prepared to meet your mistress.'

Bodres slapped him on the shoulders, helped to gather the panniers together and threw them over Priedeux's horse as they remounted and then he led the way through the gloom in a westerly direction, into the setting sun.

'Not far now, we should reach it before nightfall,' explained Bodres. Priedeux was relieved. He would prefer to see his captor in daylight, get a clear view of her, and her quarters. He did not relish arriving at wherever he was being taken in the dead of night when he could not gauge the extent of what could be a gaol.

They rode out on a frost-hardened path and Priedeux took the time to notice his surroundings now that he didn't have to be always on the alert. He was resigned to being, for the present, the prisoner of these men and thought it might even bring him to the one he was seeking. Why else would these vagabonds have followed him and attacked him? Chester was the King's town, it was well known, and they knew he rode a horse belonging to the King. He was sure they had had time to see the brand beneath the saddle, before he'd left the shop in Chester.

Priedeux had been in many tight spots before and had learned that there was only one time to die and it would come with an awful inevitability one day. He had received wounds which had healed and remembered pain and knew he could deal with it. He had been prisoner and slave in the past and had stood the bond with resignation and ingenuity until, a trusted servant, he had found means to escape and be on his way again. He would not fight if there was no chance of success and would let the day drift and take his chance and luck. If it was to be his last day, then so be it.

'God be with me and I with him,' he muttered to himself cynically, not meaning the God of the monks and priests who had tried to brainwash him as a child in the one Apostolic faith. No, Priedeux's god was more international than that. If he died today, he would have failed in this mission but there would be no-one to grieve for him, and Gaunt, once he found out, would send another or, if he thought it necessary, more soldiers to weed out the rebels. It would make no odds to Priedeux then, an unknown spirit, gone from this solid earth. Even so, the winter smell of cold bracken and leaves, made him look up and revel in his very aliveness today, even though the sting of his wrist chivvied him slightly as he held tightly to the reins, for Gringolay jibbed at the sedate trot of the others around him.

Now they were passing neat strips of cultivated land, bordered by wooden fences as markers. Some had been dug over into neat rows, awaiting the ice of winter to break down the heavy sods. The earth was a deep red rust colour. Other strips had brilliant rows of winter greens or the scruffy leaves of turnips rising from the hard ground.

Gradually these feudal strips became fewer and were interspersed with common land on which pigs furrowed, a bundle of rags with a stick, perhaps a child, tending them. Then there were groups of evenly spaced saplings, obviously deliberately planted to provide firewood for the future, and on the horizon Priedeux could see the bare bones of winter trees, through which the reddened sun striped its way. Even further, to the right of the road, there were sombre uneven shadows of rough hills. This was where they headed as the road snaked round the last of the serfs' fields.

They rode on, towards those dark hills. The countryside became bleaker, the common land scruffy with stubby grasses and large lumps of granite rising up like crooked teeth. They were climbing and the air was becoming colder. Priedeux pulled his cloak closer around him, once again grateful that he had purchased a good thick one before setting out. He wished they could move faster.

'Why do we travel so slowly?'

Bodres turned to him from where he led the party: 'We could gallop all the way but your horse would be lame by the time we arrive. Soon the road will become rutted and stony, 'tis best to take it steady.'

His prisoner nodded, in thanks for the sensible explanation, and he slowed his horse, patting him on the side of the neck, to placate. The horse tossed its mane in acknowledgement.

Yes, the road was roughening now. Large jagged granites jutted out of the ground, and the middle of the rude pathway, where no wagons' wheels rolled, was raised with great clumps of grasses, grey dandelion leaves and other weeds which would run riot in the summer, but now were stiff in the winter ice. Gringolay began to step delicately, and Priedeux imagined he could hear the horse muttering to itself, watching out for its step. The others slowed down also, despite having used this way before. Priedeux thought about this and realised his companions and their beasts must know how dangerous it was. He would take his lead from them. A lame horse could well be left for dead, especially in winter, where the cold would preserve it for later butchering with the good cuts sold to innkeepers in the town to be fed to unsuspecting travellers and the innards fed to the dogs. He shuddered. It would not be good to lose his horse. A walking man could not hold his own in the world. With all this in mind, he concentrated on the track ahead and allowed the horse to step his own way.

Soon the track became so narrow that only one animal could pass at a time, and high banks on either side hid the view. Nobody spoke, and the silence seemed to be a darkening shadow around them. Priedeux could smell the dank earth clinging onto the sides of these banks, held together by the roots of trees and climbing weeds that were a mass of rotting leaves at this time of year. In summer it would be a riot of colour, white, pink and blue, tiny flowers mingling. But now it smelt like the dead. Then they stopped climbing and the path turned sharply to the right and the landscape cleared before them. Priedeux felt as if he had passed from civilised land into a truly wild place.

Bodres stopped and pulled to one side, to allow the others to catch up with him. They were on the top of an escarpment from which they could view the next valley sloping away to the west. The setting sun now shone horizontally directly at them and Bodres said nothing as he pointed at the blunt dark building before them. It seemed even more sinister because the sun, slanted as it was, did not touch it and it looked like a black crouching creature in the valley. It was a fortified homestead built of granite, stunted into the valley.

'Storeton. Your destination.'

'Aye, but who owns it? It means nothing to me.'

'The Stanleys, the Lords Stanley. No, you'll not see them at court, they're too *fine* for the Court of King Richard II.' Bodres said it derisively. 'Wait and see, you have been summoned.'

Before Priedeux could question Bodres further, the man had urged his horse on and led the party through a thicket of dead brown bracken where Priedeux could vaguely make out what he thought was a sheep's walk. Gringolay was slapped from behind and he was forced to follow.

As they trotted down, there were rocks hidden in the dry undergrowth and Priedeux realised he would have to keep to the winding path the leader set if he were not to graze himself or lame his horse. The gathering gloom made it worse. Then, as they rounded another bend, the bracken stopped, as if it had been chopped back by a giant sickle and small fields of cultivation began again.

'The home village,' explained Bodres succinctly.

From the escarpment, despite the lack of trees, Priedeux had not noticed the collection of hovels which now spread out before him. He saw small one-roomed huts of wattle and daub, with bracken roofs and heavy woollen rags for doors. They were so lowly built it was as if they were reluctant to emerge from the earth. Priedeux realised that the bracken roofs had hidden the village from the casual glance of a traveller and also guessed that, for warmth, each dwelling had an earthen floor which was sunk into the ground; otherwise they were not tall enough for a man to stand inside. This was totally unlike the hamlet they had passed through before, or others Priedeux had seen in England. There, the serfs tended good strips of land, the houses might be wattle and daub but they were well kept, even, in some places, washed white or another, brighter colour. Here the rough abodes spoke of only one thing: the people did not care or lived such hard lives that they barely existed.

There were perhaps twenty huts, altogether, in a small circle with some trailing up towards their master's castle. Fires were now being lit outside the structures, with one large brazier blazing in the centre of what might be called the village square. Here a man, significant by his huge waist and a frayed liripipe wound round his head and shoulders, was forking meat twisting on a spit, a dog in a closed wheel operating it. He was attended by several skinny curs who slavered, watching the cooking meat intently. A few children crouched nearby. In the dusk, Priedeux was hard pressed to notice the difference between the dogs and the humans.

'The cook,' explained Bodres. 'No point in each family having a large fire so our lord allows enough wood for the cook to roast whatever they want on one spit. Their own small fires will dwindle soon for lack of fuel, even though they use dried cows' and pigs' dung.'

As they rode into the place there was a general murmuring and suddenly out of the huts came people, men with women following, urchins ducking under arms to dash out to see the parade. All were badly dressed and some had the misshapen limbs of early leprosy. Priedeux was surprised they were allowed to stay in the village. For the most part the inhabitants were small and stocky with dark skin as if it had not been scraped clean for many months. Most were hidden in layers of rags and none had leather footwear. They all wore, for shoes, thick rags banded with strips of flax. A poor hungry village. Priedeux had seen many such in parts of France and in the states along the Rhine where wars and plague had ravished the countryside and its people. It was usual for such groups to rush out and assess passers-by. Were they beneficent with a surfeit of silver to shower on them as alms for the good of their souls, or would they demand ransom and fleece the land of its corn and animals? In this village, the occupants kept their distance, watching silently. Priedeux was surprised they did not greet them. After all, Bodres and his men were known, surely. It was to be expected that the children, at least, would venture near, and perhaps ask for alms or welcome their lord's men, returning from some errand for the great lord.

Priedeux knew how much silver spoke, and hoped to be able to at least distribute a few coins as a goodwill gesture for the future. But none of the villagers came near the horsemen. They all stood near their huts and watched sullenly as the party rode by.

'Hey, cook, give a poor traveller a morsel, for I have missed my dinner two nights running because of your henchmen, these jailers of mine.' Priedeux cried as he rode abreast of the blaze.

The cook looked round, brandishing a large basting ladle.

'Heh! You'll not have none of this, for 'tis all us have and us is given and they isn't our henchmen, so get on your way, stranger.' As he looked up one of the mangy curs lunged forward to steal a chop. The cook, as if instinctively, turned quickly, despite his bulk, and whacked the dog on its nose with the ladle and kicked at him at the same time. He lifted the ladle again as the dog cringed.

Suddenly someone broke ranks from the silent crowd, a slim creature wrapped in indeterminate rags, and ran over to the cook and stood between him and the dog.

'Don't you dare do that,' she hissed in a loud whisper, anger making her voice husky but pitched so it carried to the horsemen. 'A good hunting dog is not to be mistreated.' She bent down and touched the dog gently on the snout and it pressed against her, its tail wagging slightly as if unsure whether it should be friendly or not. As she bent down, some stray wisps of hair fell from the rags that made up her head-dress and Priedeux saw in the firelight that it glinted blonde and the girl was unlike her neighbours.

A bastard offspring of the lords of the manor, he thought.

'Here, girl, silver for meat for the cur, I admire your bravery.' He threw her a coin and she looked up at him then and he saw the face. A sharp-featured but clear honest gaze, deep blue eyes. Unafraid, wondering and completely without worldly guile.

'Thank you sir, he shall have the best.' She scrabbled for the dropped coin, picked it up and then ran forward in a gesture indicating she would kiss his feet, but before she could do so, Bodres reined forward and kicked her away. In the same movement, he flicked his reins onto Gringolay so that the animal shied and moved forward. Priedeux looked around at the crowd, but the villagers were turning away now, as if embarrassed. Bodres urged his own horse forward so he led the party again, and stared straight ahead, offering no explanation this time. By the stiffness of his back, Priedeux guessed he was pressing forward, aiming to reach the castle's moated entrance before the rays of the sun finally slid away and dark descended. For there was an air of malice, of sullen, cowed malice, amongst the people, which seemed to hem in around them, even more so now he had singled out the one of them who was so obviously different, the changeling amongst them.

Priedeux smiled to himself, for he knew he had achieved what he wanted. By showing pity and horror at the tableau, he had let these people know that, if he turned up amongst them, he was an escapee from the people they obviously considered their oppressors. He also knew which hut he would head for if he managed to escape, as he watched the girl slide into one of them, nursing the side that had taken the kick. Her hut was set a little back from its neighbours, its entrance covered with a rude woven willow door, rather than rags like the others. Even if she did not live alone, he guessed her parents would care for her enough to offer hospitality, albeit of a simple kind, to someone who had been kind to her.

As they rode up the steep slope towards the entrance of the homestead, the creaking of the drawbridge could clearly be heard as the bridge was lowered to allow them in. In the last rays of the sun, Priedeux noticed the glint of metal in the thin windows and realised that armed men covered their entrance. What sort of place was this, that had to defend itself from its own serfs?

Priedeux wondered too at Bodres and his companions. He had thought they were men to respect, soldiers like him, ruthless but honourable. But Bodres' kicking of the girl seemed senseless. The villagers were cowed and uncared for, and Priedeux knew from his travels that such serfs were usually serfs of cruel, senseless owners, who rode roughshod over them for their own ends. His sense of danger was so enhanced that he could almost smell it, as if there were torturings and needless killings going on around him even at this moment.

Their horses' hooves clopped eerily on the wood of the drawbridge, the evening twilight holding the sound and echoing it back to them,

As they rode through the great portal and the door clanged

down behind them, night fell. Priedeux felt chill, the chill of a dungeon.

They were in a sanded courtyard, he could tell by the sudden silence of the horses' movements. It was gloomy and shadowed with dark now the sun had gone. As Priedeux's eyes adjusted he could see flares being lit and shadowy figures flitting about. Slowly he noticed the strong stone buildings before him. There was a slender staircase leading round the side of a tower and in front of him was an archway richly carved with geometric patterns into which was set a heavy oak door. As he watched, it slowly swung open.

'Come,' said Bodres, holding the reins of Gringolay. 'Dismount and meet your lord!' He said it sardonically and Priedeux slowly swung off his horse, but looked around for a groom.

'Leave it, someone will come eventually,'

'I'll not leave my horse until I know he is groomed and watered. Otherwise 'tis a job I'll carry out.'

'Hah, I thought someone from the King's court would never lower themselves to such menial work.' It was said sarcastically and Priedeux decided not to take up the point about the 'King's court'.

'My horse has carried me far, and will carry me farther still. I respect that and expect him to be treated as well as me, and I am surprised at you, Bodres, a fighting man and horseman, to dream of allowing any horse to be left like this, panting in this cold.'

In the bad light of the courtyard, Priedeux could not see the man's reaction to this but guessed his rough, soldier's honour was dented for he seemed to deliberately turn away, and called:

'Rob, hey, Rob, set to and see to the horses, the guest's first. Move them into the stables and make sure there's hay enough.'

A young man came running up. Priedeux patted the youngster on the back as he took Gringolay and hurriedly obeyed.

'Tend him well, for I'll be checking before bedtime and there'll be silver enough for you.'

The boy nodded and led Gringolay and Bodres' steed away while the other men took their own horses and followed.

Priedeux looked up at the entrance which showed as an oval glare from the flares inside. Silhouetted against the backdrop of light was a robed figure standing, made even larger and more imposing by the shadow thrown onto the courtyard. Obviously his host had seen all that had gone on. Priedeux could not get the measure of the man, as he could only see the silhouette of a person in a full length gown.

Bodres strode quickly up the stairs to his master. .Priedeux followed but as he moved into the beam of light the shadow moved back into the room with a graceful movement. He realised that the shape was not that of a man. He remembered that Bodres had challenged him to meet his *mistress*, so he was not surprised when the figure spoke with the high-pitched tones of a woman.

'Welcome to Storeton,' she said, ironically. It did not sound like a welcome.

The hand that was held out to him was slim and white, the nails too long for a working person.

'Madam, I'm honoured.' He used the same tone as her.

She turned and he followed her into an entrance hall, a square rough-weathered structure with no windows or slits, lit with smoking flares, and with shadowy shapes in corners which Priedeux realised were sleeping dogs, piles of cloaks and discarded weapons. He followed on after her into a hall where there were badly made long tables, already laden with food. Dogs ran amongst a group of men obviously waiting to start eating. There was a central hearth where a fire glowed. Thick acrid smoke rose from the flames, and settled in horizontal ghostly layers just below the rafters. The air was thick with the fumes of badly dried-out logs. The occupants were standing in groups, the whole company being maybe twenty or thirty altogether. Some of them seemed to be leaning towards each other as if whispering secrets or muttering plots. Or so it seemed to Priedeux who remembered what it was like at his own King's court. They did not stop as their mistress came in but raucous laughter welcomed her, as if her entrance reminded them of something they knew about her.

Priedeux could not see into the corners of the great chamber, hidden as they were by the thick greyness of stale smoke. He spotted a large fireplace at the end of the hall, where another fire roared and spluttered as fat dripped from a roasting carcass held by a spit which moved unusually quickly, even though he couldn't tell how it worked, for there was no small boy turning a handle in a corner.

Smells of warm unwashed man and dog, roasting meat and cheap tallow candles, assailed Priedeux as he was led to the daïs at the end where the most sumptuous food was laid. The centrepiece was a boar's head with a tiny bird set amongst its jaws, its wings open and jutting out between the giant tusks at either side. Around the head were set rosettes in delicate pink and yellow creating the effect that the boar was peering from a fully-in-bloom rose hedge. At the back of the head was a giant collar of bright green with gold lace edging.

Behind the high table was a hall-sized Persian carpet hanging by golden ropes, all rose and gold and jade colours. He recognised it as a prize piece from the Orient - he had seen similar booty in Italian villas and wondered how it came to such a barbarous remote place as this.

'Yes, how did it come here,' she echoed his thoughts, and he started.

'Don't worry, I'm no witch to read your very mind,' she said dryly and he wondered anew at her.

'No, all who come and see it wonder.' She paused and then explained, 'my great ancestor, Sir John, was given it by a great Muslim fighter after valiant feats in Jerusalem. I will tell you the story some time.'

Then she gesticulated before her: 'My brother, John, Lord Stanley,'

The man did not rise but leered up at Priedeux. He was already eating and his fingers were greasy with meat fat and he threw bones onto the table before him. His robes were stained as was his blond beard. Priedeux was surprised. Nobody who was a host in any powerful household would start eating until all the assembly both above and below the salt was seated. It was dangerous for a start, in case any of those still standing would lunge with a sword. Eventually he stopped chewing.

'Welcome,' he said with the family irony in his voice. 'Sit, we are all hungry and the messengers were very out with the timing of your arrival. It will be a wonder that everything is not cold. My lady sister, Gertrude, will sit at your right hand. Wine?'

The man proffered a pitcher but then poured more into his own goblet, ignoring his guest. Priedeux approached him but did not immediately sit. He and the woman were within hand's reach of the gastronomic extravaganza of the boar's head. The lady picked a rosette between thumb and forefinger and faced him. She placed it delicately against his lips.

'Taste, eat and enjoy!'

He bit the morsel from her at the same time trying to incise her fingers but she withdrew them too quickly for him. The rosette was made of sugary spices and dissolved quickly on his tongue.

'Sit, sit by the side of me and I will introduce you to the others.'

Priedeux obeyed and the lady lowered herself beside him, her hand brushing his thigh as he straightened her skirts. The company, as if this was their cue, rallied to the benches and quickly took their seats, the hubbub of sibilant whisperings fading.

The brother seemed to have slouched further in his chair, leaning heavily on one of the carved arms, fading into the background of his stronger sister.

The lady clapped her hands and servants came in with pitchers of wine, and with platters of dried bread laden with delicacies, one of which was placed before Priedeux and the mistress. Her brother already had a large pitcher before him and helped himself again after taking a heavy draught from his tankard. Priedeux watched quizzically as wine dribbled from the corner of his mouth, and turned to the sister. She looked at her brother and shrugged.

As he ate, and realised how hungry he was, she leaned towards him and said, in a quiet voice so it did not reach her brother, 'I am Lady Stanley. My brother is in charge. These men, most of them, are cousins, or in-laws, and trash.' The last word was spat out derisively and Priedeux glanced at her in surprise.

'Bodres? His companions? I wounded him badly I fear. They strike me as honourable men.'

'Aye, cousin Ector,' She nodded towards the other man who had been stabbed in the thigh by Priedeux. 'Always in trouble, always being wounded. It is a wonder he has not died of blood poisoning. But he is harmless enough! Bodres! Huh, Bodres. He is different, he will stay as long as he thinks he wants to and will be loyal while he wants to. If he decides at any time that he is not getting his rightful reward and someone else offers him something more attractive, he will be gone. Enough, ignore such trash - and enjoy the nobility!' Again Priedeux noted the irony in her voice.

As she spoke Priedeux looked across at Ector who sat below the salt, indicating his low rank even though he was a knight. He was nodding vigorously to his neighbour, holding up his thigh to view, where the dagger had pierced. He looked as if he were boasting. Priedeux turned back to the lady.

She raised a thin, well-shaped eyebrow at him. 'Yes, trash, they all eat at our table and go to wars, or hunt the stag or whatever, but are no use at all. Look at our Ector now, he is probably claiming the wound he has sustained was given in a rout where he killed ten men, and gaining points for prowess, but, if the truth were known, it will turn out he just made a wrong move himself.'

Priedeux said nothing, remembering the fight at Chester. Gertrude continued: 'For some reason my brother expects them to be here, to be fed as if they reinforced his so-called authority.' She leant forward and looked at her brother, whose eyes were half-closed now, as he sunk into a drunken stupor. 'Aah, if only I were a man.'

'You make a wonderful woman, if I may say so.'

Priedeux could now see her face fully in the bright glares from the fire and the cooking spit. He decided to be gallant. It was easy. She had the white heart-shaped face that was the fashion, the forehead high, the chin pointed, a delicate dimple in the middle of it. The lips were small and madder red, the eyes clear and blue. But there was an arrogance about the high thin eyebrows which now rose in derision at his simple compliment, and her voice, when she answered, held a cynicism in it, which was out of place for one so seemingly young. The blue of the eyes was too cold, too ice-glass blue for comfort. As he studied her, he had to look down, her gaze was so penetrating. He concentrated on his food. He really was very hungry, and the sumptuousness and smells accentuated his hunger.

She laid her soft hand on his sleeve, stopping him as he was about to bite into the flesh of a large rib that had been part of the delicacies.

'You *may say so*, if that is the way of compliments at court, for I guess you have travelled and lived well?'

He could feel the soft wool of her well-spun gown against his hand where the sleeve splayed out in fashionable openness. It was plain, with rich decorations of embroidery along the seams, and a belt of gold and rose embroidery hanging down between her legs, accentuating their shape. Priedeux eyed her up and down but, after gathering his composure, returned to gaze into her eyes, choosing to confront the coldness he found there.

'You laugh at me, Madam. A simple traveller that I am.'

The eyebrows rose again and she wiped her mouth delicately with her fingers and then licked them one by one. 'Simple? Traveller? With a fine palfrey that would trot under a king and warrants with a king's seals! Now *you* mock me.'

He nodded in acknowledgement. 'A traveller I am, and in this place I *am* simple for I know not this country and would rest on such hospitality as this I am being given, and trust it is for the King's purpose and good.'

'You are welcome to such mean hospitality as we can give.' Again it was said so cynically that he doubted she had any true charity within her. She went on:

'But we must entertain you! What are your delights? Bear-baiting, cock-fighting?'

He shrugged. He'd never had much use for such pastimes. Although he could kill a man if necessary, blood-lust was not a vice of his. He killed for necessity and forgot about it. He hated to see others' excitements when there was a killing. He remembered the condemned girl being hanged and the crowd who crowed for her to go first, and was grateful that the hangman had seen fit to end her agony so quickly. Priedeux favoured the rapid cut of the throat that ended all torment.

'Or perhaps something more?' He was brought back to this woman. He hated to hear the suppressed excitement in her voice at her suggestion of cruel sport.

Saying nothing, he stolidly chewed on the viands placed before him. She leant over and reached for her brother's pitcher of wine. He smelt the delicacy of rich roses, a perfume that reminded him of the east, as resonant as the Persian rug behind them. Suddenly, instead of being an attractive smell, it cloyed his very innards. It was too strong, too resonant of death on this woman. He did not protest as she poured more of the liquid into the large cup he had been given. She watched him all the while, and, when he lifted the filled cup to his lips and took a large gulp, she nodded, as if satisfied. A thin smile stretched her lips, a cold calculating smile. She picked a morsel from his plate, her hand brushing his, and ate it delicately. She continued to take small portions from before him, placing them on her plate and playing with them. It was like a bird of prey picking at morsels, softening them before consuming the pieces. Slowly the rich dishes stopped appearing and those on the table emptied, picked clean, so that the guests were only left with horns of ale or goblets of wine. Some men were drooping, their heads falling onto their arms, goblets a-tumbling.

Gertrude looked around the room, wiping her hands slowly with a cloth dipped in a bowl of water that was offered to her, and Priedeux was reminded of the story of Pontius Pilate. When she had done, she stood, a rapid movement, and surveyed the dinner guests. Suddenly she clapped her hands, making everyone jump. There was a silence. Some of the men looked afraid; others stared at her with obvious admiration. The flames on the fire sparked up, as if also jumping to her attention. Dogs stopped roaming and waited, fazed by the unusual silence.

'Gentlemen, we have an unusual guest with us tonight, let us entertain him royally.'

A general embarrassed guffaw arose and she snapped her fingers. Into the centre of the hall was led a chained prisoner, dirty and half-clothed in rags. Priedeux recognised the clothes of a villager, rough and grey. The man was led in by two guards, who held him up. His head rested on his chest, so that

Priedeux could not see his face. It was obvious that he had been tortured and was on the verge of collapse; dried blood caked that part of his forehead that could be seen and there was a wound on one side of his ribs, which was sunk in, indicating that he had been kicked until bones broke. He was barefoot and his legs were darkened with what Priedeux recognised was the beginning of gangrene in his lower limbs.

'A trial, we will have a trial,' declaimed the lady. 'Who complains of this man's crime?'

Lord Stanley did not protest as his sister took charge, and Priedeux was disgusted to see that he had wet himself and was now deep in a drunken coma.

A heavily bearded blear-eyed lord struggled up. As he spoke, he revealed lascivious lips, answering his mistress. 'My lady, with your leave, I bring complaint against this man.'

'My Lord Roland. 'Tis you again, with your ready tongue! Go on,' she sounded as if she were threatening him. The accused slumped further forward as if the very words were another assault upon him, but his guards roughly hauled him up to a semi-standing position.

The 'prosecutor' swaggered forward and stood before the accused, turning his back on him.

'My lady. This man stands accused...' The crowd sniggered, as if they knew what was coming, 'he stands accused of being a poor man.' The guests guffawed as he continued, 'who refused to look me in the eye.'

The whole crowd laughed now, the lady smiling grimly. Priedeux turned to her.

'Why is that so funny?'

She patted his knee, as if to console him for being outside the joke.

'And who would want to look you in the face, ugly as you are, Lord Roland?' asked the lady.

'This one must, when I order him, for he is my serf, as you well know. I accuse him and my evidence is that he would not look at me.'

Again there was loud laughter.

The prisoner slumped between his guards once more and again they pulled him upright. Gertrude stood up and slowly, sinuously, moved from her place at the top table and stepped from the daïs. As she moved she slid her hand along the back of Priedeux's chair and his hair stood on end at this almost nothing touch. He could not help admire the sensuality of her slim body as it moved in a leonine lope towards the group in the centre of the hall, while at the same time feeling a great repulsion.

He could clearly see the shape of her buttocks through the woollen cloth, pulled tight as it was by the belt. She approached the sorry prisoner and stood in front of him for a second.

'And why would you not look at your lord, cur?' she spat out.

'Look at *me* now!' And she lifted the head so that she was face to face with the creature. Priedeux realised with horror that where the man's eyes were supposed to be were blackened sockets. He stood up in disgust.

'The man's eyes have been gouged out, for God's sake! What sort of game is this?'

She turned back to him.

Smiling, she said: 'Our guest doesn't like our little game. Are they all lily-livered at court then?' She paced the room like a cat. 'Shall we show our guest what our Storeton maids are capable of, so he should fear you men?'

The diners had risen slightly at Priedeux's outburst but now they all sat down again, looking sheepish. Priedeux realised the man next to him, his host, was oblivious to the proceedings, still slumped in his alcoholic haze. Priedeux felt like shaking him, to admonish him for allowing his sister to take charge in such a cruel and bizarre manner. Before he could act, the one she had named as Roland came forward, brandishing a large dagger, a cross between a knife and a sword.

'Here, m'lady, you show him what Lady Storeton can do, if serfs don't obey their masters.'

The graceful female took the proffered weapon and turned slowly back to the prisoner. There was a sudden, hungry silence in the room. The fire subsided, and Priedeux realised the room was clear of smoke, as if the entrance of the guards and their prey had left an escape route. This meant he could see quite clearly what was going on. There was a deep sigh beside Priedeux and he saw that the seemingly comatose lord was awake. He was craning forward now, his face taut and all the languid cynicism and drunkenness held in abeyance.

Gertrude raised the dagger high and before Priedeux could jump across the trestle to stop her she had plunged it into the sagging serf's belly, held it there for a fraction when Priedeux swore she twisted it as if she were trying to spear a wriggling worm, and then withdrew it holding the bloodied knife aloft. Priedeux looked down, knowing that the man's guts would be falling out of him.

There was a deep sigh from around the hall and when Priedeux looked up again the guards were carrying the body out. Dogs scampered forward to lick the remains from the floor. Then there was a hubbub of cheering and clapping and excitement. Priedeux, against his better instincts, felt it too, the excitement of the chase, of the bloodied cheek, of conquering a protesting virgin.

Gertrude returned to the place beside him and he felt her hot hand on his thigh. Her brother was again seeking more wine, but this time his eye was bright and greedy looking, and he watched his sister walking back to them with what Priedeux could only describe as lasciviousness.

'Was that good entertainment?' she asked huskily, ignoring her brother. Priedeux stared at her and noticed her eyes were dark and hooded, the clear blue turning to the muddy azure of a turbulent sea. He could feel the sensuousness of her like rich wine. He wondered what would happen next.

Chapter Seven: A romantic interlude

'Now quickly you are caught! If we come not to terms
I shall bind you in your bed,...here fast I shall enfold you'

There was a slight tap at the door of the bedroom to where he had been led shortly after. He was expecting it. The light tap of a woman who would enter without being invited, who knew what she wanted and would take it. A woman who didn't care if she hurt those she hated – or loved.

He pulled the door open, backing off quickly and standing against the heavy panels of the wall behind the door. Gertrude stepped rapidly into the room, and shut the door behind her.

They gazed at each other in the flickering light from the flare held high in a sconce in the wall. The flickering made their faces mobile and she seemed to be smiling, but it was a smile that made Priedeux very wary. There was a strange pause. Had she come to murder him? Or to reveal something to him? He stood watching her, she watching him. It occurred to Priedeux that she too, although in her own home, might wonder if this evening would end in her murder by this stranger's hand. But why had she come? Her eyes, which he could just see in the wavering light, were opaque, still with the darkness of the kill. She still wore the woollen dress and he could see her breasts moving as she took quick sharp breaths.

Then they fell on each other, hungrily, she grabbing his vital parts and manipulating in a way that no innocent unmarried lady should know how. He stroked the topmost part of her spine, testing her reaction. She arched towards him, and, in response he slid his hand down, pressing her body to his and undoing the buttons all the way down the back of the dress, slowly, gently, feeling at the same time, the curves of the shoulders, the waist, that part at the small of her back between the well-shaped buttocks, feeling for her warm moistness. Then the dress was loose and he pulled her to him so that she stopped her manipulations and grasped his shoulders, gasping with desire. For a moment they looked at each other and she stepped away so that the dress fell down. She stood naked before him, no shift or petticoat to protect her. He stepped away from her and surveyed her body, which was as shapely as the Greek statues he had seen in eastern ruins, glimmering like gold in the candlelight. Then, as if she was magnet and he iron, she pulled him to her again and their mouths met.

He lifted her so that her head swept back in an ecstasy of surprise and carried her to the richly covered bed. He threw her on it as he unbelted his jerkin and with a quick movement he pulled down his hose. She lay there watching him, her eyes resting on his erection, her legs writhing together to try to satisfy her own lust until he took her by the knees and separated them, kneeling himself now between her legs. She lifted herself up so her face was level with his member and tried to take it in her mouth but he laughed:

'Oh no my lady, I'll not trust your hungry mouth with that,' He pushed her back on the bed, aimed and thrust as if his penis was a dagger striking her pliant belly.

He writhed inside her and felt her tauten, using muscles to sing him into climax. She was moist and warm and there were ripples of delight for him within her that he had never experienced before. He couldn't control himself.

But then she stopped, abruptly. Pulled herself away from under him as if she were a slippery succuba and crouched at the end of the bed where he had to turn to see her. In the dim night light skimmering from the sconce her face looked skeletal - all concave eye sockets, sharp chin and skull. He pulled her to him and saw she was grinning.

'Oh, no, my Lord,' she said ironically, 'You'll not take your pleasure that easily!'

He held her by her shoulders and kissed her, hard, pushing his straining member against her belly. She went limp and he pushed her back on the bed and penetrated her once more. Again her tendril-like rhythms began to tighten against him and he moved with them, feeling his way to them, joining with her until they writhed together and their movements became as one dance.

Time seemed to stand still or at least was not part of this episode in his life.

At one point he opened his eyes and realised she was astride him, mouth half open in ecstasy, her eyes staring into another world.

She was muttering: 'Faster, oh faster, deeper, oh, deeper,' and he thrust upward in response. Her thighs gripped him and he knew she was a good horsewoman, the thought flashing through his mind like an irreverence. Still she rode on, forcing him to join the ecstasy of her ride, although he knew she was oblivious to him. This excited him even more; a woman who could lose herself in such a gallop.

Then he knew he could hold back no longer and at the same time she arched to suck in his throbbing manhood even deeper and they climaxed together.

There was a pause where both of them seemed to be totally still, and it was as if his whole life flashed before him, as if he were dying, as if his very guts had been ripped from him by this woman.

She fell on him in a spasmodic movement as if she too had died. He felt the cold sweat on her but then came peace and they relaxed. He fell asleep immediately.

He woke to find one arm dead where her weight rested on it. Somehow a rich coverlet of embroidered damask had been pulled over their naked bodies. He realised it was part of the curtains of the bed which had been ripped down, as if of no consequence. Priedeux could not remember how both of them had become stripped of their clothes, it had been so frenetic. The wax had burnt low now and left only a dim glow but he could sense she was deep asleep, her breathing rhythmic. By the burning of the candle he knew it must still be dead of night.

He felt rather than saw the softness of her breasts, his fingers rounding to the dark nipple which stood proudly erect and gently he fingered it, to be rewarded by a soft sigh and her backside being pressed into his body. He caressed both breasts and moved his hand down her belly to the soft down and played with this, feeling its edges. It was soft short down. Then he swung her round and looked closely in the dim light, and saw she shaved the hair there into a delicate shape that looked like the head of a deer.

She was wide awake now and laughed as he looked up at her face.

'Aye, 'tis well done, is it not? A fashion I heard about from cousins in the Ile de France.'

'Indeed, 'tis most fascinating , I haven't seen such before.'

He continued to play with it, moving further into the softness between her legs and she opened them and lay back as if in pure luxury.

This time he entered her gently, playfully, but soon there again was that strong urgency that made them exert themselves to a mutual agony of orgasm.

She went back to sleep as if he hadn't woken her. As her breathing became deeper, accentuating his aloneness, he started to think. This was a rich place, and the occupants seemed to be rebellious, a law unto themselves. Could this be the court he was looking for? He remembered what Chaucer had said: 'An educated man, very educated. He knows his Latin and his Greek. A hunting man? A man with many books. A man who loves materials, the touch of them, the cloth of gold, the silk, the soft wool. A man who knows what good food is and knows his hunting lore.

'And, finally, a man who knows the courtly rules of love but also enjoys celebrating his yuletide in style.'

Certainly this place was a place of love, but courtly love? There *was* good food and fine materials of silk, Priedeux thought, as he remembered the Persian rug hanging on the wall behind the daïs, and he fingered the damask covering him. He noticed now the fine hangings of brocade in this room. Someone here liked good materials. And he remembered how she had ridden him.

'You like hunting, my lady?'

She woke immediately, and turned to him. He could not see her face, in the darkness, but heard her laugh. 'Aye, I find it most erotic. I dressed in my brother's garb as a young girl, when I was, as they say, just blooming, and the thrill of the hunt and the hard chase! Aah, 'tis impossible to describe the feeling. I still go now - my vassals accept that I play the man's part in my country. No silly nag for me and half-following.'

She spoke excitedly. If he *was* looking for someone who knew their hunting skills then this place would certainly fit, even though her brother seemed a weakling. Could it be a blind, a trick to curb further investigation? He considered the other criteria. A bookish man, who knew Latin, and many old tales. The brother had said hardly anything and it was only the killing of the serf that had aroused him. Priedeux could imagine the brother enjoying seeing heads chopped off and men being teased and pushed to endurance as Gawain had been. Yes, Priedeux could imagine him gloating over that. He had to find out whether there was a library here. If there was, and he could find out whether these seemingly unholy siblings took delight in books, he would have further proof that this could be the place he was seeking.

When Gertrude woke in the pale dawn she was softly

pliant, only half awake, when Priedeux said gently, almost as if he too were still half asleep. 'Your family must be great to have such fine hangings?'

'Oh, all brought back from wars, as trophies, stolen,' she said scornfully, lifting herself on one elbow. 'My ancestors were great pillagers, not like the half-bake you saw last night, my brother!'

'Why, he could be pretending, or bored. Maybe he is a bookish man who hides in his library?'

She laughed aloud then and stroked his face from eye to chin as if she were taking the measure of him: 'Oh, stranger, *my Lord,* you truly disappoint me. I thought you had travelled the world and had good knowledge of human nature, but now I know different. Surely anyone could tell that the drunkenness my brother portrayed last night was habitual?' She continued to stroke his face, and then moved her finger down to touch the collar-bone that stood out from the skin. She went on:

'As for reading. Huh, he could barely drag himself to the monks to be shown his alphabet - I learnt quicker than he at my mother's knee. Why do you think all obey *me* and not him? Why do you think he soaks up the wine each night and says nothing as I rule here? 'Tis because *I* can read and no-one else here can. So I do the books, send out orders, receive the king's messengers when they come, even though that is infrequently. *I control here.'*

As she said this last she was stroking his member into attention.

'So,' he said, trying to ignore the gathering need of her again, trying to remember his mission, to keep his train of thought. 'So, *you* are the one with the library, with the Latin and Greek?'

She continued to play with him, looking down, but then turned quickly and climbed on top of him, falling exactly into place so that he thrust directly into her. As she writhed, as if riding on an early morning gallop, she answered: 'Library! Huh, with all my activity,' with this she thrust down extra hard, 'with all this activity, what time do I get to read books? As for Latin and Greek, I know enough of the legal words to make sense to send out orders and to run rings round our scrivener who is always trying to cheat us. *I* was the one who had the hunger to know, so that the clerk of works taught me the book-keeping and the record-keeping; I was even taught the new accounting system from Italy.'

'Books.' She stopped, agonisingly for Priedeux, and sat still, he still high inside her: 'Nay, I learn all I need to learn by practice, by doing,' and with this she thrust away again.

He smiled up at her, for there was humour in this lovemaking of hers and she smiled back. They began to laugh then, he at the incongruity of this animal of a woman poring over books for hours.

She played with him, moving gently, clutching and unclutching at him in the movements he remembered from last night.

'And where, pray,' he gasped as he moved with her, 'where did you learn such lovemaking?'

And as he climaxed inside her she too stopped and gripped him, as if this was for him and not her, but when he opened his eyes her face was in a spasm of climax and he could feel the continuing contractions still, gripping and pulling at him, even though he was spent.

They lay there for a while, he not believing she would answer his question. When at last she did it turned him cold.

All she said was: 'I was indoctrinated by a cousin, but he is dead now.'

Chapter Eight: Escape

'First he was found faultless in his five wits.
next, his five fingers never failed the knight...'

'We will breakfast here, for I need to talk to you now I know what kind of man you are.'

He responded by looking at her mockingly as he finished his toilet that had been started when she left the room to give orders. He had not wanted to dress in front of her, to reveal the padding and other secrets of his attire. He hoped that the wild activity of the night before had not given her an opportunity to see the padded shirt he wore inside his jerkin, nor the small weapons tucked into boot and sleeve. She had returned quietly and was now clothed in a different fine woollen gown, this time of soft cream, and her hair was coiled up around her ears and held by a stiff netting. Despite the change of clothing, she smelt of the odours of sex, a musky acrid smell and he noted with mild disgust that she did not have the practice of regular bathing. She had not taken the opportunity when she left at dawn to wash away the aroma of their lovemaking.

'So what kind of man am I?' he asked lightly.

'After last night, I know,' she smiled. ''Tis a true test of a man's nature, to bed him and try him out.'

'And what have you found out about me?'

Instead of answering, she turned and ordered him to sit and he obeyed, balancing on the corner of the bed, leaning against the elegantly carved post, his legs astride. She turned her back on him and sat between his legs in a position both trusting and secret, looking away from him so he could not see her features, to avoid giving away any secret emotion, he guessed. He remembered how she had turned away when she had mentioned the cousin.

'Let me tell you a story,' she said by way of answer, 'This is an Italian tale, let us say from Perugia or Florence. There was a man called Vinciolo, who liked to play his tune with men rather than with women. Oh yes, I know of such things, you just have to watch my brother, although he will go with a woman as well.

Vinciolo however decided to take a wife for society's sake and the need for heirs, and chose a buxom redheaded wench whom he thought all his friends would admire and envy. She was called Rosamonda. Soon Rosamonda realised how matters stood and was angry and disappointed at first, but like most women she was practical when it came to such things. After looking around for some time, she approached a much older lady friend of hers and confided in this woman as if she were a priest. She arranged with the older woman for her to procure young men whom Rosamonda approved of. The lady friend would bring these young men to the house as guests and thus allay any suspicions of Vinciolo. It was as if Rosamonda was ordering her very own love playmates.

'This worked very successfully for some time and Rosamonda became quite content. She was happy to use the men as studs, never losing her heart to any one of them. Then she saw a youth of great handsomeness, so handsome that both men and women swooned over him, whom I will call Pietro. Pietro was duly propositioned and visited her. They found the arrangement to mutual satisfaction so that Pietro became her regular lover.'

'What is the reason of this story, Gertrude?' interrupted Priedeux, who found the facts arousing, but Gertrude removed his hands from where they were manipulating her nipples

103

through the cloth of her dress and, taking a deep breath, continued. 'One day her husband was due to go to dinner with a friend and as soon as Rosamonda knew this, she made the necessary arrangements for an intimate supper with Pietro. Her husband left, Pietro arrived and they commenced their hors d'oeuvres before supper. But the summer heat and their exertions sent them to sleep and they did not hear Vinciolo return unexpectedly because of a domestic problem at his friend's house. He came to search for his wife so she could prepare supper for him but found instead the two wrapped in sleep. He took one look at the boy and lust filled him.

He waited behind an arras that separated the bed from the toiletries in the chamber and in due course lust woke his wife and her lover. He watched as they entwined and made love again. At one point they were spooned together with the lad entering his wife from behind. This was too much for Vinciolo and he crept to the bed and carefully entered the boy from the back.'

Priedeux remained perfectly still, waiting for the story to finish. His face was impassive. Gertrude turned now and faced him.

'The boy, who had been taught most of his knowledge by Rosamonda and being in deep passion thought she had somehow managed to reach round, and to tell the truth he found it a further stimulus to the point where his thrustings became urgent. All three on the bed became so excited that what seed they had was sown at one and the same time with a great concerted orgasm. Then the boy fell back and realised there was a man behind him. He was so confused he said nothing believing that Rosamonda had perhaps arranged it and that it was part of their game. After that, many times Vinciolo joined them in their couplings, so that it could be said the husband and wife truly did consummate their marriage, even though it was through an intermediary.' She ended up laughing, and the laughter was cruel.

Priedeux found himself smiling with her but said, 'and the moral of the tale?'

'As I said, I can tell what sort of man you are. Shocked at nothing, you would go to the outer bounds of such things if it pleased you...'

Priedeux jumped up then, leaving Gertrude stumbling to retain her place on the bed.

'Madam, you are wrong. I know men do such things and I know that many crusades were organised so the men had an excuse to leave their womenfolk behind to follow their own pleasures. But I'll have none of that, I assure you.'

Again she laughed and it was a cruel cackle, unsuited to her beauty and more seeming of an old hag.

'Thank you. Again I know what sort of man you are! I like to try and test before I commit myself. I try it on, that story, every time!'

'Commit yourself? Try it on?'

'Aye, I know I must some time, and I will always try out my lovers and strangers....'

'And you have had many?'

'For the sake of my family, you understand,' she answered, turning to the window and looking out upon a grey scene, where there was a soft drizzle dulling the outside world, so as to ignore his gaze upon her. 'I must wed, I know that, but I will not be wed to some lily-livered local lord who will abandon me at the first opportunity.'

'Wed?' Priedeux was surprised. She had turned and was facing him and had her head on one side, assessing him, as if he were a prize stallion.

He shook his head. 'Madam, I am a knight of fortune, you understand...'

She moved towards him as if to take him in her arms, a persuasive gesture. Her movement was interrupted by a tapping at the door.

'Come in,' she said imperiously, turning away.

The door was flung open by an invisible hand and in marched lackeys with a table and benches which they positioned near the narrow gap of a window; then followed wenches who laid out platters of fruits and cold cuts from the feast last night. Others brought pitchers of ale and goblets.

When they had gone, Gertrude gestured for Priedeux to sit, in the same imperious manner she had used earlier. When he was opposite her she cut slices of hog and beef, tore off a leg and wing of fowl and placed them before him.

Priedeux decided to eat and eat well and wait for this woman to start talking again. He would give nothing away.

'As I was saying,' she eventually continued, wiping her mouth with the back of her hand and licking it clean. 'I will choose my own husband, if he is to be lord and master of me. My brother is not strong enough to control the others and I would have someone who can fight, like you, someone who has experience of the world, like you, and, if possible, someone who knows the intrigues and the ways of the Court. Like you?' The last was definitely a question and Priedeux wondered how much she knew of him. The equipment he carried, and the mark on the horse would indicate he was favoured by the highest in the land. Had her servants heard the bowmen maintain that the seal was false? Or did these people still believe him to be the true emissary of the King? Best to accept that she thought he was a high official working for the King, with the attendant rank. Her lackeys had seen him arrested by the Chester men, and then he had been released, so what had they made of that?

'Like me, Madam? What makes you think I am of the King's court?'

'Aah, well, that *is* a question.' She looked away and licked her fingers again, which had become greasy with the food she was eating. As she removed each finger from her mouth in a deliberate sucking motion that made Priedeux shudder, she listed various points. 'Well, there is the Royal mark on the horse, but that could be stolen; the pass that you carry; but rumour has it that this is false. If that is so, how did you walk out of the Chester dungeons? Truly you are a mystery man, and I care not whether you are the King's man, or a fraud, or your own man. I would have you on my side rather than fighting my men. And killing one of them For which I ought to punish you.'

When she had finished speaking she took a cloth and wiped her hands in the Pontius Pilate movement she had used the night before, showing she would eat no more.

Priedeux said nothing. He took a leg of chicken and broke it carefully and bit into the thin meat along the bone. She watched for a while and then continued, her voice softening: 'So, I would suggest an alliance between us. I would use your skills and experience of the world. If you marry me, you will have an interest in this land, and can live the life of a nobleman.'

He shrugged. 'True, I have experience of the world but that experience has taught me that I am not a marrying man.'

'But you are offered good hunting. Your own domain. A warm bed of a winter's night and a warm woman to bed with. Surely that is all a man wants?'

He carried on pulling at the tender flesh of the chicken leg and stuffed a portion into his mouth and did not answer. He could see she was impatient with him, but he stayed silent, thinking about it.

She continued, persuasively. 'And there is the little matter of the ferry at Birkenhead. The Prior – yes, those henchmen belonged to the priory - has beaten us once too many times and I need someone who can either convince him with a little force, or with diplomatic good sense, to persuade the King to lessen his powers. The Prior, in the name of the King, or so he claims, charges too much to pass from the lands across the water and this is stopping those who would come from Wales into my lands, and we are then losing our tolls. You could lead my men in a visit and I am sure you could persuade him to lower his ferry price?' She paused and added. 'Or perhaps use your influence at court?'

He laughed at this, for if he had any, it was a behind-the-scenes, shadowy influence, and he did not know if any petition made by him on such matters would work with his lord. He considered her proposition, as he continued to enjoy the food.

His standing at court was precarious, shadowy, he was called by Gaunt when he was needed. Otherwise, he sat below the salt and pretended to be a knight. In reality, he was a nobody who knew many secrets, who had access to the highest in the land but only at their bidding and usually behind closed doors. He might have ambitions to marry an heiress but he knew it would be unlikely.

He considered his possible future, which could not be foretold, but he knew for sure there would be no manor house for him to retire to when the time came. Even if he succeeded in his present mission, his reward could just as well be a bag of silver as a manor house. It depended on the importance of the poet, he supposed, to his master, and the necessity of being rid of him. The least he could expect was his living expenses and free board and lodging at his master's houses. This was the first time he had ever thought of the future, expecting to die in battle or by some unforeseen assassin's knife. He had seen action in the field and plagues and knew he lived only to die and was not one to think of a future of old and dependent age. Most of the men he knew, he knew but briefly, before they were killed or died of their wounds, plague or some other disease.

On the other hand, if the need arose, he had laid up a few favours with many and he could call on them. He remembered the knight he had fought with in Portugal, Sir Hugh...but the surname would not come. Now *he* certainly owed Priedeux some favours and when he had retired to the country, he had invited Priedeux to visit. Priedeux had saved his life many times in battles, if he could remember where he had gone after he'd retired from court, he was sure he would be given a home with him. Never mind, Gaunt was more accessible. Priedeux was sure that even strong royal Gaunt would pay a pension if he petitioned him.

Even so, when he fully contemplated it now, he realised his future was uncertain. This woman was offering him a home, position and herself. He looked at her as she stood over him, and smiled. She was eyeing him, her head on one side. The company at the feast of the night before convinced him that the brother was indeed weak and most of the others could be controlled with diplomacy and tact. The place *was* comfortable with rich hangings and the food he was eating and had eaten last night was tasty and well prepared. The orgy of lovemaking with this woman convinced him that his sexual appetite would be satisfied, for she was an inventive, lascivious and greedy lover. What else could a man want, after all, as she so rightly said?

'I am a travelling man, it would be difficult to settle in one place, I am sure.'

She smiled, 'there is good hunting here, for a man who likes to ride hard.'

'Aah, but that is always with others and the excitement would be marred by the boundary of beaters.'

There was a silence. They understood each other well. She was offering him a pleasure prison. He would no longer be a free man.

She confirmed this by saying, still with a smile but her forehead was creased, making the eyes seem smaller. 'Yes, there would always be my men watching you. That is true. For I would not live the shame of an abandoned wife, no matter what the excuse be, crusade or service at court.' She stood, her long hands resting on the table like crab's claws.

'But the matter is not negotiable. You are here now and you saw how my men claimed you. In this part of the world I am all powerful My spies are always watching and alert me to a man that fits the type I seek. They bring these men to me. There have been many but none have passed the test like you. Stay with me.'

It sounded almost attractive, until she added. 'You cannot escape. So, the choice is yours!' The last she said so cruelly, that he knew that death awaited him if he baulked her.

He dropped the remainder of the bones that he had gnawed as she spoke, satiated. He too stood and moved away from the table, taking his drink with him. He knew she would stay silent while he thought over her offer. Taking a draught of the ale, he looked out of the slit of a window and saw the dull heavy sky of cloud, and the drizzle, which misted over the horizon. With the bitter weather outside, it would be easy to accept her offer.

However, he remembered the job he had been sent to do. He might be able to stay in this unholy place, and, if he were really lucky, he might discover that this was indeed the court he was seeking with the renegade writer. All he had to do was to kill the writer, find a way of reporting to Gaunt, and he was free. For the moment he was in the dry, and safe, which, for a fighting man, was all that could be expected. In his long travels with Gaunt, he had never worried about the wet and cold before. Was it because he was nearing the age when most men were well married and settled? Was he changing? He could not see far but he knew there were forests hereabouts where there would be good hunting, if that took his fancy. He knew he could ride fast if he had to and reckoned he could evade any who gave chase if the need arose. Could he bluff his way and remain here, enjoying the comforts but also ensuring his job was done and then escape?

Then he remembered the so-called entertainment of the night before. The way the woman had bandied with the serf, the way she had tortured him, strutting and crowing over him. The cruelty and needless stabbing and the laughter which echoed in his head now, the day after. He recalled the story that had been the start of his quest, *Gawain and the Green Knight*. Although there was the beheading of the green knight at Arthur's court, and the teasing of Gawain at the end, there was no needless cruelty and the whole story was based on the concept of courtly manners. He was sure that this house, with its dissolute lord and this unholy woman, could never be a haven for the one who had written *Gawain and the Green Knight*.

And the story she had just related, where did a woman hear of such things? And store them for future reference? Indeed, she was cruel and corrupt beyond measure and Priedeux, never one for worrying about his soul, worried now, for he thought her a very she-devil.

What he found so horrifying was his need for her after the cruelty, after the story. Suddenly he put his drink down as if the ale had burned his mouth. He returned to her.

'You sound like the very devil himself, tempting our Lord,' he said laughing, and carried on in the same bantering tone: 'If I am to be your consort, perhaps we should find out more about each other?' And he stretched over and gently stroked her breast through the soft wool. She smiled at him, the hardness in her face melting into the softness of a person ready for sex.

'But first, my lady, the privy, I need the privy for what I have will fill the piss pot.'

She laughed. 'Outside, at the end of the corridor, I have a good privy.'

He gathered his cloak around him, for he was aware of the cold of such places, and left the room. Outside there was an armed servant, sword and dagger well in evidence, but he nodded as Priedeux passed.

Somehow he had to escape. The windows were small and it would be impossible to jump out. There were probably other armed servants at doors and exits. He would not be able

111

to leave easily, and as he opened the door to the privy, he was beginning to think it would be impossible.

The privy was gloomy and cold, with bare stone walls and stained smelly straw on the floor. The seat was of wood, well shaped and polished and Priedeux smiled, realising that Gertrude really did think of her own comfort. As Priedeux sat with bared buttocks he realised there was cold air breezing its way from below. When he had finished he looked down and could see specks of light. He realised this privy had a large outlet beneath him, where no doubt serfs would clear the human excrement and use the muck as compost. He was impressed for not many houses had such a system, although Richard, with his namby pamby ways, had introduced them into the Royal household, along with the effete handkerchief. Priedeux had last seen one of these new types of privies in a knight's house in Kent a few years ago and the method had been explained to him by the owner.

He returned to the room to find his hostess wrapped in the brocaded coverlet with one bare foot extended which she gently rotated, beckoning to him. He needed no other encouragement for, despite his reluctance to make his present situation a permanent one, he still found her exciting and enticing.

In spite of this, he knew he did not want to stay and even as he entered her again was thinking of ways to escape.

Afterwards he watched as her eyelids fluttered and she fell asleep. He felt her body relax and grow heavy in his arms and he gently pulled away from her and rose. He had not undressed and quickly buttoned himself up. Stealthily, as he had trained himself, he filled his panniers, grabbing at some of the food off the table, and then, watching her sleeping all the while, he strapped the panniers around his waist, each one hanging down the side of his hips. Then, after checking the tightness of the knots, he flung his cloak around him again.

He gently let himself out and nodded at the guard

muttering: 'Too much wine and good food.' He made his way to the privy once more.

When he reached it, he inspected the wooden seat. As he suspected, it was a loose slat of wood placed on top of a stone-built shelf, the revealed hole being much larger than the gap in the seat. He pulled it off and slotted it under the door handle for there was no lock on the door. That would stop anyone but the most determined visitor for some time. Then he looked down the hole. He could see nothing but a tiny speck of light, so tiny he wondered for a second whether the hole which let in the light would be large enough for a man of his bulk. It was only two storeys up and he was not afraid. He only hoped there would be something soft, albeit smelly, to cushion his fall.

He stood for a few seconds astride the hole. He loosened the panniers and threw them down.

'So, now I'm committed or I've lost all,' he muttered to himself. He tied his cloak between his legs so that it remained tight against his body. Then he levered himself into the hole, so that his whole body was hanging down, only his fingertips holding him there, said a short prayer and let himself go. He kept his arms above him to keep as slender as possible, so that his whole shape was straight as a Cheshire bowman's arrow.

For a second he wondered what had happened, the force of the fall leaving him dazed. He stayed still but a moment, recovering his breath. From his crouched, fallen position he could see the courtyard of the manor house. He had landed in muck but it was not as bad as he had thought it would be, for the cold weather had frozen over most of the shit except for what had been deposited in the last few hours, which was damp and slimy. He screwed up his nose against the smell but felt that a covering of shit was a small price to pay for the first stage in his escape.

The courtyard was empty. From where he stood, he could see that the rain had changed from drizzle to heavier pounding sheets. He guessed that most of the lords were sleeping off the excesses of the night before and the servants would all be indoors, hiding from the downpour, believing that none of their so-called superiors would yet be awake and abroad. Priedeux pulled himself out of the mire and stood against the wall and surveyed the area. He was quite content to let the rain and the heavy drips from the overhang of the wall soak into the material, which was spattered and stained with excrement. The gate was closed and for the moment he could see no way out of the courtyard, bounded on three sides by the house and barns. He decided to remain nonchalant and head towards the stables. If anyone saw him he would be just a visitor checking on his horse.

He found Gringolay in the first stall and the horse stamped and nodded its head as if in recognition. There was plenty of fodder left for him and Priedeux was satisfied that he had been rubbed down well. He checked the horse's hooves and stroked him gently.

'You and I are leaving this hell hole as soon as possible, despite it being comfortable.'

He whispered to Gringolay, who seemed to eye him and nod in understanding. ''Tis a very hell of a place.'

He looked around the stables and found his tack and dressed the horse in preparation, keeping an eye out onto the courtyard all the time.

Then he heard doors opening, shouting and bangings.

'Find him, find the stranger,' he heard Gertrude shouting imperiously, her voice raised to a high-pitched screech which sent shudders through him. He was reminded of stories he had read of beautiful siren-like creatures who lured men to their lairs where the men discovered the creatures had changed into serpents who crushed them to death for the eating. It made him more determined than ever to get out of the clutches of the woman.

He glanced around for a suitable hiding place as he saw

men spilling from the main door, with swords a-ready. Looking up, he saw a low thick timbered rafter from which hung various pieces of horse's tack. As some of the men ran through the drizzle towards him, he swung himself up, using a length of leather, and stretched himself along the wide timber support. The men ran into the stables and one of them yelled: 'He's been in here, his horse is saddled!'

Others came running and they inspected the stables, stabbing into piles of hay and fodder, pulling out the hay from stalls and bays and moving barrels by rolling them on their sides and stabbing them through their lids.

Then he looked down on the head of Gertrude.

'Fools, can't you see this is a clever trick! He's left the horse like this and gone by now. He could be miles away.'

'But my lady there's no other horse missing, how could....?'

'He's probably run for it. We know but little about him. He may have accomplices waiting with another horse. I want him back!' She was still screaming, the pitch grating Priedeux's ears in the enclosed area. 'I have not finished with our stranger yet.'

'We'll not get to him then, my lady, if he has another horse,' said another of the lackeys. Priedeux saw Gertrude walk towards the man and slap him hard around the head so that he tumbled.

'Oh, for God's sake, open up the gate and ride after him, for he must be soon out of our valley. Use your sense. How can he hide in here? This is a decoy, he's a clever man, and all the while he's on his way!'

The men rushed to their horses at her command and started preparing them. She stood there, stroking Gringolay's neck in a hypnotic manner. He heard her muttering: 'Truly your master was the man for me. Leaving a horse such as you behind was a master stroke, for most would not believe he would leave without you. Such cold-hearted calculation means strength. What a man.'

She strode out, her sentimentality gone in the second she was in the courtyard. He could hear her shouting orders outside as the creaking of the opening gates could be heard. None of the men attempted to use Gringolay or remove the tack and saddle, which was what Priedeux feared. Several men led other horses out and he heard galloping. He waited a while until the hubbub had died down. He prayed no one would think to shut the gate again.

After a while he slid down from his perch and looked out. The courtyard was again empty. He untied the horse and led it from the bay and turned him, all the time keeping an eye out onto the courtyard. He waited, but no one came. It was raining even heavier now, the rain like icy needles on his face, for which he thanked God, not only because it would wash the woman's shit from his cloak but also provide cover for him as he rode away.

He jumped onto Gringolay and spurred its flanks so that the horse almost leapt out of the stable door and clattered across the yard, through the gateway and down the slope.

He was sure he heard a satanic screech behind him.

As he rode he tied the panniers across the saddle. Before he reached the hamlet he pulled off to one side and galloped through strips of bare land, where in summer the serfs would grow their food. He rode so hard that great clods of reddish earth splattered behind him and the rain bounced off the horse causing steam to rise. Through the misty downpour he could see the grey shape of hills on one side and decided to head for them hoping for some shelter from the contours of the land.

He had no idea where he was going and for the moment he did not care.

Soon, he knew, he would have to stop galloping to rest his horse.

'The woman could never know me if she thought I would leave a steed such as you,' he whispered, slowing down as they reached some woodland.

Soon he reached a thin coppice which bordered the village. He pushed the horse through the branches, which dripped great dollops of icy cold rain on his face and soon there were large droplets running down his neck and chest as well as the dampness now penetrating the inner clothes. Soon he was in an ancient woodland of oak and ash and beneath him he heard the crunching of acorns. Even if he had wanted to he could not go fast through the wood for the gloom of the downpour was accentuated here in the cover of the trees and he could hardly see. He had to rely on sound and he was tempted to wrap the horse's hooves in cloth to stay the noise from his footfalls but he realised this would be no good; it was the scraping of their bodies through the trees that caused most of the noise.

Suddenly he saw movement ahead. He stopped and waited. Yes, through the trees there were shapes moving around. At first he could not make out what it was. He edged closer, thinking they were strange humans snorting until he saw the grey-pink four-footed creatures, and realised that it was a herd of pigs. From this distance he could not make out whether they were wild boar or domesticated. He edged Gringolay forward but stopped again as he saw another movement which surprised him. It was a slight human figure, heavily wrapped against the rain. The creature was bent over a stick. Priedeux realised he had come across the village pigs with their keeper, probably one of the lads. He approached slowly and the figure straightened up in surprise.

'Oh, 'tis you, the stranger,' said a low-pitched girl's voice and he realised it was the blonde girl who had defended the dog. She spoke quietly and Priedeux guessed from the husky voice that she spoke infrequently. She went on. 'You escaped? They have been this way, scattering my pigs as well.'

'Which way did they go, girl? '

She looked up at him and he knew he could trust her.

She pointed beyond her and then added, 'if you go the opposite way you will come to the sea so I have been told. The

117

old man says so when he tells stories of great events - and that way,' she pointed behind him, 'are the wild men of Wales who eat little children.'

'So, which way shall I go, child?' He looked down at her and she smiled, a knowing confident smile, 'where do you want to go?'

'I want to go where I will fulfil my mission, on the King's business.' He explained seriously for there was something about this miniature adult that commanded respect.

'Then head that way, towards the land, away from the place they call the Wirral, deep in the woods and out the other side and you will find what you seek.'

'Thank you, I will follow your guidance, and I will not ask how you know what you know.'

'The people think I am a witch. It is because I listen to the stories of the old ones, and I listen to others talking and I go to the big house in the mornings and talk with the blond man there who says he is my father but that I cannot believe because he is sad and silly.

'Then I come here with the pigs and I think about what I have heard and I try to make sense of it all. I try to make stories and make those stories follow on from what I have been told.'

Priedeux looked down at this child and wondered about her future. He could recognise the truth of her parentage but would it profit her for it to be confirmed by him? Did it matter? What he saw in her was an intelligence such as he had had as a boy and knew she would be like him, a wanderer, an outsider, one that would walk her own road. But she was a girl and could not follow the fortunes of war or patronage. Her best chance was to go to a nunnery and learn to pray eight times a day. As he looked down on her, Priedeux thought that would be a terrible waste, for her intelligent face to be surrounded by a hard wimple and that blonde hair shaved. He could see Gertrude's beauty in her face, untainted by cynicism and cruelty.

He dismounted and felt for the sealed stone. He had not had time to dispose of it. Some instinct told him it could only be for the good, and in his dangerous mission it might compromise him, whereas with this girl, it might help her one day.

'Child, I will tell you something now that you will treasure. Always listen to your own stories for they will be the only truth along your hard path. Oh, and here, take this, and use it wisely. You will know when to show it and when not.' He gave her the stone, and she quickly stashed it inside her sodden clothes without looking at it. It was as if all who touched it needed to inspect it in secrecy. Then he added:

'And if you ever see a group of serfs with their lord, sheep and pigs, travelling the country, go with them, show the lord the seal, for they are of your kind.'

'Sir, thank you and I will remember what you say. And if the men from the house return I have never seen you. God bless you.'

'And you, my child.'

Priedeux rode past her and slowly moved through her herd of rootling pigs. He turned and waved, but only saw a misty figure disappearing in the rain like a wraith.

Chapter Nine: Travelling on

*'At every bank or beach where the brave man crossed water,
he found a foe in front of him....'*

Priedeux was well versed in the art of navigation and always knew instinctively which way he was heading provided he was not preoccupied with other matters. Even if he didn't know the terrain he was still confident. Now, travelling alone and moving into flat countryside, he felt safe. He was out of the Wirral and some miles from the Storeton lands. He could relax.

As the girl had advised, he was travelling east. He planned to find a small hamlet, with a good inn, where he could hole up for a while, read *Gawain and the Green Knight* again and look for clues. He could think of nothing else to do. It would be useless to return to the court without the news that Gaunt wanted; the certainty that the writer was dead.

The rain slowed and then stopped, and the sky cleared with long washed out clouds thinning until they disappeared altogether, leaving a cold clear sky with the dull winter sun lying low to his right. It was now mid morning but it barely lit up the region. He was riding through a grey expanse, with silhouettes of trees like bony men breaking the sky. Here there were wide marshy regions where a man could see for miles but he knew he also could be seen. He kept the horse to a trot and maintained a good eye about him. He wrapped his cloak tightly against his body for it was dry inside and the rain had washed away any stink from Gertrude's latrine.

Her men might follow him but they would not venture outside the country they knew, he was sure.

He was travelling back into a more civilised land. The road was well defined, with flat sparse scrub and stunted trees dotted on either side. He passed through small hamlets where the people kept to their homes although he sensed he was watched as he went through the main street of each place.

For half a day he rode without seeing more than a frightened serf with a basket held on his back with leather ropes, gathering wood in this sparse landscape, who hastily nodded as he passed by, afraid of the solitary horseman. Then, in a dip to one side of the straight road, he saw the roof of a church, ruddy red in colour and with a small hamlet of lesser roofs surrounding it. The road he was on would not pass through the small place and he guessed it had been built away from an older village that had been destroyed by the black death, the great plague of fifty or so years before. Indeed, now he thought about it, there were grassy humps and crevices along the side of the road, evidence that there had once been buildings. He turned Gringolay and jumped over one of the hummocks, heading towards the new hamlet.

When he reached the church he stopped and looked about. A long low wall, newly built, stretched from one side of the churchyard, from the lych gate, and surrounded a graveyard with only a few new wooden crosses scattered about. All looked fresh and orderly. He decided to investigate, for the sun was lowering behind him and new clouds had gathered to diffuse the early evening rays. He could tell that the bright day would end with more rain, if not snow, and as he rode it started to drizzle again. Also, Gringolay needed fodder.

The church and its surrounds were imposing and too large to be the hamlet's place of worship. Priedeux guessed it was part of a college or monastery. Behind the church he now saw the high walls that surrounded cloisters, and the walled gardens of a brotherhood. Behind these, he knew, would be the living quarters of monks and, more importantly, a refectory which, he hoped, would welcome and feed strangers. As he reached the church, he heard the chant of monks at evensong and knew that, even if he had been followed, and challenged by Gertrude's men, he would be safe, given sanctuary which most men would not breach.

Reining in his horse, he looked around him. He saw neatly marked fields and a road new laid up to the church with good, well shaped paviers. He walked Gringolay to the south side of the church, saw a fish pond and led Gringolay to its banks for a drink, noticing it was well stocked. He could see trout, salmon and carp and his mouth watered at the thought of a well-cooked fish, straight from the pond. Away by the far wall, now hiding the last of the day, was a young yew tree, which darkened the rest of the yard. There was an air of peace and tranquillity.

He waited for the monks to end their chanting. He would have none of that; it woke too many emotions which he did not want to acknowledge. Music, he thought, as he sat there, was a strange and wonderful thing. He had seen great princes cry over some tunes, and when the troubadours sang soft songs of love he would see women's eyes melting. He had experienced those emotions too but, even as his eyes filled with tears at the sounds, he resented the music, as an insidious creature trying to infiltrate his armour.

Because religious music was usually accompanied by the thick smell of the incense the monks used to hide the smell of the bodies of their congregations, he found it even more cloying and unpleasant. The swinging censor sent out sweet odours, that tickled his nose and stirred uneasy memories.

One of his older brothers had been left at a monastery, the lame one, the one who could not work the land, and Priedeux, as a child, had been sent to the place many times with bundles of food as a thank-you gift for taking in the useless boy. That same sickly sweet smell always wafted around his brother like an apology for him being alive.

Now the monks' chants, evocative and insistent, made him think that there might be a God and Priedeux feared that he would be judged one day for the killings he had carried out. He would rather not be reminded. For now, though, he waited, and his thoughts turned to practicalities. He needed a bed for the night, fodder for Gringolay and, if he had been followed, sanctuary. All the evidence around him showed that here there was a rich landowner who could afford a good benefice for the new church and had given alms for the monastery to be created. A monastery which was well endowed, no doubt with a good refectory where strangers would be accommodated.

The church was in the latest style, copying the new buildings at Westminster built at the order of the King, except that this was in the local pinky-red stone and not the pure white of Westminster. He was sure that, given the air of the place, strangers would be welcomed.

He spurred Gringolay on to the entrance of the monastery behind the church but a movement attracted him, as if there had been a disturbance amongst the mounds of the dead. The light was fading fast but Priedeux could still make out the grave markers, skeletons of trees and the yew in the corner of the yard. Something had flickered between the yew and the graves near it. Priedeux did not believe in the supernatural and from the sounds and size he knew it was no animal. He could also sense someone watching him. He guessed it was a child.

'Come out from there,' he called peremptorily and stared at the mound he was sure was hiding the watcher. Slowly a dishevelled head appeared.

'Who are you?' he asked in a kindlier tone and the child stood up and twisted his hands together in embarrassment.

'Tom sir, Tom the son of Tom the smith, sir. I was admiring

your horse, sir. Indeed, it is a grand horse, sir, a fine palfrey. It rides well, sir?' As he spoke in a broad local dialect that Priedeux could only just understand, he was sidling forward.

When he was about a sword's length away, he stopped.

'Aye, Tom, it's a goodly steed, that has brought me far. But I must rest soon, for we are both tired. What place is this?'

'It be called Bunbury, sir. Bunbury and the church is new, sir, just been built and I wanted to help and be a mason and carve like up there.' He pointed to a fine gargoyle's gaping features.

'But the masons said there was no room for such as I to train and I should stick to my father's trade but I don't want to be a smith, sir.'

The place name seemed familiar to Priedeux but for the moment he could not recall why. The boy stretched up and stroked the horse's head as he spoke. Priedeux saw he knew how to handle horses, which, bearing in mind his father's trade, was natural. He had probably been holding nervous horses since he was a toddler. Gringolay nodded, as if understanding that the boy was a friend. Now that Priedeux knew he was safe, his previous need for a place for the night became pressing. He realised the chanting had stopped and decided to enter the church to see if there was a memorial to some local lord, a sarcophagus or brass which would give him a clue as to why the name of the place seemed familiar. It seemed to raise memories of fights, helping others, a resonance of camaraderie, but the memory would not surface except for such vague concepts.

He dismounted and handed the reins to the boy. 'Hold her for me, young Tom whilst I see the inside of your great church.' The lad swelled with pride and led the horse away to a clump of thick grass at the side of the new-laid path.

Priedeux swung open the heavy wood door, its fittings new-shining and entered the gloom of the chapel. The monks had gone. There was just enough light to see the tall arched nave painted brightly and, at the end, a sarcophagus, as he suspected, but surprisingly protected by railings. He walked slowly down the nave, his sword clanking eerily. There was a smell of resin, of new wood, of damp plaster, and he realised the church was so recent it probably had not stood a winter. He walked around the oblong structure and found the Latin inscription.

'Sir Hugh Calveley a true knight and a good one 1394 he died and this college was built because of his great beneficence'.

Calveley - Bunbury. Of course. Priedeux shivered. Only yesterday he had thought of his old friend Sir Hugh and thought of the debt that was owed. It all came back to him in a rush. The fighting in Portugal and hand to hand battles against the infidel in the east. And whom had he fought with, side by side, back to back in many cases? Hugh, his old companion. Sir Hugh Calveley. There had been one such sortie when they had indeed stood back to back, their shields forming a tortoise-like structure while they each hacked away at their attackers. Hugh had come out of it with a bloodied arm and he with a bloodied leg and they had joked that now they were a two-footed tortoise and needed to be cared for. They had bandaged and creamed each other and Hugh had taught him the garlic cure. They had fought on all the campaigns together since then but when Gaunt and his men had returned to England, grey-bearded Calveley had said: 'Time for me to return to my home. I'm too old to learn new tricks at court - but you, Priedeux, keep your wits about you and serve well and surely you will be rewarded.

'If your destiny ever takes you to my part of the world, come and see me and I'll look after you like you've looked after me. We'll talk over our old campaigns and I'll fatten you up with the good sheep on my land.'

So they had parted and now here he was, standing before his tomb. Too late now to ask for Sir Hugh's help to provide a good living. Priedeux sighed, and knelt, head bowed, well aware that the sadness he felt was somehow connected with his current quest, and its lack of any substance. He felt he was just drifting around the country not achieving anything, unlike the battles he had fought with good Sir Hugh. At least they had obtained valuable bounty.

Sir Hugh had made good use of it. He had been well laid down, for the effigy of him was a good likeness, even though the masons had carved him a good foot taller than he really was, Priedeux was sure. The stone was richly painted in reds, pinks, yellows and greens. He lay there depicted in full ceremonial armour, the type he would never have worn on the battlefield, and his hands were together in prayer. Candles flickered where they had been wedged on the top of the railings that surrounded the tomb, casting shadows on the effigy so that it seemed as if Sir Hugh smiled and then frowned. Priedeux continued to kneel, his hands similarly clasped in prayer. This was the end for all men, lying in a grave, but he knew he would not have such a great tomb, or such a great monument.

The church was icy cold and there was a faint odour left by the priest's censor which blended with the new-wood smell, accentuating Priedeux's sense of doom, reminding him once again of a family not seen, his roots, those things he never usually thought about. The cold eventually got to him so that he realised he ought to find his lodgings. There was an earthy smell as well, as if the church had not yet impressed itself on the old foundation of mud and stone it stood upon. He suddenly felt totally alone.

'If I were a superstitious man I would swear you had woken at my coming to talk with me, old Hugh. Ah well, if this is how man ends, let us live to the full while we are here, say I.'

And he rose and strode out of the chapel without a backward glance, to where Tom waited.

126

'Tell me boy, where is the entrance to the monastery?' The boy pointed:

'Behind the church, sir, and they will let you in before dusk and no later. They lock up and no-one seeking shelter is let in after dark, for there have been troubles since our Lord Calveley died. Hurry, I'll show you.' The boy handed him the reins and scuttled away across the mounds. Priedeux could just make out the way from his movement against the shadows.

The boy ran out of the churchyard and to the left and as Priedeux followed he stopped by a heavy wood door in the new reddish-pink wall. By the side of the door was a long chain-pull.

'Here it is, sir, and if they won't let you in come to the smithy - just beyond there, and my father will put you up for the night and check the horse as well.'

Priedeux rewarded the boy with a coin, as he yanked at the chain, and listened to the echoing sound from within. Shortly after the door was pulled partly ajar and a young new-tonsured monk peered out, 'who is it?'

'A traveller seeking shelter for the night. I am a knight who fought with Sir Hugh Calveley. My name is Thomas Priedeux.'

The door was shut and he guessed there were hurried whisperings and discussions on the other side. He waited, for he was not too concerned. He could sup at the smithy as well as here. But then the door was swung wide open and the monk said: 'Enter, traveller, and rest.'

He found himself in a courtyard surrounded by an open cloister with cells off this. In one corner was a larger structure and beyond that there was a walkway which he guessed led to the church and perhaps the refectory and guest quarters. He was led that way, Gringolay clopping loudly on the new stone pavement of the cloisters.

They reached stables and there a servant took Gringolay: 'I

will rub the horse down well, sir, fear not; any friend of Sir Hugh's will have good service here.' The servant held a flare in such a way that he could see Priedeux's features.

'I recognise you, sir, you did indeed fight with my old master. 'Tis sad though that you missed him.' He said it as if Calveley had just set out on a journey.

'Indeed, I would have liked to sup with my old friend again, but he is handsomely remembered in the church.'

'Indeed, sir, he was much respected.'

Priedeux nodded and turned away to where the priest was waiting, who gestured for him to follow, leading him to the corner building.

In the refectory he was the only one who ate. He guessed the monks had eaten before their chanting. He was given a trencher and placed before him was a large basket of good bread, and a fresh trout on its own platter, its tail hanging over one side. As he ate, serving monks glided around him, pouring good ale into his beaker. They moved without speaking, but with total politeness and small smiles on their faces. When he wiped the wooden trencher with a last chunk of bread, all was cleared away. The young monk who had led him in said: 'this way, I'll show you to the cell where you can sleep, where our night prayers will not disturb you. We are still singing masses for the soul of our benefactor, Sir Hugh Calveley.'

He was led down a side corridor and shown to a cell. It was simply furnished, but had a jug of something and cups beside the truckle which was heavily laden with good quality wraps. There was a large beeswax candle burning and Priedeux guessed it was designed to last him through the night hours if he so desired. No cheap lamps here, made of smelly animal fats then. It confirmed his original belief that the monastery was well endowed.

He thanked the priest and unloaded the panniers which he had kept with him all the time.

Strange fortunes, he thought wryly. Where last night had been one of lust with a beautiful yet dangerous woman, now he was alone in a tiny cell in a celibate monastery, just as well fed but in a much simpler manner. He was also just as well cared for but with more courtesy, with just as comfortable a bed with less sumptuousness. The only thing missing...but he thought he could manage the night without a woman.

As he inspected his load, the manuscript of *Gawain and the Green Knight* fell out. He had never really studied it in detail. In the excitement of escape he had almost forgotten his quest, the reason he was on the road, but the site of Sir Hugh's sarcophagus had brought it back again; his duty to his masters.

He flicked over the parchment and read patches of it.

He found those parts which implied criticism of King Arthur, and remembered that Edward III had set up the round table, in memory of his 'ancestors'. Picking out one particular piece, he muttered as he read it:

'It would have been wiser to have worked more warily,
And to have dubbed the dear man a duke of the realm'.

Or this:

'Who supposed the Prince would approve such counsel
As is giddily given in Christmas games by knights?'

Was this, - could it be, - a criticism of Richard II with his love of pageantry, his lack of diplomacy when he was arguing with the dukes and lords of his realm?

Compared to these snide remarks, Gawain's greeting at the castle in the west seemed to be one of courteous and dignified welcome:

'With a hoste of well-wishers to welcome the knight.
They let down the drawbridge in a dignified way
They came out and did honour to him by kneeling
On the cold ground courteously,'

Priedeux continued to read. All at the western place was kindness and benevolence and dignity, a place where it would be good to live. He could understand as he read more, why

Gaunt and Chaucer would be suspicious and believe it to be an insidious political tract, albeit in rhyme. The contrast between the two courts was so striking that, if Priedeux had wanted to choose sides, he would choose the king of the west rather than the court at Westminster with its intrigues hidden by false gaiety, drunkenness and debauchery.

As he carried on reading, he was interrupted by a short tap on the door, as if someone hesitated to wake him if he were indeed asleep. Priedeux jumped up and swung the door open. There stood a man, who with a large cross resting on his chest, could only be the Prior. Priedeux could see the monk's habit was made of the finest wool, thickly woven, and the belt that split his bulging body into two was made of gold. The cross also was of dark gold, as befitted the head of a rich house. He bowed slightly and his chubby hands were held together over his capacious belly.

'Forgive such a late hour for a visit,' he rasped in a peculiarly husky voice.

Priedeux waved him in. He entered but stood, not moving his hands from the crossed position in front of him, and they faced each other for a few moments. The flare was behind Priedeux so he could study the features of his visitor. It was a keen intelligent face, but rounded with too much food and the tonsure was white with age. The Prior spoke first: 'You fought with our benefactor, Calveley.' It was a statement, not a question. Priedeux acknowledged it with a slight nod of his head.

'It has been confirmed by Sluesh, his page, in any event, who now serves in our stables and he added that you were a brave companion but one who stood on his own.'

Priedeux smiled slightly. Said nothing, and waited, for he knew this was leading to something.

The Prior seemed to sway from side to side, like a ball made of cloth. 'May we sit? I have something to discuss with you.'

Priedeux moved the stool he had been sitting on towards the Prior and he himself sat on the edge of the bed. The Prior at last moved his hands and edged himself down carefully as if long periods at prayer had stiffened him.

'I have been assured that you are the King's man?'

Priedeux said nothing. He watched as the Prior placed his hands across his ample belly again, the tips of his fingers just touching.

'If you are the King's man, I can trust you. Let me explain. We have great troubles hereabouts with bandits from the wild lands to the west and we would hope you could perhaps organise a sortie for us. The King's men are losing their grip in this part of his realm. Law and order is becoming scarce. Calveley left us without a lord and our lands are constantly being ravaged by these bandits, who have no respect for God or man. They have raided our crops for two seasons running now and the people are starving. We do what we can but we have our own work to do and have many orders for missals and books of hours to work on in our scriptorum. And besides my monks are not fighting men.'

'And you wish me to petition the King for help?'

The Prior looked at him sharply and nodded.

'Have you not consulted the law at Chester? Can they not help?'

The Prior sighed. They are too worried about their own situation. They consider us too far away from them, although it is but half a day's ride.'

Priedeux nodded and realised he had ridden well, in having avoided Chester. He would not have wanted to pass that City again. Neither could he afford to be caught by the officials in the town nor by Gertrude's spies. He could offer the Prior little comfort, and explained:

'I may not return to Court for many months. I am on my way to claim my own lands.'

The Prior interrupted sharply: 'And where is that?'

Priedeux realised he had been made a mistake. He had made up the lie on the spur of the moment, not wishing to tell the Prior of the real reason why he was travelling in winter. Now he thought rapidly. He would not be able to make up a fictitious place, or give a real one. These monks had ways of communicating between themselves and were everywhere. He would be discovered as an impostor.

He took a deep breath and said, 'Prior, I am going to trust you. But I swear on the body of my old friend who lies in your church that if you betray me I will return and far worse will happen to you personally than ever happens at present in these lands.'

The Prior did not blench but bowed his head, as if to accept the curse. Priedeux took a deep breath and went on. 'I am on a mission for the King. As you say, law and order seems to be breaking down. I have been sent to find out why. If I succeed I could be well rewarded. As part of that reward I could ask for leave to bring a party of the best knights to rout these bandits but I know not whether I will succeed in my quest. Indeed, my very life has already been endangered. I have no idea where I am going next or for what I seek or how long it will take me.'

He finished lamely and there was a silence between them, the Prior watching him keenly. Then he said, 'child, I thank you for your honesty. I had heard of a stranger in these parts seeking, for we are well respected by our people and they know we like to be informed of what goes on in the outside world.'

He paused, and looked around the cell. He lit on the parchment, which Priedeux had thrown on the bed when he opened the door.

'I see you have a manuscript you study.'

Priedeux did not reach for the book and nor did the Prior. He explained: 'My lord believes there is organised revolt being planned. It is supposed to guide me to where the insurgents' centre is based. I am studying it.'

As he explained, the Prior leaned forward to see more of the book, but Priedeux took it up and riffled the pages, not handing it over. The Prior did not attempt to try to reach for it. Instead he answered, 'if you need more information from such as that we have a large scriptorum here and there are many such as these. My scribes are the best hereabouts, forgetting Glastonbury which is some miles away. How can we help you?'

Priedeux studied his companion and guessed that, with the books he had and his information system, he probably had a good idea what Priedeux was doing although the details could not be known. Priedeux was cynical enough to know that the Prior, for all his kind looks and offers of help, had only his own self-interest at heart. At this moment this self-interest stretched to helping Priedeux because he recognised he might get what he wanted out of it; help from the highest power in the land to make his own domain peaceful again.

'I would like to see your collection of books. Also you could help. I have here a tale told in rhyme, which is a good tale but may be not the sort that monks would transcribe, concentrating as it does on romance? But it has been transcribed by a learned man so it may be that you would recognise he who wrote it?'

The Prior laughed. It was a guttural laugh that ended in a short rasp, and he held his chest as he took a deep breath before recovering. Priedeux guessed he suffered from a breathing problem that would take him to his lord shortly.

'My monks undertake such commissions but I entrust them to a few older ones whose loins are shrunken so they will not be tempted by lewd words.'

Priedeux interrupted. 'This is not lewd, but sumptuous and rich and concentrates on the courtly romance style.'

The Prior nodded, 'I have seen such a definitive book on this courtly style of love, it is called Romance of the Rose.

'Twould be good if all could follow such high ideals of love. But our Lord would frown on such earthly pleasures as the garden of love and its revelries.'

Priedeux shook his head: 'No, I too know of that one - it comes from France and is well used at our King's court. This is something written in the dialect hereabouts, or so I have been told, and as I read it I see it mocks this courtly love idea.'

The monk's face seemed to tauten as Priedeux spoke. Then he tried to relax again but not fast enough for Priedeux, who knew he had to tread carefully.

'You have heard of Chaucer?'

The Prior nodded. 'Indeed my monks have transcribed *The Parliament of Fowls* which is his work.'

Priedeux nodded and part-truthed. 'Chaucer has said this work is a great work and he would like to know who the author is so I have been sent to find out, as one of my tasks whilst I travel.'

The Prior used that sharp look again and Priedeux spread out his hands in front of him in a gesture of openness but continued, before the Prior could ask more. 'Here, look at this manuscript. It is called *'Gawain and the Green Knight'*.

There was a great silence, as if the cell grew into a great room which had no windows, no walls, no contours where echoes could abound. The silence of a million secrets, thought Priedeux. He felt excited, that old feeling he had when he was near his quarry. *This Prior knows something about the book,* he was certain. Now he held it out so that the Prior could take it. He half hesitated before he took what was proffered.

Holding the book in both his chubby hands, the Prior started to flick the pages, stopping to look at the small pictures but Priedeux knew he was not interested in studying them as a man would do if they were new to him. Priedeux watched both the chubby hands and the round face and it was as if their owner was touching something he had known years ago and was re-familiarising himself with it.

Priedeux waited. He knew it would be wrong to hurry the man and also knew that any answer he received would be contrived but the more contrived it was the more Priedeux would be able to guess different.

Then the Prior said slowly: 'You swore if we helped you, you would help us?'

Priedeux nodded.

The Prior took a deep breath and Priedeux heard again the rasping in his chest as he explained: 'One of my scribes copied this. He copied it but last year for a lord but two days' ride from here. The lord sent a lackey, an ignorant man who knew not what he carried but was sent a few months later to collect it. We knew not exactly where he came from except it was in the eastern peaks.'

He gasped for breath, then carried on. 'Although we tried to follow the servant, to make sure it arrived with the lord, you understand, our people could not follow the tracks into the high peaks and through rivers and we lost the trail. If you wish, I will give you the wordings we wrote down and you can go as far as we went. Maybe you will find the channel that leads through the peaks to this lord's manor.'

Priedeux knew he was telling the truth and leant forward to pat the man on the shoulder: 'My thanks, Prior, and eternal indebtedness.'

The Prior took Priedeux's hand from his shoulder and held it in his smooth chubby fingers. He croaked, 'my son, I am sure there is danger attached to this book but I cannot tell why. I read it and enjoyed it but the tale did not tell its moral to me, for I am versed in the ways of the Lord, not mammon. I know I should not have enjoyed it for the Green Man was an ungodly creature and the Lady was a witch and so our Lord Jesus would not have sanctioned such stories in his House.'

He slowly pulled himself to standing.

'Enough, it is late. We will visit the scriptorum tomorrow in daylight for candles are forbidden in such a place. God grant you rest.'

Then he was gone.

Chapter Ten: Journeyings

'Let him lie there still,
he almost has what he sought;
so tarry a while until
the process I report'.

The next morning Priedeux woke suddenly, totally refreshed as if he had been given a magic draught to induce sleep. Which he probably had, he thought.

He checked the panniers that he had placed underneath his head for a pillow and was sure they had not been touched. He rose and straightened his clothes, pulled the cloak around him for he knew the corridors would be cold, and went in search of food and a privy.

There was no one in the refectory when he arrived and he assumed that, like last night, he was the only guest. On the table were hunks of bread, ale and herrings and he helped himself. The bread was fresh and the herrings were tasty without the usual stuffy smell of pickled fish at this time of year.

As he chewed through the thick bread, dipping it into the herring oil, the monk who had ministered to him the night before entered and waited. Priedeux continued eating, and nodded and the monk stayed standing respectfully at one side, until he had finished and wiped his mouth.

Then the monk stepped forward and said: 'Come, the Prior has asked that I take you to him in the scriptorum.'

The voice was harsh, through lack of use. Priedeux was

surprised he had spoken and was about to ask a question but the monk turned and walked away, tucking his hands into the sleeves of his habit, and Priedeux realised this was an indication that no more conversation would take place.

He was led out of the refectory into the deeper parts of the monastery and Priedeux followed until they reached a spiral staircase and he was led upstairs. They passed through another long corridor until they came to a long hall-like room with many windows on one side. These were too high for the occupants to look out and admire the surrounding countryside. Priedeux realised the windows faced north. Underneath each one, and set diagonally to it, was a desk with the sloping desktops hidden by manuscripts and beside each stood a monk, with head bent to the parchments before him. Nobody looked up as he entered and all seemed to be working diligently at the parchments before them. The room was chilly and each monk seemed to be chubby but Priedeux realised this was because they probably wore several habits in an attempt to keep warm. Some wore gloves with the fingers cut away to help them hold their pens more easily. There was an odour in the room of soot and apples which, Priedeux recognised, came from the ink. Next to an inner wall was a long trestle table with unfinished pages of manuscripts in orderly piles. Hanging on lengths of wood jutting from the wall, above this table, were large uncut sheepskins, waiting to be cut into the vellum pages of new books. At the end sat another monk at a flat table and he was using a needle to bind the vellum pages together. All this Priedeux took in at a glance and he realised this was an industrious and important book-making place.

Just inside the door stood the Prior, his arms rounded on his belly, the fingers entwined, in the now familiar fashion. He moved towards his guest as he entered, the monk disappearing at the door.

'Come, I will show you our library.' He walked along the room ignoring the working scribes.

He said in a low voice, 'you note the age of these scribes. I have a theory that God does not take those who find a vocation that helps the world, like these dedicated workers, until their job is done. What say you?'

Priedeux shrugged as they reached the end of the gallery, where there was another door, similar to the one through which he had come. The Prior went in first and Priedeux followed him and the Prior closed it behind him with an almost secretive movement. This room was turreted and there were windows all round. There were shelves all round on which there were books piled up, some of them chained to the walls. Others were hidden by dark un-dyed curtaining. Priedeux scanned the shelves and read various titles. Most were in Latin, including a large Latin Bible. The Prior had turned his back to Priedeux and was seeking something. Priedeux lifted the curtain nearest to him, and peered at the contents. One of the books was a Bible in English. Priedeux was so surprised he took it off the shelf and started leafing through it. The Prior turned back to him but said nothing, although he must have known what Priedeux was looking at. Priedeux exclaimed:

'I thought such things were banned by the Holy Church?'

The Prior took the book from him and answered: 'It is for research, you understand, I do not allow the younger scribes to read it.'

He put it back from where it came. Priedeux carried on moving around the room, his fingers tracing the edges of the books as he went along.

There were the usual devotional books, books of hours and missals. But Priedeux was further surprised to see many secular books as well. There were the tales of Sir John Mandeville, an Italian version of Marco Polo's travels and other travel books.

Priedeux said nothing and the Prior did not explain.

When Priedeux eventually stopped and turned to him the

Prior smiled, obviously proud of his library.

'Yes, our benefactor left us well-endowed and I have ordered books from monasteries across the Christian world. I believe the Lord gave us intelligence to find out about his great creation and we can do that through books. Enough, I have something to show you, pertaining to your search.'

He moved to one corner and then stretched up, his middle flab wobbling and his fat toes showing. He brought down a large flat book and opened it, turning the heavy parchment. The pages were so large that Priedeux guessed they were the size of half a calf. He leaned forward to read what he thought was tightly woven writing. Instead he saw lines and waves in black, blue and red, with fantastic creatures emerging from behind pointed shapes. This was a book of maps.

The Prior eventually stopped his thumbing through and tapped one chubby forefinger on the page before him.

'This is what I think you must see. It is a map of the land hereabouts with its contours. Here, you see our small college, added on recently, and the boundaries of our lands. There you see that cross - that is the church next door to where you stand now.'

He pointed to some squares, and others with green circular shapes on them, and added: 'There are our woods, our fields.

'But I wanted you to see where you must head.' He pointed, his chubby finger hovering over a mass of crags. 'North-east from here, up into the peaks that are shown. Rough ground and bleak they be, and the serfs enter not for the wild monsters. We know the lord's rider came from that place, and disappeared back into those parts with his copies of the story you are reading.'

Priedeux looked over the priest's shoulder and saw black pointed peaks depicted, with dark green monsters twining between them and behind, a fantastical character half-animal, half-man, with horns, a tail and a gigantic chest with eyes in its centre. Here it was that the Prior's finger hovered.

'Copies?' queried Priedeux as he looked down at the picture of the land.

'Yes, we were asked for five copies, the lackey said something about for all parts of his master's lands.'

Priedeux pondered on this. He knew five was a magic number standing for the five wounds of Christ, for the five points of the star, and for the five fingers on a man's hand. And in the Gawain poem there was a description of the hero implying he was perfect because he fitted the perfection of the five-point system. Now Priedeux wondered if 'five parts of the land' related to England, Ireland, Scotland, Wales and France, totalling his King's dominions. If so, this would make sense. He was beginning to think of the poet as Gaunt and Chaucer saw him; a dangerous man. If a small local lord had written such a work with the deliberate intention of subversion and insurrection and intended to send it to the different parts of Richard's kingdom, what would he not do to a wandering adventurer who was trying to stop him?

Such thoughts would be best kept to himself and he decided not to confide in the Prior, so he said nothing. Instead he studied the map, and then looked up and closed his eyes, to ensure the details were indelibly fixed in his mind. He did this several times, and on one occasion when he opened his eyes, he realised the Prior had moved, silently. He turned and saw him peering out of the window. Neither of them said anything.

After a while he faced the Prior and said: 'Thank you for the guidance and I will make good use of it, even though it seems I need to travel in strange lands.'

He continued, looking around him at the feast of strange and varied books: 'I am not a learned man but I honour the information in such things. It would be good to spend my old age in such a place as this if my eyes don't fail me.'

The priest laughed: 'We have a bargain already, friend, but if you complete your task and grow old bones I will note it in our records and you will be a welcome resident, although I will not be here when you need the shelter of my House.'

As they left, the Prior stopped and placed a chubby hand on Priedeux's arm.

'My son, I know now what you seek, but again I would warn you that you go to strange lands. None have returned, you only have that memory to guide you, trust in God and all will be well.'

Priedeux looked down at the be-ringed chubby fingers on his arm. His only thought was that his trust in God might well be rewarded if he also followed his lord's command and found the insurrectionist who had written the poem. Then rich rewards might follow, from his lord, Gaunt.

With that they left the library and returned through the scriptorum, none of the scribes taking any notice of them knowing that in winter their working day was short.

The Prior handed Priedeux back to the monk who acted as guide and servant:

'I will leave you here, and wish you God speed. Your horse has been well fed and rested and the smith insisted on coming this morning to check the shoes, for he felt you treated his son, Tom, with kindness. All is well, he asked me to tell you, and the horse is fit and rested, and will carry you far, so he says.'

Priedeux thanked him and insisted on giving a silver coin from his now reducing purse for alms for the poor.

'You are a good man, you know, I can see in your heart. Don't pretend otherwise.'

Priedeux laughed cynically as he was led to the stables. He, good? When he had only ever carried out others' instructions to kill or spy? Gringolay was ready, and there were new panniers already in place. He noticed they were bulkier than before and the monk saw him patting them:

'Yes, we have provisioned you for two days, by the Prior's orders.'

As he passed the churchyard, Tom stood high on a mound

and waved at him.   Priedeux waved back and spurred Gringolay on, over the brow of the hill, eager to continue his quest, excited that he was so close to his prey.

Chapter Eleven: Finding the castle

'...a mansion he marked within a moat in the forest,
.....it shimmered and shone through the shining oaks'

He had ridden into rain clouds which misted the hills in front of him and for some hours he had been drenched through. It was icy cold rain, reminiscent of the downpour that had washed away the memory of Gertrude. Now it had stopped but it was still a gloomy day with lowering clouds. He rode north-eastwards checking his direction by noting the moss on the side of the trees. It was an old trick; moss only grew on the northern side, the sun burning the delicate soft stuff off the sides that were warmed by its rays.

The terrain was much like that which surrounded Bunbury, low rolling hills, some pasture around some hamlets. He rode all day, encountering a few peasants and no-one else. All the time he headed towards the hills in the distance but never seemed to reach them. Then towards dusk he knew he was climbing and the landscape began to change, it became steeper and the deep green of gorse spotted the slopes. The flat fields, drenched with the sheet rain of the last few days, now waiting for spring crops, sloped away behind him but there were few cultivated pieces of land in front. The dark hills now seemed to be lowering before him, a barrier to his view but he knew that was the way he had to go.

The trees became fewer and more bowed, twisted as if the winds and rains of this region battered them, trying to force them to kneel in submission, and the land became scrub, fit only for hardy mountain sheep or goats. As dusk fell, Priedeux felt a strangeness about the land and realised there were no birds, not even a crow cawing their raucous evening warning.

Large outcrops of granite started to appear and Priedeux felt a tingling under his ribcage. He knew he was getting close to his quarry. When he had ridden into battle, he had had the same feeling. He recognised it as a sign of impending danger. Now that feeling was pervading him and he knew he was entering perilous country, not just because of its mountainous terrain but, he suspected, because of its inhabitants. He did not really believe in the strange creatures depicted on the Prior's map, but did believe in enemies.

Gringolay was stepping gingerly as he clambered up the rocky path. The darkness was overtaking them, and Priedeux realised that with this sort of countryside he could easily lame the horse on an unseen obstacle so he decided to find a sheltered spot to rest for the night. Somehow he knew he would not find shelter with humans, friendly or otherwise. He edged forward carefully looking for an overhanging tree or some rocks he could rest against. He also needed water but again his training told him that in this sort of country he would soon find a spring or running water for granite seemed to crack open and spill out its secret flow, like a wounded animal spilt blood.

He moved on and then on but it was another hour and blue black dark before he found what he was looking for and then only because it stood out as a blacker thing against its surroundings. An outcrop of the stone, rising high above him and a solitary skeleton of a tree leaning over it like a guardian. The stone formed a natural roof and he could hear the sound of running water nearby. He dismounted and held the reins as he stepped forward and led the horse to the running stream of bubbling water. Gringolay moved surely, as if he knew he was being led to stabling, even though of a rough sort.

Priedeux waited while the horse drank his fill, then he tied him to a branch of the tree. In the dark, he felt for the panniers and slid them off. He found flares and tinder. Indeed the Prior was a thoughtful man. Priedeux lit the flare and sought wood. An abundance of old branches had fallen from long-gone trees and he used dried moss to start the blaze. He soon had a good fire going. Then he found the food and settled down for his feast. He turned to the horse and while the fire was tindering into flame, rubbed him clean with dried grass he found under the overhanging cliff. He stroked him and stroked him until he lay down and his head drooped. He hoped the light from the fire would not be visible to others but it could not be helped, it was too cold to remain outside without man-made heat.

He settled down, the panniers beneath him to stop the earth's chill from penetrating his bones and leaned against the broad side of Gringolay who seemed to tremble slightly at the unfamiliar weight on him.

'Steady, my friend, we must huddle together for warmth, for the chill will get to both of us.' He felt the horse's hot breath on his forehead, and continued to talk, as if the horse was a hesitant woman who, if he spoke softly enough and tenderly enough, would yield to him. Slowly the horse relaxed, the breathing became slow and heavy and then Gringolay slept. Priedeux curled into the beast's flanks and, with the fire before him, managed to keep out the freezing cold of the night.

The hours passed slowly, and it was uncomfortable for both man and beast. At first, they slept little, Priedeux constantly on guard, trying to keep the fire going. At one time when he awoke he heard the howling of wolves. Gringolay neighed, showing his fear and Priedeux had to stroke the horse rhythmically to calm him. The cold penetrated and he wrapped his cloak around him even tighter, speaking gently to waylay the horse's fear.

Sometimes there were shufflings of small wild creatures going about their business but Priedeux was not afraid, for he knew such animals feared the scent of man or tamed beast and would not venture near. The noises of the animals and the whispering of the air as it forced its way through the high rocks meant that the night was full of noise. It spoke to Priedeux of his solitude, almost taunting him. No one knew where he was. He had no one to return to. He had to go on into the unknown. Again he considered his own mortality. *I am half way through my life if a man reaches three score years and ten. What is to happen in the next half?* He shifted again and tried to sleep but the panniers were lumpy. He pummelled them into more even shapes to provide better cushioning. Eventually he fell into a deep sleep and only awoke as the light of dawn touched him.

The night left him stiff with cold and aching. He was glad when it became lighter and he could look around him. The fire was but ashes now. He stood, and stretched, trying to warm himself, and gazed down into a small valley where two rivulets flowed through a flat plain. There was no habitation and it looked as if the valley was inaccessible from his vantage point. Towards the end there was a dark area, thickly wooded, he guessed from the skeleton shapes of the trees, with oaks and silver birches. The sun rose in front of him, touching the tips of hills. The white of the birches shone in the morning light.

If he had been superstitious, he would have said it was mystical, the cool opalescence of the early morning sun shining on the quiet valley. It was as if he was entering a magical realm, far away from the harsh realities of his life.

Even though the valley seemed inaccessible he realised he had to find a way down, through the water and towards that distant woodland. He left the horse tethered and reconnoitred. He had climbed the promontory from the south-west and he tried to see if there was a direct route down the other side but it was impossible, being a sheer cliff drop. As he looked down all he could see were some trees growing precariously at an angle from an invisible vertical cliff face.

He climbed to the top of the precipice and looked westwards, the way he had come but his view was barred by a higher rock promontory behind him, which he now realised, he must have skirted around before climbing to this point. There the sky was a lowering black, heavy with storm. He smelt the snow coming from the west. Even as he watched, the sky divided into two parts, one tangerine and ochre with streaks of white and blue; the other with wave upon wave of grey and stone and granite colours as if the earth itself was being wrapped in un-dyed black sheep's wool.

He would have to go down the way he had come and then skirt this awesome cliff. He quickly breakfasted on the now dried bread and herrings and broke open one of the sealed pots of ale and drank gulping. Then he scattered the ashes of the fire and found some animal dung, which he rubbed into it. If there was anyone stalking him with dog or alone, he hoped this would mean his scent would not be traceable.

He led Gringolay down, for he realised now the way was covered with large stones and loose shale where the granite had broken. Shattered branches and other debris made the way perilous. Beneath his feet the earth cracked and he knew the dampness from the day before had turned to ice in the night. He also needed to move to loosen his rigid bones and he wondered if this was how age began, with the stiffening of the body after a day's hard ride and a night's hard uncomfortable sleep. Again he thanked God for making the horse so sure-footed as he saw now that he could easily have stumbled last night.

'You must be able to see in the dark, my old friend. Another of your talents I will boast to old Bondon about.'

The horse tossed his head as if to agree and Priedeux patted him. Somehow he felt that he and the horse had become true partners in the long night.

Eventually he found an easier path and mounted and rode down. He kept on travelling downwards, using narrow pathways only fit for animals, until he was in the river valley. Once on the flat, he realised he was vulnerable. Anyone hiding above could plot his every move. Every bone in his body was tingling now and he knew he would find something in the woods he was heading for. It was as if the brilliance of the sun-dappled silver birches called out to him of strange promises. Whether of life or death he cared not, for he more than most knew that life was but a shadow. 'So long as I am known as a brave man, I care not for death,' he said aloud and it seemed to echo around him.

The air was warmer down here, the cliff structure that he had descended from and the hills around protecting this valley from the elements. But he could see the western clouds rolling more and more across the sky and knew the snow would fall soon.

The valley was longer than he thought and it took him the best part of the day to reach the end. He saw no-one, no animal, no bird, not even an encircling eagle or falcon high up on currents created by the surrounding hills. Even so, he felt exposed. Was he being watched? If so, they did not reveal themselves. He crossed one of the streams where there was a stony ford and rode between them, reasoning that, if any riders came from nowhere they would at least have to cross one of the rivers before they reached him. This gave him a feeling of some security, perhaps false. Eventually he found himself riding through young oaks where the woodland touched the sandy grass-covered river edge. He followed the course of the stream into the woodland and, as the trees closed around him, he realised it was becoming dusk and it wasn't just the darkness of the wood encroaching upon him. It had taken him all day to ride down from the crags and through the valley. He had eaten most of his provisions as he rode along. He thought that even though he must eat well, the Prior did not know what a hungry man could eat if he imagined that would last two days.

Then the first pads of snow fell, like miniature ladies' handkerchiefs from the King's court. They settled on branches around him for a second and then seemed to dislodge and fall gently on again. There was no wind to swirl them about and they seemed to keep falling, falling onto the hard earth beneath. At first there were just a few but the silence that fell around him told him that more was coming. Sure enough, before he reached the deep parts of the wood, it was snowing so thickly he could hardly see his way but a few yards. The snow settled on him and Gringolay and he could feel the stinging cold of it.

Oh, I truly do not want to spend another night in this bitter cold, he thought and pushed on.

Then he caught a shimmering between the trees which accentuated the darkness descending as if the snow made the time shift and the night come faster.

The shimmering effect seemed to turn solid but at first he thought it was the silver birches he had seen from the cliff top. He rode towards it but it shifted and he wondered if mirages could be created in snow like they could in deserts. Gringolay became hesitant and Priedeux had to spur him onward.

They moved forward slowly, Priedeux ducking and weaving to avoid the low branches of the silver birches he now found himself amongst. The snow was settling, and tiny ledges on each branch of the trees made them stand out. It rose before him into a solid mass that could be nothing but man-made. Priedeux headed for it as if it was his destiny. He did not care whether it was for good or evil. He spurred the horse forward and it was as if they came to the end of a tunnel and he stopped, for they were in a gigantic clearing.

In the opening the snow was being whirled by a soft wind,

as if the air was being sucked out of the clearing. Sometimes the structure before him seemed to move and he had to stare hard to make out its shape.

Before him through the whirling circles of whiteness, he saw a magnificent white castle and knew that this was what he had been sent to find. He remembered the description in the poem, so contradictory, so beautiful, like a table decoration he had glimpsed at the French king's court, all elegantly-rounded turrets and pointed castellations. Here it was, exactly like that description with the shape accentuated by the settling snow, each ledge and turret shadowed by its layer of even deeper white.

There was a silence however and Priedeux wondered. Was it enchanted? He didn't believe in such things but the unearthly silence, the picture before him and the way he had come on it made him wonder. He knew that snow dulled footfalls and noises and made the world seem unearthly but there was little movement except for the swirling storm. The new snow had not been ravaged by prints of any kind. He sat on Gringolay and stared. No flags waved on the battlements and he could see no faces at the slit windows.

'Well, my steed, let us go forward for we may find something here, and if so I shall thank the Lord. Another night like the last and I might become a monk.'

He spurred on the horse and found himself before the drawbridge which was closed. On the other side he could make out a studded closed portcullis which would surely bar his entrance.

He called out. 'Hello. Is there anyone to let me in?'

His voice seemed to swirl and then fade away in the snow flickering around him. He waited for some time, immobile, not knowing what to do. If he had been a praying man, he would have prayed for the gate to open, whether of its own accord or by fearsome men at arms, he did not care. After a while, he looked down to find snow settling on him and the horse. Soon, he thought, he would blend into the scene. A peculiar deadness took hold of him.

Then, as he waited, he heard noises. Creaks and crankings. The drawbridge started to lower towards him and the great gate was lifted upward. As the bridge moved so showers of snow rose in the air and swirled around, like so many fussy servants surrounding him. There was a smell of sour animal grease from the pulleys and weights that operated the structure. He waited until it was fully down. He hesitated realising he could be putting his head in a noose from which he would never be let out except as a corpse. Through the gateway he could see a snow-covered courtyard and smaller thatched buildings surrounding it with a backdrop of tall battlements of granite. At first he saw no one.

Then a man ran out, dressed in a green livery which Priedeux had never seen in any court or great house before, and bowed.

'Welcome, stranger, enter and be not afraid, for we have hospitality for strangers and they are few and far between.'

He stood before the rider and, as Priedeux nodded, he took Gringolay's reins and Priedeux allowed himself to be taken into the castle.

Chapter Twelve: Good food and company

Then squires and knights descended ceremoniously
to bring the bold knight blithely into hall...

His horse was halted in the middle of a spacious courtyard, surrounded by thatched outhouses. In front of him was a great hall with beautifully carved gothic windows, the stone elegantly patterned. Gringolay was held still while he dismounted. The servant repeated. 'Welcome. My master awaits you, you are truly welcome. Trust me, stranger, with thy horse and he will be well rubbed and fed. Yonder lies a house servant to lead you into my lord's good company.'

Priedeux looked to where he had pointed and there was another green liveried servant waiting in the entrance to the hall, with the door open behind him. Priedeux could not see inside because a thick curtain hid the way. He took the panniers and slung them over his shoulder and crunched across the already freezing snow.

He cared not what situation he was in, his overwhelming feeling was one of relief at finding shelter for the night, especially with the weather settling in. His uncertain life had led him not to think of the future or the past, like other men, or believe in the order of things, like other men, but to accept life as a daily passage so whatever happened on that day would suffice. He had also developed a keen sense of self-preservation and knew that if he had had to sleep out in the cold that had fallen over the earth, he might not have survived.

He did not know what this castle held, but it was at least going to be warm with food provided

The house servant held open the door, pulling back the curtain, while bowing deferentially, and, as Priedeux stepped in, a deep draught of warm air assailed him. He found himself in a spacious hall with a well-carved new hammer-beam ceiling. The long walls were broken by tall narrow windows, the carving inside even more elaborate than outside. There were floral patterns with carved faces at each of the points of the windows.

The room was full of people, all elegantly but warmly dressed in rich lawn and fur-lined clothing, the colours vying with each other for attention. Ladies wore bright crimsons and blues, and there were ochres and deep moss greens. They were standing facing him, in groups of two and three, smiling a greeting. Their evident eagerness showed him that a stranger in their midst was a great treat.

The plastered walls were richly decorated with swirls of leaves and flowers and coats of arms. On the wall behind the high table was a painted carpet-like picture with medallions, each medallion richly decorated with hunting scenes.

A great fire blazing caught the glint of the jewels and gold that the assembly wore; chains around their necks, gold belts, rings and amulets. As he came close to them he could smell a perfume strong and sweet, that he recalled from his days in the east. Refectory tables, totally bare, lit by flares, ranged the whole length of the room. More flares in high brackets caused shadows to dance in the intricacies of the roof. The whole picture was one of wealth displayed, but displayed with artistic thought.

Priedeux stood and waited. The servant came from behind him and stepped forward, gesturing for Priedeux to follow. Priedeux, so engrossed by the richly dressed assembly had not noticed that, at the end of the hall, was a daïs with a long table and high-backed and cushioned chairs. Even here the people stood and, as the servant led him to them, an imposing giant of a man with a heavy ermine-edged purple cloak came forward, his hand held out in greeting.

The whole room seemed fitting, friendly and at one with their lord. The only point that grated, was a cowled figure at the end of the daïs who scuttled away and disappeared through a swishing curtain, as if he did not want to be part of the welcoming party. Priedeux, while noting this, quickly dismissed it, as he concentrated on the large man who was so obviously his host. He seemed to gain height as Priedeux watched him, and repeated his servants' original greetings in a deep imposing voice.

'Welcome, stranger, truly welcome, for you must have travelled far to find us. You must partake of all the hospitality at my disposal, and rest awhile especially at the festivities we are now starting.'

Priedeux said nothing. The man's welcome puzzled him; why did it sound as if he had been expected?

'How long have you been travelling?' continued the man, 'For 'tis yuletide and the turn of the year will be but three days' hence. Have you travelled through the Christmas when all good folk should be with their families?'

Priedeux was even further confused. Surely he had not been travelling for so long? He tried to calculate, but the warmth in the room and the unfamiliarity of being in a crowd made him feel tired and addled. At the same time he felt relaxed, it was not now important where he had been or how long he had journeyed. As if reading his thoughts, his host boomed:

'You are tired. Come, you have had a long ride: you must bathe and make ready for the feast we will have prepared in your honour.'

Then Priedeux spoke. 'Where am I? What castle is this?'

'All will be revealed but first we must attend to your bodily comforts.'

He clapped his hand and another servant appeared and bowed. Priedeux was led away to an antechamber where the furnishings were as sumptuous as the clothes of the host and his court. In the centre a bath had been placed on a wooden platform, steaming and sweet-smelling of sandalwood and roses and other aromas which Priedeux did not recognise. Beside it stood a great barrel with more steam emitting from it. Luxury indeed, that extra water. On the bed were laid a robe and an undershirt of soft wool, and a servant indicated they were for him. Priedeux dropped his panniers by the side of the richly carved and curtained bed and took off the heavy padded shirt and leggings he had worn for days. As he started to strip the servant moved discreetly away, busying himself with his back to the guest. Priedeux had learnt to bathe in the east and recognised it as a good way to keep fleas at bay, and irritants that might get at a man's skin. The aroma from the bath told him that soothing herbs had been sprinkled in the tub. The room was warm and his natural instinct to keep covered and always ready for attack was abated. In any case, he thought ironically, it would be a good way to die, warm and clean in a bath. Ready for my shroud. He grinned to himself as he levered himself into the steaming waters. The servant who had been busying himself discreetly approached and started to scrub his back.

As the servant scrubbed at the grime of many days and the flesh became exposed, he must have noticed the battle scars around the shoulders where Priedeux had sustained the hackings of swords and knives. The scars were old but deep and there was the new healing wound on the wrist and in the crook of the arm. Priedeux offered no explanations and the servant asked no questions, but he touched them tentatively. Priedeux could tell he was wondering.

After the bath he was helped to dress in the clothing which had been left out. This was as richly coloured as the other clothes he had seen. The soft woollen undershirt was warm and fell around his dried body as if to caress him. Over this, the servant pulled around his shoulders a long robe of patterned damask with an outer surcoat and a great belt which was so long, that, after it was tightened by a great elegant clasp, left enough slack for some of it to fall nearly to his knees. Not unlike the clothes King Richard favoured, he thought; so courtly fashions reach this remote place that cannot be found even by monks. To go with it there was a great ermine lined cloak, which, in the warmth of the room, Priedeux did not need. As he finished dressing the servant clapped his hands and three lackeys came in, as if waiting outside for their call, lifted the bath and the barrel and marched out, leaving the room empty of all bathing accoutrements. No one spoke a word and Priedeux was too tired to question them. The bath had relaxed him to a point of lassitude, an acceptance of his surroundings.

As he continued to dress, strange memories came to him, a feeling of déjà vu, as if he recognised the clothes. He knew he could not possibly have worn such expensive items before, not in this life anyway, but as he pulled on the rich woollen leggings, so fine that they clung to his calves, and the soft leather boots, he knew exactly how it should be done. When he was finished he knew he would leave the chamber and return to the great hall, as if he had read a script of what he should do next.

Suddenly he remembered and grabbed the pannier, pulled out *Gawain and the Green Knight* and started to hunt through the pages. Yes, there it was, Gawain too had met sumptuous people, been bathed and clothed and fed.

Priedeux decided to follow the script but he also thought he should hide the original. Some instinct told him to be as careful as possible about the reason for his mission. He stowed the book in the capaciousness of the gown. He would go along with this charade and see where it led and if he found the man he was seeking then so be it; it would be a comfortable way of carrying out his mission.

He left the chamber and followed the noise of laughter and the strumming of musical instruments. When he re-entered the great hall, the conversation stopped but not in an unfriendly way. It was as if the party awaited his return and now he had come they paused, waiting for directions from their lord.

Their leader rose from his throne at the centre of the head table, and passed behind his companions to reach Priedeux and led him back to the high seats. On one side sat a haggard crack of a woman, all wrinkles and white hair slipping from her wimple. Her cloak was rich brown and fur-lined and almost covered her tiny frame, the sleeves falling around her wrists leaving small crabbed hands exposed. They rested on the table as if they were too tired to be left on their own. She was bowing and nodding either in greeting or senility Priedeux could not say. The lord introduced her.

'My dear mother, ancient as she is.'

The old woman pulled herself to a standing position, her face screwing in pain as she did so, the crabbed hands holding on to the side of the table but eventually she stood beside her son. Her head just reached his chest, he was so tall. He ushered her forward. Priedeux kissed her on each cheek and stood back. As he did so, his host turned to one side and added.

'...and my wife, my lady.'

Priedeux had not noticed her. He was sure she had not been there when he first entered the hall. Had she just emerged from the curtain behind the daïs and sat down quickly? The candle flame caught her face as she stood, and illumined it as she looked down modestly while she curtseyed. He saw a fine brow and straight nose and well shaped mouth, the upper lip slightly pouting. As she rose however she looked straight at him and it was as if he had been pierced.

The look was penetrating, shy and bold at the same time, Priedeux did not understand how. A smile played on the lips as if she recognised his puzzlement. He could not bring himself to greet her by taking her by the elbows and kissing her on both cheeks as he had done with the old woman. He felt troubled in her presence as if she could read his lascivious thoughts, which were somehow inappropriate in this place. She made him feel ashamed of all that had happened in the past, the killings, the seductions, the abandonment of family, his lack of regard for his lame older brother.

He looked away, merely bowing to acknowledge her. It was probably considered incredibly rude, but he was sure that, if he took her in his arms, he would betray his emotion. In order to compose himself, he remembered his story, his inspiration on this quest. This woman was as beautiful, dignified and elegant as the poet had described.

She moved closer to him, a movement as graceful as a willow bending to the water, and so he forced himself to greet her politely. He took the slender hand she held out to him, a tiny form with finely shaped nails, hardly large enough to be seen in the wide brim of the ermine that surrounded the sleeve of her gown. She did not proffer her cheek, as if she knew this would be too much for him. Her husband had stepped back, leaving her and Priedeux facing each other, and as he took her hand, he felt a shock. It was as if they were alone in this great crowd of her people. She smiled at him, a confidential calm smile but her eyes were dancing. It was the eyes that hypnotised, rimmed with dark lashes, of a dark pool colour that reflected shapes and shadows that made promises to him of such unimaginable pleasures that he eventually looked down. For once he truly felt embarrassment in front of a lady. He felt she could read his very soul and knew his roughness, his way of living, but did not mind, would accept that and mould it to her own ends. It was all over in a few seconds but he felt as if he had lived another life. She stepped away and, in one graceful sliding movement, returned to her seat.

He turned to his host. 'Surely she is most beautiful and I thank you for your hospitality and courtesy.'

The lord guffawed loudly through his thick wiry beard. Priedeux saw gaps and black teeth and wondered at the contrast between the couple. The older man slapped his guest on the shoulder and Priedeux nearly fell forward. 'Sit, my friend, for I am well pleased with your speech. Sit on the right side of my dear wife and keep her entertained for she would hear from whence you came. We have but few honoured guests and she would know your story. As I would, and, I am sure, would all my host.'

As the lord sat so did his company and, as if by some hidden signal, food was brought in on huge platters. Music wafted from some hidden gallery. A servant handed Priedeux a large flat bread for a plate and other servants stood before the long top table in a row, all of them holding a tray of delicacies.

'You take first pickings, as guest of honour, please,' said his host and Priedeux was proffered the choicest portions of minuscule fowl, pigeon, fish of all kinds and beef. There were tiny side dishes of quails' eggs and rare cheeses and curds. He ate until he was full and little conversation took place within that company while they ate, as if they all wanted to concentrate on the good fare before them and listen to the music.

Wine was served in delicate gold rimmed cups, and when Priedeux raised it to his mouth he was surprised to smell a rich aroma of fruits which brought back memories of the warmth of the south, of the Spanish sierra and Portuguese terraces. No rough wine, this, but strong fortified richness.

He turned to his host and the great man, his face half hidden in the beard which covered his cheeks almost to his eyes, was grinning. The grin split the beard and made the eyes into tiny pinpoints surrounded by a whole crows' wings of wrinkles.

'Yes, my friend, we have good wine here and good food. And when we are finished we will have a good tale from you, I'll be bound.' The man took a great draught of the liquid in his beaker and then poured more from the jug the servant had left before him.

Priedeux realised it would be considered the height of rudeness to enquire as to the name and antecedents of his host but knew he would have to give good account of himself. As he ate he surveyed the crowd below the salt, trying to see the cowled figure who had disappeared from the hall on his arrival. *Could he be the poet?* But there was no sign of him among the laughing and jovial crowd, who were all tucking into the good food. If he had been there he would have stood out; a dark figure in all that colour.

His thoughts turned to his own situation and he weighed up what he would be able to say, what tale he could tell. The mark on the horse would have been seen by the stable hand - no doubt it would be reported to his master. His panniers could even now be rifled although the incriminating poem was on his person.

He thought of the Prior and his knowledge and remembered what the Prior had said about not being able to find this place. Priedeux guessed that this lord would have a bevy of spies and that Priedeux's approach had been well known despite the lack of snow-prints into the castle. Priedeux decided that only the truth would do.

Then he heard her soft voice for the first time and it sent another thrill through him for it was deep and sultry, reminding him again of foreign sun.

'You have eaten your fill? And you are not tired? We will not force your story out of you if you do not want to relate it now.'

He turned to her and saw her softly-sympathetic eyes watching him. He then realised her white, delicately formed hand was on his arm but it was so light he had hardly felt it. Now he looked at the be-ringed fingers and tenderness towards her swept over him.

But he smiled to hide the feeling.

'My lady, I am indebted to you and will repay such debt with the tale of my coming, if you wish it.'

She smiled at him and said, just as softly: 'I do wish it for these parts can be lonely and a new tale would be entertaining.'

Others below the salt were still eating and the lord waited, looking around to command attention, without saying anything. Soon there was a hush as if all realised there would be some entertainment and the lord stood, pushing his bulky weight up with his fists on the table before him, in a gesture which oddly mirrored his mother's crabbed claws.

'My ladies and gentlemen, we are all pleased to welcome a stranger to our midst at such a time as this, for it is the very devil of a time to travel.' He said, and the company nodded in agreement, some of them smiling sympathetically towards Priedeux.

'So now I would ask our guest to tell us his name and his business and where he is going.'

The whole room clapped and each face was smiling at him with such good nature that he felt he had nothing to fear. None of the company had drunk so much that they were slumped over the remains of their meal; none had turned away to hand a morsel to a dog. He had not noticed any lascivious gropings of the maid servants who worked alongside the men. Even these servants leant against the walls behind them in a relaxed manner which indicated they were staying, to hear the stranger's story.

Priedeux stood and looked around at them all, waited and said: 'I am overwhelmed with the welcome you have given me, truly it is thawing the winter snow outside.'

The company laughed at this witticism. He continued: 'I come from lands afar - from King Richard's court. But before that I travelled in all parts of this earth, even to Jerusalem, seeking my fortune as a knight. Many adventures have I had which are too many to tell but never have I seen such a castle as this and such good company, and I thank the good Lord for leading me here. I have been sent by King Richard to find a very special person but perhaps you have heard of him - The Green Knight?'

There was a great roar of laughter and men banged on the table, and Priedeux heard comments from those nearest them, 'Oh, a wag, a funny man from the Great Court down south.' Priedeux turned to the master but he was laughing too, so much so that tears were squeezing from the corners of his almost closed eyes. Even the old woman was cackling in a hen-like manner. Priedeux felt the soft hand again of his hostess, and sat, leaning towards the lady:

'What have I said? Why is it funny?'

She too was smiling broadly. 'Aah, you have truly touched the hearts of the people. The Green Man is a story told hereabouts, of a great knight who is part of the forest and half magic, half man. My husband adopts his livery to please his people. And now you come along and ask to meet a mythical man.'

'Tell me more about him.'

She laughed then. ''Tis not my tale, it is my husband's.'

Priedeux turned to the man but he was still laughing. Then he saw Priedeux watching him and his laughter subsided. He explained in between gusts of laughter: 'If you want to know the Green Knight, you must play games, my friend. Do you not know that?'

Priedeux nodded and said grimly: 'I have heard.'

The lord looked sharply at him. 'So be it. We will play the game, shall we not? Drink, drink again and we will be merry!' He filled Priedeux's cup and they both swigged back the rich liquid. Then he went on.

'The game is about tokens and honour, is it not?'

Priedeux shrugged. He would be led by events. The feeling of déjà vu was becoming very strong, and he felt as if he were within the story of a story, as if he were being guided. If it meant he could achieve his mission, with the promise of more gold at the end of it, then so be it.

'So, for the next three days we will wager stories with stories, we will swap experiences, what say you?'

Priedeux gasped, the similarity with the poem was becoming farcical. He realised that if indeed the similarity was not coincidence - and how could it be? - then his very life was in danger. If Gaunt and Chaucer were right and the poem had been written to incite rebellion against the only true King of England then Priedeux would not be allowed to escape from this place with the knowledge of the name of its creator. Or even the name of the place. Everyone knew how vengeful King Richard could be. Priedeux was sure some trumped up charge to satisfy his advisers would be made and this knight, with his friendly court, would be the subject of a campaign to wipe out traitors to the King. Already Richard, with his Uncle Gaunt goading him on, had proved a revengeful and cruel monarch to those who crossed him. Priedeux had played some part in some of their plots and had also seen Richard being criticised by his barons for what they saw as misjudgements. Richard had haughtily dismissed their concerns and it was his uncle, Priedeux's paymaster, who had pulled them back into seeming loyalty. Richard was a man who, at court with his favourites, could seem effeminate in his enthusiasms, but, if the need arose, when there was rebellion, he could ride out, make promises to allay the rebels, and then break those promises. Priedeux, thinking all this, did not have time to reply to his host, who, assuming his silence was consent, nodded.

'Good!' He said. 'Tomorrow morn, I am to hunting and you will stay at home, and refresh yourself. Tomorrow night, at the feast, we will exchange the tokens we have won during the day.'

Chapter Thirteen: A visit

'The lady in lovely guise came laughing sweetly,
bent down o'er his dear face, and deftly kissed him.'

Priedeux woke early before light penetrated his room, and listened to the sounds of preparation in the yard. The saddling of horses, stamping of impatient hooves, hounds whining with excitement, hushed orders being given.   He remained luxuriously wallowing in the rich down of the coverlet, knowing his script.

The night before, by the light of a rich candle flame, he had read through the poem again, concentrating on the scenes in the castle. If he was right that somehow he had to follow the story of Gawain then he needed to stay in bed and await events.

He was not to join the hunting, he'd already been told last night. He didn't mind, it had never been to his taste to force a horse into galloping, to watch the kill and the stripping of skin and chopping of flesh for the eating. He preferred a clean quick despatch, coldly carried out for need or reward and wanted none of the social etiquette which went with courtly sport.

He read again the description in Gawain of the lord's day and grimaced. Surely the man who had written this revelled in the sport and had seen enough killings of deer to know exactly how it was done. Priedeux could almost smell the warm bitterness of discarded offal. He hid the book beneath the pillows, and waited.

Eventually he heard the drawbridge being lowered and the clopping of the horses as they rode over the snow-bare boards of the bridge, and faded as they reached the snow covered woodland, accompanied by the calling of the followers, and horns of the hunt as it left the castle. Then the drawbridge was raised and a silence seemed to settle over the place, as if the remaining servants had slunk off, back to their quarters to warm themselves, to snuggle against their loved ones.

Priedeux settled down again. He too was cocooned in a curtained bed, warmer than he had been for some time. He felt the material of the curtains, and revelled in the softness of the embroidered damask, wondering at its rich and contrasting colours, with its border of gold-braid. There was a warmth in the curtained-off bed from his own body. His pillows were thick and luxurious and the covers were of expensive damask of a different pattern to the curtains. Truly there was wealth in this castle, wealth he had rarely seen outside the court of Richard and of his Lord Gaunt.

He had dozed off again when the slightest of noises shot him into full wakefulness. He did not open his eyes. He had read the poem; he knew what was to be expected. He felt the cool breeze from the outer room, as the curtain was lifted and the slenderest of bodies gentled itself onto the side of the bed. Priedeux still kept his eyes shut and deliberately regulated his breathing as if he were still asleep, and waited, just as Gawain had done in the poem.

He knew he was being watched as if the watcher was forcing her presence upon him. He could smell the slight scent of her, of lavender and of body heat inside musty winter clothing, which was not unpleasant to him. Her breathing came regularly as if she too waited.

He lay there thinking. It would be unwise, he was sure, to seduce this woman until he was more aware of the situation, even though this quiet entrance suggested she expected him to. In his world no lady would visit a man's room alone unless she hoped to be bedded. Although he felt his manhood rising, he knew he had to follow the poem; courtly conversation only.

Last night she and her husband had seemed on the best of terms, and, knowing his guidebook of a poem, he suspected a trick. He decided to keep cool, even though, he had to admit to himself, the mere softness of her presence on the bed was playing havoc with his resolve. He remained immobile as he thought wryly that this was probably the first time he had ever been alone with a desirable woman and was not going to...

Priedeux realised he would have to show wakefulness eventually and mimicked the situation he had read in *Gawain*. He stretched himself, opened his eyes, and looked astonished as his gaze fell straight on the lady.

The look of surprise was not feigned by Priedeux, for her appearance was not what he expected. He thought she would be dressed as she had been the night before in rich but formal clothes. Instead her hair was falling about her shoulders with cleverly woven gold braid twisted in it as if the rich hair was caught in a huge fishing net. She had discarded her cloak at the bottom of the bed as if that was where she saw the boundaries between coming to him and relaxing in his domain. She now revealed a fine dress, cut low on her shoulders and tightly fitted around her body, so that her sharp little breasts were forced up into rounded shapes which contrasted with the narrowness of her waist.

She was smiling down at him and one hand was resting on the edge of the bed not a few inches away from his thigh, as if with one movement she would reach out and caress him.

'So you have woken, at last.' She smiled, 'a man must have travelled long to be so tired.'

'Indeed I have, Madam, and the experiences of the last few days have been many.'

'Tell me about your experiences, for you say you have travelled far.' She said it with a lilt, as if she was laughing at him.

'Where do I begin; what would you have of me?' he fielded.

She looked away as if pondering but soon looked back at him and, her face seemingly serious, countered: 'Tell me of courtly love, of the pure love of the knights and their innocent ladies at the court you have come from.'

'Madam, you mock.'

Still with those arched eyebrows that belied her words, she answered: 'Indeed I do not. All I know of such places are what I have read in a book called *The Romance of the Rose* and such-like treatises. I truly believe the highest court in the realm must be governed by the courtesies that I read of in that book.'

As she spoke she seemed to move closer, and her arm rested on his hip bone. She was either deeply innocent as she said despite her being married, or she was giving him obvious signals that he could bed her before the winter sun reached its daily zenith. He could feel the lightness of her as the featherest of touches, a mere hint of nothing. Or of all. But he would not fall for her wiles and began to think her a witch, a cruel temptress, even more cruel because she seemed so innocent. Such conflicting thoughts dampened his manhood. Even so, on an intellectual level, he wanted to penetrate that archness, that ironic coldness that created a barrier as strong as castellated turrets. He told himself it was to find out more about her husband, his retinue, whether there was a cleverly-wordy poet in his pay.

He said cruelly. 'Huh, *The Romance of the Rose*. A true fairytale indeed. Madam, if knights behaved in such a way with their ladies and only worshipped from afar, they would never get pricked with the stabs of that love which helps man to procreate, would they now?'

'Aah, but it is a subtle art form which I understood helps to seam the fabric of society, so that all is kept on the right path of decency and kindness and honour.'

He sat up so that he faced her with only a few inches

169

between them. His hand brushed hers as if he would take it but he did not.

'Decency? Kindness? Honour? Such things are tempered with deviousness and cruelty. For a man could not survive wars or the court if he were decent and kind, and as for honour...' He let the word hang in the air between them for some seconds before he continued: 'Yes, we all have our tune of honour which harmonises with the lives we choose, or the tune which is thrust upon us.'

'So, I have riled you.' She stroked his hand then, as if calming a wild beast. 'Now tell me what your honour is! Would you bed another man's wife?' She asked with her head on one side, her face shaded in the gloom of the chamber. The question sounded objective, as if she were asking a priest a theological question, not related to herself at all. It still took him off guard, although his training stood him in good stead for he made sure his face did not flicker.

Instead, to cover himself, he laughed and this time he did take the tiny hand, and turned it over, as if he would palm-read. He stroked the narrow channels of the lifeline, the loveline across the palm. That way he would not need to meet her searching gaze, and it gave him time to think.

He said quietly. 'It would not depend on who the other man was or that the woman was a wife. It would depend on the lust I felt for the woman.'

She pulled her hand away and held it to her ribs with her other hand as if it had been burnt. Then she spat out, 'lust! Is that all you can think of? Yes, I could tell when you strode in last night, that you are a man of strong urges, but I believe you must also be capable of great loves, are you not?'

This time he leant on his elbow so he was looking away from her but his body was enveloping hers, his legs curled around the curve of her buttocks. She seemed undeterred by the intimate closeness of their bodies, as if she did not appreciate any sensuality between them. He was puzzled by her. There was a silence.

Then he said dismissively, 'I know not what love is, if what the troubadours sing of is love. But I could pleasure you and you would enjoy it and so would I. That is the truth of the matter, Madam.'

She backed away as he said that, in what he interpreted as mock horror, her face pale.

He threw back the covers and moved quickly to the window to get away from her before he broke his resolve and seduced her. He wore the soft white nightshirt that had been laid out for him, which reached to his knees. He looked out at the winter scene, all white and grey and skeletal woodland. He stood like that for some time, almost expecting her to join him, perhaps stroke his hair or press herself gently to him like a dog seeking forgiveness, but she did not. She remained on the bed. There was no movement in the room.

For once, he felt uncertain of himself, his calculations of femininity being incorrect. He could feel the cold penetrating his feet and his hands where they rested on the thick granite ledge and he welcomed it. The knee-length shirt he wore was of little help outside the warmth of the covers. The cold air filtered through the narrow gap of window, and smelt of tangy bitterness. He turned and leant on the wall and looked back at her, absorbing the cold of the wall like a punishment to cool his ardour. She was but a dim shadow now because his eyes were unaccustomed to the room's gloom having been dazzled by the whiteness outside. He smiled, a friendly smile, hiding all feelings of the lust which simmered within him. His self-control restored, he repeated:

'I know nothing of love, but I know when I wish to bed a woman!'

He strode towards her and cupped his hand under her breast, feeling its lightness, a virgin's unripened pertness about it. 'And you, with those wonderful breasts pointing at me, you I wish to bed.'

She backed away and stood up, her arms crossed before her and looked at him so sternly that he knew his wish would be thwarted, at least for now. He remembered the poem; he would bide his time. He would not force her for he had never had to force a woman and had no intention of doing so now. His enjoyment was in the woman's response, the power he had over her as she submitted to his every thrust and movement.

'By that you have forfeited my goodwill for you are a guest of my husband and it is required of you to be honourable to me, if only as a stranger should be.'

His eyebrows rose then and he answered: 'Madam, you come into my room and speak of love, ask me if I would bed another man's wife, and touch me gently. It reminds me of one such as you in a book, and I would not so be teased.'

'But I am not one in a book, I am as I am; a woman who is curious about the world, who wishes to know. I have led a sheltered life and rarely come across such as you and I would know, so I need to ask questions.'

He raised his eyebrows. 'Do you not know 'tis dangerous to enter a knight's room on your own in such manner?'

She smiled. 'I guess it and imagine it, but cannot know it. I want to know it, and I thought you would be the one who could explain... I have no-one to ask.'

It was an admission, spoken sadly.

'Why do you not attend Court? Why do you not persuade your husband to go on pilgrimage? Then you would find out.'

'My husband! You may well note he is older than I, grizzled but strong. You do not think that such is a love-match or what the troubadours sing of and drive women wild with the longing for? I will tell you enough now and then we must end this for today. He will not leave this lost castle of his now that he has nearly all that he wants. There is one thing however that he has not got.'

'And pray what is that? Nobility? Wealth?' Priedeux felt a quickening interest, perhaps this conversation would lead somewhere. It might be useful to him in his quest. He felt he could ask and find out more about the husband, for she had become confiding, but she stepped back again, as if withdrawing from him not only physically but mentally.

'You think he wants power? You have not listened to anything I have said.'

'Nobility then?'

She said nothing still backing away. He went on: 'He cannot want wealth, unless all this is but a dream?'

Still she stayed silent.

'Wealth!'

He repeated the single word sure he had the solution. She stepped back again, still looking at him, still saying nothing, as if to escape from physical blows and soon reached the door. Then she answered:

'I'll say no more now, for 'tis late and you must arise, and eat. Then we will walk together, in my arbour, my sheltered place, and you can tell me what you would give my husband as a token this night.'

She suddenly stepped forward and brushed his cheek with soft lips so that he felt the kiss as a feather stroking him and, before he could pull her to him, she had gathered her cloak around her and was gone. Priedeux realised this woman was as slippery as a trout in a monks' pond, for no other woman would have escaped his clutches after kissing him in such a way.

Suddenly he realised he was chilled through, and dressed quickly. Even though he did not relish the hunt, he wished he could be in the saddle, away from these feminine wiles. It left a bad taste in his mouth, for all he wished now was the good healthy laying of a woman. Even though he could bandy words, he had grown bored of such ways and usually kept with tried methods of seduction which did not tax his emotions or intellect. Now he found himself in a situation not unlike a hunt where he had to stop himself from being cornered by clever words. He had continued with it because, at the back of his mind, he thought he could find a way for her to tell him about her husband. Priedeux was sure he was on the track of the Gawain poet now, and wanted to find out if this castle had a library, if the owner, whose name he still did not know, was well versed in Latin and ancient myths. He certainly loved hunting.

That night at table the feast was as good as the first night and served as courteously. Priedeux was silent but polite, watching his host and his wife who sat back in her chair as if she wanted to be unobtrusive. Even so, the couple seemed quietly devoted to one another. As the last of the rich wine was poured, his host turned to Priedeux and raised his full cup. The woman beside him leant forward and smiled, as if to encourage what her husband would say.

'Now we will exchange our tokens.' He clapped his hands and lackeys brought in the deer, which Priedeux was expecting. He had started using a phrase: *And so it is written*. He was sure now that he had to be in the castle of the Gawain poet. Priedeux as guest accepted graciously and, with some trepidation, moved towards his host and gave him the lightest of kisses on his cheek, a mirror of that he had received from the man's wife earlier.

The lord roared with laughter. 'So you have been toying with the wenches all day. But you do not seem to have got far, if that is all you have acquired! Better luck tomorrow. Do you wager with me again for tokens?'

Priedeux realised he could hardly refuse and solemnly accepted the game for the next day.

As he climbed into bed that night he realised he had some hard thinking to do. If Gaunt was correct and the poem had been written deliberately to incite rebellion against the King, then Priedeux was right in the enemy camp. He was convinced of it. He took the flare from the wall and lit the small candle provided, balancing it precariously on the cavernous bed. He pulled the curtains tight for he did not want any chink of light to shine from the narrow window as a beacon of his wakefulness. He needed to read his opus magnum again, *Gawain and the Green Knight*, to see how the enemy would use their wiles to trick him. He was sure too, that they knew who he was but he had still not discovered the name of his host. Every time he had tried to lead the conversation towards that, it had been deflected. On one such occasion, the lord had leant across him and filled his cup and ordered him to drink again. As he lifted the cup to his lips the lord began a long and convoluted story of hunting experiences.

Priedeux was also puzzled about the general merriment which had erupted when he mentioned he was looking for the Green Knight. In the poem, he was the lord of this manor, disguised so Gawain did not recognise him from their encounter the year before. In the book he was a mythical giant. It was not mythical creatures that he was concerned with in this place, he was sure. His host, and, more importantly, his wife, were flesh and blood creatures. It was the descriptions of royalty and its air of corruption that he wanted to investigate. Even so, he wondered if the laughter had been because they thought he was so off the mark? Or the myth of the Green Knight was used as a cover? Could they guess that he had been sent to sniff out rebellion? If so, why did they play with him in this way? Perhaps they thought he was one of a horde sent to wipe them out and hoped he would tell them more? If so, why treat him so well, why not just take him to the torture chamber and extract all he might know by beatings? His thoughts now also turned to escape, if the need arose.

He had not had a chance to inspect the castle and had no way of working out an escape-route, so, for the time being, he decided to play along with the farce, and let it take him where it would. But, he thought, forewarned is forearmed.

So he took up the book again. He read through the parts where the lady visited. She made three visits, and Priedeux knew enough about the way such poems were written, from listening to Chaucer at court, to realise this might have mystical significance, perhaps representing the Trinity - the all-seeing, all knowing God split into the Father, Son and Holy Ghost. This was something most men would understand and appreciate. He considered the banquet scenes where tokens were exchanged and then read on, to where Gawain finally leaves to fulfil his quest, to meet the Green Knight again.

As he fell asleep, questions rose before him. Would he have to leave to find the real poet? The real incendiarist? Or would the answer be inside this castle? And what about that cowled figure? The slight glimpse he had caught of the person, with the dark robes, had been so at odds with the bright colours, courtesy and openness of this court that the thought of that person now haunted Priedeux. That night, his dreams were vivid.

Chapter Fourteen: Further conversations

'It gives me great happiness, and is good sport to me,
that so fine a fair one as you should find her way here
and take pains with so poor a man, make pastime with her knight...'

There was blood, a thick viscous river of it flowing towards him like the lava he had once seen flowing from Vesuvius towards the foaming water of the bay, overpowering all in its path. The blood was hot and he knew, in the dream, where he stood in the centre, that it was fresh but he couldn't make out whether it was flowing because of something he had done or whether it was his.

Even in the dream Priedeux tried to reason with himself. He knew it was not his, but the blood of someone he had murdered coming towards him. It flowed and in the centre it split and channelled around a rock which, as he looked, seemed to grow and become *a cowled figure.* It was bending over so that its face could not be seen and, as the red flowed around it, it became darker, blacker, more defined, uncurling. Priedeux knew that the figure was staring at him and he expected an arm to be raised and an accusing finger pointed at him. So much blood on his hands, so much to atone for. He felt sad, as if something or someone had made him realise what he had been doing wrong. Even as he thought this, he rebelled. He was a soldier, a man of fortune. If he did not kill, he would be the one to die. It was nature's way. Like hunting. He wanted to accost the cowled figure, explain, but he could not reach him because of the river of red hot liquid which flowed between them.

The baying of excited and eager hounds was part of the dream and visions of boar hunting and viciousness, of kill or be killed, invaded the scene. Now he was standing on a promontory away from the red river, watching it moving inexorably in front and pass by where he stood as if he had stepped to one side to avoid it. There were figures below him, in the midst of the red, trying to run rapidly but not succeeding as the liquid slowed them like glue. Some were chasing the others. He recognised it as a hunt. Suddenly one of them, small, four-footed but rounded with huge tusks which glowed whitish brown in the red, turned and charged back at his pursuers, facing Priedeux.

He forced himself out of the dream but the noise of the hounds continued echoing in the enclosed courtyard below. The noise of the start of a hunt was only too real. Priedeux found himself shaking with an uncontrollable fear, and closed his eyes again only to find the colour red still flooding his dream vision.

Whilst not superstitious he did have a belief in dreams and he tried to remember all the details of the vision as he came out of the deep sleep of exhaustion, good wine and a late night.

He almost expected to see dark red curtains, a bloodied sunrise. Instead the room was grey with a winter dawn and he listened to the hounds barking excitedly outside, and now knew that he had not dreamed the sound. He opened the bed-curtain. Bitter cold greeted him. Another freezing early morning he thought. He pulled the fur-lined cloak he had been given around his shoulders, and, moving to the slit of a window, he surveyed the scene in the courtyard. It appeared that all the host of the night before were gathered, their horses champing to be gone on the hunt. The keepers of the hounds were goading their charges, thick necked and strong creatures, as the drawbridge was slowly wound open. Priedeux, relying on the omen of the dream, was not surprised they were the particular hounds bred especially for boar hunting. He wondered if the memory of the story of Gawain was haunting him, as he remembered the second hunting expedition was for wild boar.

Their leader, the lord, was riding round and round the group, laughing and talking to each of his guests. One he clapped on the shoulder, with another he exchanged a large tankard from which they both drank. Suddenly he looked up at the window as if he knew Priedeux was there. He waved a thickly gloved hand and nodded. Surely he had eagle eyes, thought Priedeux.

Priedeux waved back but doubted if the gesture could really be seen and then watched as the retinue galloped out of the battlemented exit. As the drawbridge was pulled up again with a great clanking of chains, he turned back into the room - to find milady standing there, arms folded, smiling.

'So today you are awake, but I would have preferred it if you were still abed for I would talk with you more and I would prefer it if you were defenceless, still in your night shirt.'

He strode towards her and taking both of her hands in his, smiled at her, as if she were a bosom friend. 'Madam, I would do what you would wish, I am at your mercy.'

'Aah, no, I would not presume, I would never wish to have anyone in my mercy. I would wish all to want to be with me, to love me, to be my companion, because they would wish it, of their own free will.'

'Free will, what do you know of free will?'

She pulled away from him, and walked around the room, as if testing her own thoughts. He watched as she wrung her hands together. Then she turned and said: 'Have you said mass today? Yesterday? This week?'

He laughed. 'Mass? That is for those who wish to exhibit their belief or for those who know they might die soon. I would hope to receive the last rites to make sure of my place in heaven but if it is not to be, I shall trust in the God that my mother spoke about who is all-wise, all-forgiving, all-good. And with the intercession of certain saints to whom I pray I trust my afterlife is assured.' He said it ironically for could such as he worry about an afterlife? He turned, threw off the cloak and climbed back into bed pulling some of the covers over his bare legs. She came closer and sat at the end of the bed and surveyed him.

Eventually she spoke. 'Then you would know that I have been reading the good books not only in Latin but also your English Wycliffe and I find what he says wonderfully true for me. We all have free will to do good or bad, and we must exercise it according to our conscience and not according to what the monks or priests would tell us. We all have God within us.'

Priedeux began to feel uncomfortable. He did not know what to make of this woman. Yesterday she spoke of love and troubadours' songs whilst ignoring the overt sexual overtones in their discourse and today she spoke like the worst heretic he had ever seen burnt. She had said she knew little and wanted to know more but she spoke with authority as if she had indeed read many books. Not only read them but understood and appreciated the arguments. Priedeux guessed this from the way she spoke, for he had no time for such reading. A thought occurred to him but he dismissed it. He would look at his poem again. He was not interested in religion; it seemed irrelevant to him and he had no use for it in his life of fortune. He wanted to change the subject. Anyway, how would talk of religion help him to find his quarry, the man who wrote *Gawain*? He picked up on something she had said : '*Your Wycliffe.*' Did that mean she wasn't from these parts? He had noticed the slight lilt in her voice, but wondered if it was part of the local dialect.

'Maybe so, Madam, but I am of this world and do not know of religion or of this man Wycliffe. I prefer to think of those I am with,' and he pulled himself into a sitting position and moved closer to her. She did not shy away.

'And what are you thinking of me?' She asked innocently, as if she wanted to know, again, in the same objective way she had asked him yesterday if he would bed another's wife.

He decided to risk asking her direct questions. 'I am thinking I know nothing of you, where you come from, your name, your status, although I can see you are a grand lady and I wonder why you are not at court.'

'Your English court you mean? I would like that, to see how great knights - for they must be great to be at the English court - behave. I imagine it is with great courtesy and ceremony?'

He laughed at the wistfulness in her voice and mocked her, but did it with an overlaid kindness. 'Indeed, it is with *great* ceremony. Our king, Richard, enjoys *great* luxuries in food and wine and loves *great* company. He has been known to feast for twelve days and nights and the food has been so rich that most of the court would fast for a month afterwards.'

They both laughed at this and she played with a strand of her hair that had wisped out of the coiled braid. 'But the food, describe it to me. I would know all this in detail and I can then serve my Lord with such delicacies.'

So Priedeux described the foods and the subtleties. The celebratory show-pieces made of sculptured sugar or pastry models, sometimes of ships, sometimes of fancy castles or even strange creatures. He hummed the tunes played on trumpet and drum, he sang snatches of songs although his memory did not serve him well. Even as he jumped off the bed and mimed the antics of mummers, he hoped he was putting her at her ease; that way, he believed, if she was like every other woman he had ever met, he would be able to penetrate her defences. Soon she would be so comfortable, she would start to tell him everything about herself. He had discovered at a very early age that women needed to confide, to share likes and dislikes, to tell about their families, as they grew to want and like a man. Now, he hoped, all he had to do was to tell her something of his life and she would be his. He described how Richard had dressed as a lion, albeit still with crown and sceptre, and chased his retainers around the long hall in the twelfth night ceremony.

'And he was most particular to ensure he held his handkerchief to his nose when he caught one of them, for he is a pernickety man'.

He told of conjurers and story tellers who entertained the mass of diners. He explained that such things were now commonplace and described the exotic presentation of foods at Storeton Hall. The memory of that place made him think of Gertrude's lustful honesty, which he could do well with now. He did not say he had lately come from there, not knowing whether this woman knew much about her nearest neighbours, even if they were several days' ride away.

'You understand such things have now spread across the country, for Richard's court travels from place to place, and such tales as his luxury and exotic ways go before him to places where he would never venture.'

He did not tell her of the squalor and intrigue behind such ceremonies, of the dirt and filth of many men which became so stenchious that the court moved on, leaving the mess to be cleared by serfs. He did not tell of the quick couplings in corridors that led to a hastily organised 'stately' marriage to ensure legitimacy for an heiress's babe, nor of the secret disappearances of those who displeased the King. Or even of the public humiliation of banishments within the King's own family which had lately occurred.

'But the money? Where does he raise the money for such things?'

Priedeux suddenly tensed; was this now going to lead him where he wanted? Would he now find the rebellious questioning that he had been looking for? Had this wife been indoctrinated by a jealous spouse who resented the revenues raised for such luxuriousness? He remembered what she had said the previous day about her husband lacking one thing, and Priedeux had guessed it was wealth; was he now lusting after Richard's revenues?

It was true, as Priedeux well knew, that there were mutterings, even within the Royal household, of resentment against the costly extravagances of the blond Richard. Those closest to him even complained about his namby pamby favourites. Priedeux knew these things but did not imagine that those outside the court would also know. Supposing rumours had spread to this outermost part of the kingdom? That they too felt the yoke of high taxes, and she was now forcing him to acknowledge this was a problem? Or was she just interested as a householder in how the money was obtained?

'Why should that worry you? Surely you have never worried about such things?'

She put her head on one side then, as if surveying him, and answered with a question. 'And why should I never have worried about money? Should I not be concerned about it? Is it not *womanly* to think about raising funds, or how taxes should be spent? Should I just spin and embroider and while away my time with strangers as you are?'

'Madam, I apologise, but at the court I come from it is unseemly to talk of gold and how it is spent unless it is behind closed doors by chamberlains and such like.'

'Is that so? And your great ladies concern themselves not with how they are finely decked in gold and silken robes?'

Priedeux laughed then, thinking of the spoilt Lady Beatrice, a great heiress, finely clothed and groomed as she was, who would never think of how it had all come about. All she would know was that the man she would marry would be her equal or superior and hold a position at court and she would want for nothing except freedom and he doubted whether that lady, with her downcast eye, would know anything about freedom.

'Madam, the women do not have to concern themselves, for that is man's work. And special men at that. I, for instance, do not worry about the use of money, except to pay for good food, a bed for the night and fodder for my horse. Others, more versed than I, concern themselves....'

She interrupted him.

'Oh, 'tis only stories I have heard of ladies who run castles and estates when their menfolk are away and I would know how they do it. You can see my lord is grey-bearded and I often wonder about how I would cope with a lonely future. Do you think I could manage such a place myself? How would I find out how to do such a thing?'

Priedeux smiled, remembering the Lady Gertrude, aggressive and cruel and grasping, so different from this lonely lady who was curious about everything and seemed to know hardly anything. He was tempted for a moment to suggest to her that indeed he did know a woman who could teach her all she wanted to know, but something about this woman stopped him. She could never meet Lady Gertrude, who would corrupt her, Priedeux was sure. And he did not like the idea of that. He suddenly wondered if he was becoming soft in the head. He realised he felt *compassion* for this lady, so beautiful, so curious, so *innocent.* How else could she ask such searching intimate questions? He had not felt such compassion for another, certainly not a woman, for many years.

He tried to recall when he had last had such feelings. It was on the few times when he had remembered his mother as he'd travelled further and further from her and he imagined her anguish at losing her favourite last born, the one who was healthy, the one she had doted on, after abandoning her older, lame son to the monastery. As he had found himself even further away, and learnt about the hard life of a mercenary, in the retinue of Hawkwood, sometimes, in the deep of night, he had anguished over her not knowing where he had gone. He had thought to send a message that he was alive but then there had never seemed to be an opportune moment and the excitement of his life had carried him through such thoughts. By the time he had joined Gaunt's household such feelings had completely faded.

'Madam, do you have no fine sons to take over when your lord dies?'

She blushed then, a soft pink on the unnaturally pale cheeks, and looked down, hardly shaking her head.

'Nay, that has not happened and I know not why.' Then she looked up at him, suddenly straightening her back as if with resolve. 'I will not speak of such things, the time is not ripe, I know you not too well.' She stood up. 'There may come a time, not too distant, when I will tell you all but the hour has not yet ripened into total revelation.' She drew away from him as if to leave.

He caught her hand and tried to pull her back down, looking at her beseechingly. 'Surely you are not going to leave me now, when I thought we were conversing so easily?'

She smiled. 'I will go. Before I do, what token can you give my dear lord as exchange when you are asked?'

He returned her smile, for this time he recognised that she was deliberately flirting. He was also fairly certain that she was familiar with the Gawain story. Why else would she worry about tokens? He answered quickly. 'Well, Madam, the most acceptable thing seems to be a kiss; will you give it willingly?'

He sat up and looked at her where she stood, still poised for flight. He realised he was in a defensive position, and there was no way he could force her to stay but she bent down, holding his shoulders and kissing him fully on the lips, before moving away so quickly that he could not reciprocate. He caught the flavour of sweetness on her lips.

She stood at the door, half turned from him and smiled. 'There. That is something to pass on to my lord.' She said something else too but he could not catch it for the door swung shut and blocked out the rest of her words.

'Damn! Damn! Cursed be that woman.' He muttered aloud as he jumped out of the coverlets and quickly dressed. He was full of unsatiated desire. He had always found solace in action when troublous events overtook him and now he strode round the room as he pulled on hose and shirt and tunic and cloak. He felt trapped in a situation that he could see no way out of except to play his part.

He did not know the castle, except for the view from this room and the few corridors leading to the great hall. He looked down on the courtyard, which was so far below, that jumping out of the window would probably mean a broken neck. In any event, the slit was far too narrow for his broad shouldered shape even if he were to consider launching himself over the parapet. He had no idea of the layout of the castle, its back entrances for servants, the way to the kitchens. He could see a rudely built thatched apartment attached to the other side of the castle courtyard, and guessed that this was the kitchen. It was always so in the palaces of the King's court, to make sure that, if there was a fire from the cooking, it did not ruin the whole building. There was a long covered walkway leading from this to below his chamber, where, he guessed, food would be ferried to the great hall. From this, he calculated that the great hall, where he had entered the castle, was directly below his room. If he could find the entrance to this covered walkway from the hall, he might be able to find an escape route through the kitchen. He decided to watch from where the meal arrived that evening and to mark that place as a possible escape route.

Now he had developed a plan, he left the room to find food. When he opened his door, he found a polite lackey, who gestured to him to follow. As he strode along he realised that the vision of the dream of blood and retribution, had faded, but with that realisation came the memory of the cloaked figure.

* * * * * *

The evening's feast followed the sequence of the night before and Priedeux drank and ate as if he had no worries at all except to enjoy himself, even though all he could concentrate on was the exchange of tokens. Soon the sweetmeats were all that were left and there seemed to be a hush as if some hidden master of ceremonies had raised a hand to indicate to the diners that the time had arrived.

Priedeux's host turned to him with a full goblet in one hand and jug of wine in the other: 'Let me fill you again, for we will have a merry time of it with our exchange of tokens.' He poured and then handed the empty jug to a servant who quickly arrived behind him. Priedeux hardly listened as the lord explained about his hunting prowess of the day. Instead he watched the lackey back away and glide along behind them, almost touching the back of the wall behind the daïs. Then he seemed to disappear behind a rich carpet of Moorish colours of orange and blue and pink in the lozenged patterns of the East. So, that was the way out, he thought.

'So today, we have this for you.' The clap of the lord's hands made Priedeux come to attention. Into the hall from the same way as the evening before, came another servant carrying a large silver salver upon which was a dressed boar's head, 'a symbol merely, but your token from me is the great boar I fought and killed.'

Priedeux took the salver and placed it before him, and stood. He raised his glass and proclaimed to the host: 'Indeed

187

this is a great gift and I would share it with you all. I request the right to oversee the roasting of such as this and will dress it in a royal manner straight from the King's own chefs, if you would but let me.'

The lord laughed and nodded. He said: 'But in exchange? Your token for me?'

Priedeux looked down at the lord, and wondered if he could kiss him as he had been kissed by the wife. She was sitting the other side of her husband and looking at him expectantly. He knew he had to do it if he was to stay loyal to the poem, and he was following that poem as if it was a signpost to the end of a great quest. So he took the man by the shoulders and bent down and kissed him, on the lips, quickly, and then stood away and looked the lord squarely in the eyes.

The man had risen as if to meet him half way and had stayed still as he had been kissed but now his face broke out into the familiar wide grin. There was mirth and surprise, and Priedeux was relieved that the man was not angry.

'Well, my Lord,' he said quietly, 'is that what you would have expected?'

'Expected perhaps not, but neither am I surprised, for I too have been in the world and would expect a lusty man of your experience to have a way with the wenches. Will you not tell me who?'

Priedeux shook his head, and they both sat then. 'I would not spoil the honour of anyone in your domain, my Lord.'

'Oh, I love your sweet words. Indeed, tomorrow we will have one more exchange of tokens but you must swear to me that you will tell me who the wench is and if she is worthy of you, we will see a betrothal. What say you?'

Priedeux sighed inwardly, everywhere he went it seemed people would marry him off. He explained. 'I regret I am not the marrying kind, even though proposals have been many. But I will honour your ladies; that I promise.'

The lord nodded then, giving him a searching look and said no more. The answer to Priedeux's questions would have to wait till the morrow.

Chapter Fifteen: Foxhunting

'Now indoors let him dwell and have dearest delight,
while the free lord yet fares afield in his sport!
At last the fox he has felled that he followed so long...'

The next morning she was there before he had fully wakened, like a wraith who had arrived by air and not passed through doors. Priedeux was convinced he had been drugged for, like most veterans of crusades, he slept lightly and the slightest noise would have woken him. He came sliding up from a deep, but this time dreamless, sleep, sensing her presence as a slight indent of the covers.

'Wha-a..?' He opened his eyes and she was smiling down at him, an indulgent kindly smile. She was sitting in her usual position half-way down the bed. For a second a window opened for Priedeux and he remembered his mother doing the same when he was but a small child. He did not like thinking that far back. He forced the memory away but the strangest of emotions stayed, like a dimly recurring dream. Anyway, this woman was nothing like his mother, who had been wide-hipped, earthy and full of common sense with the good humour of a person at home in their world, no matter how small their horizons. Compared to her this woman was intriguing, an enigma. Now she seemed to guess the closing of his mind to the pleasant memory but took it personally, for she said gently, 'don't shut your heart against me. In your face, for a second, was the true face of honour and kindness, as I thought I could see in you the first time I saw you.'

Her eyes dampened with the sadness of her speech.

'Madam, you must allow me time to waken. I do not like this entry of yours into my chamber before I am dressed.'

'But it is the only time you are defenceless, is it not?'

'Exactly.' He tried to rally his thoughts. 'I am defenceless in a castle where I know not the name of my host and hostess, where my horse and weapons have been taken I know not where.'

'But you are free to leave at any time except that it is cold and bitter outside and we celebrate a merry season here and we are honoured by you as our guest.'

'And can I see my horse, to ensure he is cared for?'

She nodded, smiling. 'Of course, why should you not? But first, I would ask you questions. Please indulge me.'

'So long as I can ask some in exchange?'

'Sir, I do not bandy tokens like my husband and I would honour you with truth, so I cannot promise to answer your questions, for the simple fact is that I may not know the answers.'

'But you would know your own life story?' He asked. 'You cannot pretend not to know that.'

'My life story' She said it wistfully. 'There is not much to tell. It is a life governed by others and I would not have it so. I should have been a man for I have a curiosity that cannot be satisfied by being locked up here. I would travel back to my homeland, and further, to the great places of the world, to see such wonders as the Pharos of Alexandria.'

He interrupted her: 'Madam that you can never see.'

'Pray, why not? I know about it. It was built by Alexander the Great and is 440 feet high and built of solid stone and can be seen for many miles, some say as far away as the island of Cypros.'

He interrupted her with a laugh and took her hand. 'So you have read the ancients?'

She looked down, as if ashamed. 'I have a great need to know. While my husband is out hunting I use the books in his library.'

So, there was a library. Now he had to find out who else used it. She had implied her husband used it if she could not when he was in the castle. But first he felt he had to tell this woman the truth, of what he knew from his travels in the crusades. He had been as far as the Alexandria she mentioned.

'I must tell you, sweet lady, not all can be found in libraries. For the Pharos is no longer. It was destroyed by several earthquakes, back in '75, some fifteen years ago. I was told it was swallowed in a great fire and all its contents with it.'

The lady looked crestfallen.

'And the ruins of Rome? The Parthenon?'

'Yes, I believe they still survive.' He wanted to change the subject now to her life, her husband.

'But tell me Madam, your husband, is he at home, does he know you are here?'

She laughed then, the ironic tone of the previous two days creeping in. 'You have no idea of my situation if you believe I would visit your room if my husband was in the castle. Nay, he left early this morning for the hunt, for he must find food for our honoured guest, must he not?'

Priedeux was even more convinced he had been drugged for he would never have slept through the clatter of the hunt preparations. He resolved to say nothing. Instead he picked up on her ironic tone:

'So, my lady, you do not always obey your man?'

She put her head to one side in the same way as yesterday. 'Of course, I obey, but...' She hesitated. 'I tell you, again, I need to know, I have led such a sheltered life.' She said it in the same way as she had done the previous day, with wistfulness, with longing.

'Tell me!' He said it with authority and he knew she would not be able to refuse.

'What is there to tell? Such a little life..' She stood up and walked around the room as if in an agony of imprisonment.

He waited, almost suspected her of trying to concoct something to keep him satisfied. He was fascinated by the way she moved, the guileless sinuousness of the lithe body, so slender at the waist that an hourglass could be fashioned by her shape. He felt desire arising again but knew he would not be able to take advantage of this woman by his normal wiles. So he waited. He felt he was coming close to the truth.

She stopped at the side of the bed, looking down at him. Her arms were folded as if in defence, below her neat pointed breasts and her face, even in the gloom of the curtained recess of the bed, looked pale. He noticed she wore a chain of gold around her waist, the knot hanging down her belly, and he had an urge to touch it, stroke it, as if she were a wild stallion that might need taming by such gentleness. As she looked down on him her eyes seemed hooded, as if she would keep her secrets.

She said, almost to herself, it seemed to him. 'Yes, I will tell.'

Taking a deep breath she started. 'Father and mother I have never known for I was to blame for my mother's death by my birth and my father was one who fell in the Crusades. My guardian, not knowing what to do with me, put me in a nunnery. I was brought up by Dominican nuns; black-robed creatures like ravens, who starve themselves of all that is right so that they became like those scavenging birds, with sharp noses and beady eyes, or so it seemed to me as a child.'

'Where was this? I notice you have a lilt in your voice?'

'Aah, one good thing those nuns taught me was to speak any language well, I learnt Latin at three, French at four, then German and later, much later, English which I find a rough and hard tongue to use. So where was this? Yes, I will tell you. This was in Spain, in a castellated closed convent high in the hills not unlike this. Almost impossible to find unless you knew what you were seeking.'

'Are you Spanish then?' He surveyed her now as if looking

at her for the first time. She was still standing and he pulled the curtains open wide and tucked it behind the bed-head to give him more light to see her by. He realised that the pale skin could be a Mediterranean olive stripped of all its colour by being hidden in a dark northern clime; the hair was indeed richly mahogany. The dark-lashed eyes that had seemed to dart promises into him the first time he had seen her looked down at him again in the same way. He thought he could see a whole vista of different worlds in her that he had overlooked before. Yes he had known she was beautiful but now the beauty was accentuated with a depth of exotic promises, layers of hidden lives.

She nodded. 'If by lineage of the father, then I am Spanish. My mother was of the English court, an heiress who was negotiated into marriage as part of the politics of a man called Gaunt or so I was told. I now know he is a great man, whose power stretches across the known world.'

'John of Gaunt?' asked Priedeux quickly.

'Indeed I believe that is his name. But, being such a great man he had many children placed under his guardianship. I thought he was Portuguese, although I know the name is not Portuguese.'

'Aye, it would be John of Gaunt. He is still alive and living in England.'

She ignored him, looking away as if what he said was of no import to her story. 'The nuns said little to me except to educate. All I learnt of my mother was that her emblem was a pentangle, she wore a star with that shape on her belt - look, I have it still.'

She showed him the belt hook, of gold, and, as she unhooked it, the five-sided star collapsed into two parts, one with three points and the other with two points. Then she twisted the pieces together again so that the clasp turned back into a five-pointed star, the belt held tight against her belly. She went on. 'A five sided moral tale, the nuns said. They told me no more about her, not of her lineage, her parents, how she came to be married, except what I have told you. I would hope...'

But she stopped what she was saying and started another sentence:

'I learnt quickly the rhythms of the convent and the times for prayers when I would walk to chapel and chant with my carers, and when I would be left alone. Then I would be off to the library which was very fine, for the Abbess was a converted Moorish princess, who had refused to marry an unconverted prince, but she still kept contact with the Moors of her childhood and knew many Arab scholars. That is how I know of Alexandria. There was a great library in that city. Yes you know that. The Abbess would receive visitors from that part of the world who would present her with new books. She also had Italian connections and was sent copies of Petrarch and the Decameron, and I read everything and anything. I led a solitary life except for my companions who jumped out of the pages of those books. And because there was little else to distract me or for me to love, I held dear those stories to me '

As she spoke, she relaxed and her arms loosened and she gestured the opening of a book and flicked her fingers as if she was releasing the words from the very pages. As she finished her story, she gentled herself onto the bed so close to him that he could sit up and be face to face with her. But he stayed reclined, resting on one elbow, so as not to scare the confidences away. He was sure that if he made any move towards her she would freeze on him.

'How did you get from Spain to this cold and inhospitable place?'

She bowed her head as if she was offended and he amended his phrase, 'To this rich and comfortable castle.'

She looked up and laughed then, a tinkling sound of joy. 'Truly you are the kind and perceptive man I thought you were!'

'So?'

She took another deep breath so that her chest rose and started again. 'My lord came for me. The nuns had never mentioned it but I was educated to be a lord's consort and they knew who this was to be. He had saved my father's life in some battle. I was never interested in such things and the nuns' tales of battles and crusades wafted over me. On one such crusade, my father told him the secret of me and promised me to him. When he came I did not mind, he was understanding, even though he seemed very old. He promised me the travel I craved for and escape from the nuns who had, even though they were kind, become oppressive to me. They discovered I crept into the library and had hidden the stories I loved, but by then I had read most of them anyway. They had expected me to pray with them at all their offices, instead of mass once a day, and I found this hard to enjoy, although the singing was something that lifted my soul.'

Priedeux nodded and took her hand gently, and she did not withdraw it. As she made the confession of her life it seemed she trusted him more.

'Go on, I beg you,' he said.

She nodded and continued. 'So we began the long journey out into the world. I could not ride of course – the nuns had never taught me - so I was transported in a covered wagon and it took many days. My lord was considerate, he knew the terrain would be hard and he knew the temperatures would change and he had provided rich cloths of lawn and fine ermine-trimmed gowns. As we travelled further north, I wrapped myself more and more in the clothes. We were not married until we reached his country and he did not touch me until after the ceremony.'

Priedeux realised with surprise she was blushing and looking down, as if confused. It was the first time he had met a married woman with such feelings. Even the court maidens did not blush at such things; why should they?

'Did the nuns not prepare you for that?' he asked, entwining his fingers in hers. She did not reject the attention but played with his hands as if such a touch would make her know him more.

'They told me that a woman obeyed her master. Many of the nuns would giggle and talk of such things as something to be avoided, the reason why they had become nuns. They seemed to have double standards to me, for they also said it was the way of the world, a necessary evil, to ensure procreation, to ensure God's chosen would continue. I knew how young are produced for the convent had its own cows and I loved the warm milky smells of their mangers, I would hide there when I no longer wanted to learn. There were dogs and bitches who had no shame and mated in front of me, even though the nuns hurried past. I read romances and guessed that man and woman were different, that we had love to sustain us and that the mating would be different to that of dogs.'

Priedeux hid a grin but could not resist asking. 'And was it?'

She stood up suddenly and turned away from him. 'No of course not, if breeding has to happen then it is just the same as dogs and bitches.' Her voice sounded muffled, as if she was trying to stifle sobs.

Priedeux gently moved the covers, slid out of the bed, and, catlike, stood behind her. He knew he could seduce her at this moment. Would he do it? Very slowly, he touched the nape of her neck, below the golden net which held her hair on the crown of her head, almost expecting her to start like a frightened doe, but she did not. He moved her then, turning her slowly to face him and she turned to him, docile. He lifted her face, his fingers below her chin, and he could see the tears in her eyes. She looked up at him, but then, as if she could not bear his gaze, she rested her head on his breast.

He whispered. 'And the breeding didn't follow.'

Her head was shaking from side to side and he could feel the wet tears through the lawn night-shirt. So, there had been no children. Only animal couplings which brought her no joy.

'Even so, you know in your heart that it is not just like dogs and bitches, for you have read the love stories - you know that it is more than just coupling?'

She rested her head on his chest, compliant but hiding. Her head moved as if nodding.

'How many years, sweet one?' He knew he could say anything to her now, she was so yielding.

'I know not. My husband keeps no sundial or hourglass or calendar, for he finds such things of no use, measuring his time by hunting or eating or managing his estates. But for the seasons passing I guess ten years at least.'

'And you have wasted all these years locked up here, in this strange castle?'

She looked up and moved away. 'You measure time by man's reckoning, of being wasted in one place? I have learnt that time is the gathering of knowledge to expand one's own soul from whatever resources can be found. To look upon a flower and consider its petals can be wisdom and calculation. To watch a bird dancing on the wind is to dance oneself.'

'But you want to travel? You said so.'

She nodded, and added. 'Indeed, but I have learnt that travelling is also knowing through sights and smells and tastes that can be had in one place. I have learnt that it is the retaining of these things and the living in them in the mind that is important, as I used to do as a child. That is my life.' She sighed and he felt that her learning was perhaps a compensation rather than an enthusiasm.

'Then someone like you comes and curiosity stifles my calm, and I want to know. I must find out if the Romances are but lies, whether the stories of great places in the outermost eastern confines of the world are true. So I would devour your knowledge of the world, if I cannot go out into it myself.'

He stroked her hair, felt its soft waves contrasted by the gold wire of the net she wore, found the edge of it and gently disentangled the wire from her braids, until the hair was loosened down her back. She did not resist.

'I need to know your name. Please, tell me now.'

'I was called Isabella, after the great Queen of Spain.'

He nodded. It suited her, with its echoes of regal dignity but also, like the Queen Isabella with her King Ferdinand, it spoke of encouragement of invention, of knowledge, of exploration, in that age of Spain which promoted such things. He stroked the loosened hair.

'Let me take *you* on a journey.' He whispered gently, knowing it was the only way he would seduce this woman who to him was worth every wile he could think of. He thought of her as virginal, as indeed she was, of all sexual knowledge, even if her maidenhood had been broken by that big man, her husband, he of the unknown name. She reminded him in many ways of Lady Beatrice, the heiress he hoped to win at court, and what he did now, he felt, would be how he would treat that girl on their nuptials, if he ever achieved the obtaining of her. For once Priedeux wanted to teach and please a woman rather than seduce her to have power over her, or just to satisfy his lust.

'Isabella,' he whispered into her ear, 'a magic name of wonderful promise.'

They stood together as he stroked her hair, her shoulders, as if wiping away all cares, his hands moving slowly down the thick wool of her gown until he reached the bare flesh of her wrists. Then he took her by both hands and stepped backwards, towards the warmth of the bed and she stepped with him, as if in a dream. She was looking at him now, a look of trust with a slight smile at the corners of her lips as if she knew this would be one adventure she would never regret.

The back of his knees touched the coverlet and he levered himself down so that his head was level with her belly and he rested it there, feeling the coolness of the gold belt she wore. He released her hands and she held his head to her while he felt for the starred clasp and undid it and let it fall with a muted clatter to the floor. Her body was leaning on his and he fell back, pulling the lightness of her on to him, so that his face was smothered in the cleft between her childlike breasts. Her body felt wraithlike above him, insubstantial, and he stroked it to feel the contours and found it pleasing, the buttocks rounded and well shaped. He gripped them and pushed them onto him and he could feel her responding, her hips moving down upon him.

They kissed and her lips were only slightly parted as if she did not know that kisses went deeper than just the exterior touching. He gently taught her and she opened up to him.

She was whimpering and he knew if he felt her in her secret place, she would be moist, ready for him. His hands moved down her thighs and slowly, oh so slowly, he gathered the skirts into his hands and drew the material up so that, gently, he revealed her stockinged legs, the bare thigh, the naked buttocks, the curly hair of her pubis. She did not resist but continued to whimper into the pillow, her hands curling into his hair, clutching at strands of it as if this was all that kept her safe.

Then he turned her onto her back and trawled the dress away from her body so that her breasts were revealed almost last. He levered the wool dress over her shoulders, her head, and she lay exposed, wearing only her stockings. He cupped one breast, then extended one finger to the nipple and caressed it. It was as if he had pressed a button for her hips rose towards him and she opened her legs so that he knew if he tried to penetrate her it would be like a ship making a homecoming into a welcoming harbour. But he did not. Instead he knelt beside her and took both breasts in his hands and caressed them with a fingering movement. She opened her eyes and looked squarely at him. Her pupils were dilated,

200

deep pools of wanting and she whispered to him: *'Please, oh, please,'* but he only smiled down at her and she smiled back uncertainly, through moistened lips. He wanted her to enjoy every moment they had together, as he knew he would for her body was pliant, her skin soft and velvety, the breasts like small piquant peaches that he had tasted in the Orient. He bent down and kissed them softly, one after the other and felt her hands in his hair again, but this time she stroked the back of each ear, took the earlobe between thumb and forefinger in a way no other woman had ever done to him. It was a gesture he had never experienced and he found it erotic beyond his control. The movement sent such signals through his body he could no longer hold back. He bestrode her and levered himself into her and her legs seemed to move automatically around his buttocks forcing him further in, deeper and deeper, so that he lost all sense of self, of time, except for the velvety grip and friction surrounding him.

But he stopped. His one aim was to pleasure her and the action was driving him towards his own climax. He stopped and breathed deeply, controlling himself and started to move again, slowly and deliberately, this time watching her face. The whimpers she had made had become deep throated and her eyes were half closed, moistness fringing the lashes. Her lips too were moist, and she licked them like a cat that had finished a bowl of rich cream. He kissed her and forced his tongue inside, playing with her tongue in a mirror image of the thrusting which was going on below. Then she was sucking his tongue hard, and he felt as if his whole body was being drawn into her in rapid uncontrollable movements which scuttled all his self control and with a loud groan he came.

They lay locked together for what seemed an age of peacefulness to him, something he had never experienced before. He remembered the coupling before he had been summoned to Gaunt at the start of his quest; with a fighter's instinct, once satisfied, he could rapidly release himself from the snares of the woman and continue his day to day tasks. Now he felt as if something had been loosened inside, a wariness, a lack of trust in any woman to fully satisfy him, he wondered? He felt so relaxed that he knew he was drifting into a doze even though he wanted to enjoy the feel of the woman for longer. In the end, he slept.

Suddenly he woke, a great fear on him. In his sleep which had started so peacefully, the memory of the exchange of tokens which would have to take place that night, had woven itself into a fitful dream that turned into a nightmare. What was he to give the lord that night?

Chapter Sixteen: The castle

'The tale of the contentions of the true knights
Is told by the title and text of their works - '

'Come, I will show you the castle, now I know I can trust you.'

He raised his eyebrows at this but his lady had already thrown off the covers and swung out of the bed, recoiling as her bare feet touched the floor and quickly pulling the woollen dress over her head. He watched in admiration as it fell over the soft curves in a gentle movement that seemed to settle on her hips and stomach as if the very wool itself would caress her. He felt excited again and tried to pull her back under the coverlets, but she turned and laughed:

'Come, enough of that. I will show you even greater delights!'

She ignored the quizzical look he gave her, collected her belt from where it had fallen, fitting it round her waist as if she would squeeze it even smaller than it was, and buckled up the pentangle, smiling at him as she did so.

He marvelled at her self-assurance. It was as if that, now they had consummated their mutual attraction, she had developed a layer of skin that protected her. All shyness had gone and she continued to dress, pulling on stockings, patting her hair, as if it was the most natural thing to do, as if he were not a stranger. He marvelled at her, thinking that, indeed, she was an enigmatic woman. As he dressed he caught himself wondering what she would do with the rest of her life, when her husband died before her, as he was likely to do. Would she return to convent, like many matrons? Take another husband? He felt a sudden jealousy for that mythical new husband although he felt no jealousy for her current one. A loveless marriage was no contest for him.

Once free of her lord, she could choose, and he felt a regret that she might choose someone other than himself. He wanted to be part of her future. He never realised he could feel such a yearning to see how another's life would develop. Suddenly he understood why people married, and stayed together until one of them died, why they cherished and cared for their partner despite the boredom of day-to-day living. It made him aware of his own body, of the scars and pocks of old war-illnesses. Of how it had roughened and toughened over the years. How it was now littered with odd dabs of grey, in the hairs on his chest, on the crown of his head. It made him feel embarrassed dressing before a woman, this woman, and he tried to turn, and pull on the hose and jerkin discreetly.

He could feel her eyes on him; he knew she watched as he dressed, and eventually he turned to face her. There was a look of pride and wonder in her face, as if she too had discovered a secret, a secret in which she revelled. He smiled, it turned into a laugh and she too couldn't help laughing as he said: 'I don't believe I will ever experience such delights as I have experienced with you today. You ought to know from the romances you have read that there is no greater delight than what has passed between us.'

She nodded, still laughing, a glow suffusing her cheeks. She stayed where she was, a stride away from him so he could not touch her easily, when he wished her to come to him and cling to him, when he wanted to feel that soft pliant body wrapping itself around his again. She stood aloof almost, but for the laughter that played around her shapely lips. That was enough to tell him she would come to him if she thought there was time for such dalliance.

When he was ready, she took his hand and led him out into

the corridor. Instead of heading for the great hall she diverted through a curtained recess and he followed her through a narrow corridor of roughly hewn stones, which, he guessed, led to another corner of the battlemented inner keep.

'Let me show you my favourite chamber, where I travel through many strange places of the mind.'

Priedeux guessed where they were heading, and, as they reached a heavy door which his lady opened, he knew he was right, for it was lined with heavy vellum manuscripts, lying on their sides and piled high.

As he followed her, he looked beyond her and caught a dark movement and a swishing sound from the end of the room and saw a shadowy figure glide out of the door that was the twin of the one at which they had entered. A hooded person clutching a manuscript book. Priedeux started to say something but his companion seemed to be oblivious of anyone else, and he wondered, by her very lack of acknowledgement, if he was imagining things. She had entered the room first and would have seen the person and been close enough to greet them. He thought her too polite, the whole court too polite, to ignore anyone. Perhaps he was so keen to find the poet that his eyes were playing tricks. Or was the elusive figure the one he had come to annihilate? He would hold his tongue now, enjoying being with this woman, but investigate later if he had the chance.

He deliberately stepped into the centre of the room and turned around twice, to take in all that he could see. It was truly a great collection, and he knew he was in a rare place. Expensive tomes like these would normally be found only in great monasteries. The room was larger, the books more sumptuously bound and there were more of them than in the library at Bunbury. Some of the books had crests, engraved in gold leaf, on the front covers. Some of the larger ones were attached to the walls with delicate chain-linked ropes, others were lying on sloping shelves protruding into the room. The walls were wood panelled in an exotic pattern of carved five-sided star-shapes, into the centre of which the chains were screwed. The room was long and narrow, and he guessed that it formed a corridor in its own right. The place was lit by high windows, glazed with plain glass letting in the natural light that shone down obliquely and, he noticed, did not touch the leather bindings at all.

'See, great books of the past - here, here is my favourite, and one of my latest acquisitions – *The Romance of the Rose*. I know it is the story of a dream, but there are pearls of wisdom in it and I know that pearls are the greatest of jewels for they come from the deep and fishers lose their lives for them.'

Priedeux listened to her as she spoke in her sing-song voice and wondered once again at her knowledge. He knew nothing of pearls except that they were expensive jewels but he was sure she was right.

He moved along the shelves fingering the rich vellum, some encrusted with precious stones. As he moved, she too followed him and watched as he took one volume from a shelf. He opened it at random and tried to read, expecting it to be Latin. The lady watched him and when he looked up, puzzled, his look questioning, she was smiling.

'Aye, 'tis strange, that one, from Wales, the Mabinogion in Welsh. I have others too, Piers the Plowman by one Langland, all in dialect. I like to study them, for I have time in abundance. Time to study each word and wonder and compare and work out the meaning not only from the script itself but from other sources. The nuns taught me well and I am grateful to them for it takes away the tedium of days alone.'

He looked at the script again but could not decipher it. As far as he was concerned this was final proof that this strange castle, with its wonderful mistress, was indeed the place where he must seek his poet. He handed the volume back to her and she stroked it, and holding it as if it were a precious jewel.

'And is there any other who uses the library like you do?'

She smiled, but in the strange downward light of the room it seemed as if she did not meet his look.

'Of course others come here, but I worry them not and they do not worry me. We keep our own counsel amidst the knowledge we find in these books.'

'But what others? Visitors? Retainers of your lord?'

'As I said, I do not know, I cannot tell, we are silent as we work.'

She had been standing still, stroking the fine vellum cover of the book she held but she replaced it in a movement that dismissed his questioning. She brushed past him in an action so provocative but seemingly so innocent that he could hardly fathom it, and he followed as she glided towards the exit at the other end of the long chamber. He watched her hips as she reached the door, a sinuous, exciting movement and realised he had never seen her walk far. He wondered if all her activities would excite him. What would she be like, for instance, riding a horse? He remembered she had said that the nuns had never taught her to ride; even so, he still wondered if she would seem at one with the animal, riding as if the very act of control aroused her? As if reading his thoughts, she said:

'Come, we will visit your horse, and you will see that he is well housed and groomed.'

She led him into a narrow stone corridor with the same rough-hewn walls as he had seen before. He could see at the end, a stairwell which wound down into gloomy darkness. She led the way to the stairs, holding her gown high and watching as she stepped down. For the first time, he thought she moved awkwardly and wondered if she usually used these stairs. Was there a grand staircase which would be her normal route? At the bottom was a strong outside oaken door and she produced a large key with which she unlocked it. He smiled to himself, for it would not cause him much trouble if he needed to exit this way in the future. The best Italian locksmiths had shown him how they devised such mechanisms and how they could be opened. A moment later, he felt the blast of the cold air and she led him into the courtyard. They crunched across icy snow that covered the open yard, towards the stables, walking side by side, not touching.

There was no-one else around, no cooks plucking at the feathers of fowl, no lackey throwing away vegetable scrapings, no saddler polishing horses' rig, in that freezing space. Except for their crunching footsteps, there seemed an unearthly silence. Priedeux suddenly realised that he had heard no birds singing in the mornings, no howlings of forest animals at night. It was as if this castle was encased in its own secret wrappings, only making its own noise of hunting and feasting and music.

As he stepped into the warmth of the stables, Gringolay whinnied and he moved towards the stall from where the noise came. He knew from the sound that his steed was well fed and treated. The animal tossed its head, recognising him and he whispered to it as he stroked its neck, the well-muscled front and legs, checking haunches and hooves. He found that the horse had been newly shod.

'Here, try this as a treat. I know not whether such creatures love it, but certainly humans do, so why not?' She held out strands of sugar, webs of woven stuff left over from the sugar-chef's concoctions of exotic centrepieces. He in turn held them out and Gringolay stretched, his mouth moving and gathering up the strands. He seemed to lick his lips as the delicate sweetness melted and then nudged his master for more.

The couple laughed and Priedeux kissed the well shaped hand of his lady, as it rested on the stable wall, acting as attorney for the horse in thanking her for the delicate treat.

'Well, Gringolay, you are indeed at home, and truly rested. We should be on our way soon though or your new shoes will be wasted with all this fine living.'

It was a deliberate hint to the woman. Without looking at her, he knew she moved away at his words. He heard her say, so quietly, as if to herself. 'I know you must go, but I will hold your soul in my heart for evermore, if not more than your soul.'

He reached out for her and spun her round and held her so close that he knew he could crush her body, if not the soul she spoke of. 'Aah, my lady, my lady, if things were different. But fear not, I will always be true to you. I swear it, on my mother's soul, which I recognise now I broke in so many pieces.'

She looked at him puzzled.

He went on. 'I cannot explain now.' He spoke sadly. 'Some day, if I have the time, I will tell you of my wicked life, and how I...'

She stopped him with a touch of her delicate fingers on his lips.

'No! I will never believe ill of you.'

Feeling thoroughly ashamed and confused he fed Gringolay the remaining strands of sugar she had given him.

* * * * * *

That night he felt as if he could not sit at the high table without betraying some emotion but somehow he managed it. He was helped by the fact that, as on the previous evening, the lord sat between him and the lady and all he had to do was to be sociable to the lord and concentrate on what he was eating and drinking. If he wanted to see Isabella he would have had to lean forward and make a deliberate attempt to do so. In addition, she seemed to sit back in her chair, as if to be invisible to him.

Every time the lord tried to include her in the conversation he was having with Priedeux, she seemed to be helping his mother on her other side. At one time she was cutting up some thick meat for the old lady; at another she was whispering in a conspiratorial manner. Eventually the lord gave up and devoted his attentions to Priedeux and kept proffering the wine, as if it was a substitute for a comforting gesture from his wife. Priedeux began to think there was some dissension between the couple that he had never seen before, but was more concerned to watch the drink with which he was being plied. He remembered the way he had slept the two previous nights and drank slowly. On one occasion when he realised his host had filled his goblet again without being asked, Priedeux deliberately caught it with his sleeve and ensured it spilt, apologising profusely as servants rushed to sawdust the area.

The feast was nearly at an end and had followed its normal good-natured course, when the lord stood and said direct to Priedeux, 'today we have had good sport with the wily old fox. We always manage to catch him at the end, even though he leads us a good dance. A lot of blood has flowed today to bring you this reward. I know it is not for you to eat but it is for you to understand what is being given you. So take it: the brush of the fox.'

As he spoke a servant came forward with the thick red tail of the fox, hanging from his hand as if it was a flag.

The lord had not spoken threateningly but Priedeux knew the allegorical meaning of animals. He now feared for his life. He was sure this large man knew why he was there and the last three days had been playing more than a game of tokens. Priedeux felt he was being told now that he was really the prey and that this man enjoyed a hunt where both sides could dip and dive and play against each other. Not for him the straight kill but a fair challenge where the prey might have a chance to escape. His host was now telling him that he was caught.

Did he know or suspect of the dalliances with his wife? Would that incense him even more? The man was waiting for

Priedeux to answer and Priedeux knew he would have to give his token. He could not exchange a kiss with this man or anything else so intimate as he had shared with the woman all day. He had known this moment would come and had had time to think about it as he bathed and prepared for the evening's feast.

He stood up and surveyed the whole company, who had been rousting and laughing, some not even taking note of the exchanges on the daïs. Suddenly there was a silence. Priedeux appreciated that the atmosphere was different from that of the first night. That had been jovial and eager, keen to please a stranger. Now the air was tense and waiting, as if those gathered knew what would happen and would be disappointed if it didn't. Like a crowd who watched a man who tried a clever trick on a strange horse that everyone else knew would buck and throw him. Everyone waited for the fall, thought Priedeux.

'My Lord, I have learned something today, and I will exchange tokens, but it is nothing tangible. Despite that, it has even more import to we who have parried such gifts these last three days. As you know, I am a wandering knight who would take the gold and silver of those who offer it and while the gold runs into my hands I would fight good and true in what I am asked to do. But for these tokens of yours I would give only what I, in my circumstances, can give.' He paused and the lord, who had remained sitting, now stood and faced him. He was a head taller than Priedeux but the lowlier man stood his ground, and continued, 'what I offer as my token, even though I would continue my journeyings and leave this place, is my undying love and loyalty to you and yours. Something that, as a wandering soldier, as you know I am, I would not normally give away. I would expect to be paid, and paid handsomely. I hereby promise to be loyal and true to you and your company as long as I live.'

His host took him by the shoulders and kissed him on both

cheeks. Priedeux looked across at Isabella, who smiled up at him, confidently, satisfied and, it seemed to him, joyous, at his answer.

The whole room then stood up and cheered, goblets raised in the air.

The chorus went on for some time and a few dogs started barking excitedly. The smoke from the fire whirled into the air in hurried spirals, disturbed by the movement of the diners. Then all sat down and started talking about the stranger and wafts of conversation came to him to show that his offer was, if a strange one, something they all thought appropriate and most acceptable.

As the hubbub of laughter and conversation continued, Priedeux turned to his host again and smiled as he said: 'Now, my lord there is one thing I would ask of you, but my loyalty will remain if you refuse, although so will my curiosity.'

His listener bowed and Priedeux was sure he could see the mouth, hidden as it was in the grizzly beard, turned up into a smile, as if he knew what was coming.

'I would know your name and your lineage and that of your mistress.'

'Of course, 'tis only polite to tell. And when you know, you will understand why it has been important to test you. Many have come this way and many have not left, their bones even now in my dungeons, for I could let none escape and tell the world lest it endanger the whole company here.'

He took a draft of his beverage and continued, 'my name is de Coucy, originally from France.' He paused as he saw Priedeux's face crease into a frown. 'Perhaps, if you have been at court for some years, the name is familiar?'

Priedeux knew the name but it was buried in the mists of his memory and would not surface. He shook his head.

'Aah well, maybe 'tis safe now. But I was one of the young French nobles who were held hostage to ensure the French king kept the Treaty of Bretigny, that was in the days of your old king, Edward III. Naturally, because of my nobility of birth, I was allowed to wander freely at your English court, treated as a noble should be, until the ransom was paid. My family had other priorities and indeed felt it was good for me to know English ways so they did not rush to pay the ransom. In those days it was probably good to keep young pretenders away from their families or so I can see now. I was treated well and served at high table like the other young squires. It was not long before I noticed Princess Isabella, Edward's eldest daughter, looking wistfully at me.'

Priedeux had started at the name *Isabella*, for indeed he had heard tales. He said nothing and de Coucy continued, 'aah, now I see you recognise my name. Let me go on. She was a little long in the tooth and indeed should have been married much earlier, but the politics of the time were liquid and I see now that her father did not know which way to run, with the hares or the hounds, so to speak. So he waited to see who would be the most suitable of the European crowns for his eldest and best-loved. Time slipped by. She was strong-willed and wily, was Isabella, like her father, and knew what she would have. In the end it was me, and her father sanctioned it and bequeathed upon me many lands in this area, and parts of Cheshire and Lancashire.

'We were married and, shortly after, my ransom was discharged, for I was now part of the English king's household. Eventually, I took my not so young spouse back to my hometown and we settled down to an acceptable way of life that did not involve too much togetherness except for the propagation of heirs and she duly obliged, being a strong and healthy wench. I carried out my duty of wars and crusades and returned to find her occupied with young knights who were energetic, if you know what I mean. She was discreet and I accepted it, so that I too could follow my inclination without scandal.

He spoke quietly and Priedeux noticed that the young Isabella was occupying herself with her mother-in-law again, wiping the old lady's chest where she had dribbled food.

De Coucy stopped and took a deep draught of the wine before him. He had been talking as if in a confessional, as if he had never revealed this before and Priedeux guessed it was so. No other wandering knight, if he had found this castle, had proved himself like Priedeux had. Priedeux realised he had probably been prepared for the rites of passage by his reading of Gawain.

'On my travels, I met a good and strong knight from Spain, and we fought together in many a battle. I took to going on crusades, I could not stay at home, I longed for a Saracen's sword swiped across my neck but, I suppose, because of my great height and horsemanship, it never happened. At the siege of Gallipoli, my fighting companion was wounded by a Turkish sword. I swear that place will be the downfall of many men in the future, for it is a sickly place, although strategically important for trade routes, as the Venetians and Genoese know. They paid their soldiers well but did not believe in providing medicines for their men and my great Spanish friend and colleague died in my arms bequeathing me his daughter, whose name also was Isabella. I felt it an omen, that I should find a substitute love in my latter years and you see her before you now, my spouse true and well-beloved.'

De Coucy continued, 'I could not live with her openly for the wrath of the English monarch at the betrayal of his daughter, as he saw it, so we travelled to this castle, for not only is it well defended, it is well-lost in the surrounding woods amid the peaks that surround us. 'Tis only the determined who make their way here. Or those I would allow in.'

Priedeux realised he had probably been 'allowed in', but for what reason? Was it to join this host, like Arthur and his knights of the Round Table?

He added quietly. 'My wife recently died of the plague, a terrible death for such as she. She apparently raged and boiled at the pustules, screaming at her servants to put her out of her misery for the two days that the disease ravaged her and finally claimed her, but I was married to this Isabella by then...'.

'The only sadness of my last years is that my young, dearly beloved, does not produce a son who can inherit these castles. For Isabella - the Princess - has poisoned my other boys against me and would have nothing to do with me. The other lands are entailed but this castle and the surrounding wild parts are free and I could pass these on to sons of this my true queen.'

He turned to the woman beside him and took her hand and squeezed it, she smiling graciously at him in response. 'It would be fitting to have a son whom I could see grow in glory for the good of me, God willing.'

As he said this, Priedeux noticed that Isabella withdrew her hand from her husband's, using her mother-in-law as a pretext, wiping her fingers for her, gently removing the crabbed hands playing with the food before her.

Priedeux said nothing, felt sad, and understood much. He remembered his first conversation with Isabella when she had said there was only one thing her lord lacked. Now Priedeux knew what it was.

Then de Coucy laughed. 'Enough of this sadness. We have good food, good company and good wine. And a wonderful wife.' He turned to her and again took the small hand which was resting on the arm of her chair. She nodded in acquiescence, ignoring Priedeux's gaze, her eyes down.

'We must to bed.' said the lord, and he stood and moved away from the table, the woman who was his wife resting her slim arm gently on his muscular thick one. The whole company stood except Priedeux.

He watched them go. Jealousy, sadness, regret and fear for his future wrapped Priedeux in confusion like a heavy cloak.

215

Eventually he stood and followed the lackey who led him to his lonely bedchamber. He swore that he would leave this enchanted castle on the morrow for such confusions of feelings he had would, he was sure, be cleared once he tasted clear air and the real world again.

Chapter Seventeen: Leaving the castle

'Oh God, is the chapel green
this mound?' said the noble Knight.
'At such might Satan be seen
saying matins at midnight.'

That night he made certain preparations, wandering around his chamber in the gloom of a sickle moon. He gathered his belongings from where they had been spread about and checked his panniers. He was sure they had not been touched. The book he kept on his person. It was early morning before he was prepared.

He *would* leave today. Yes, he would keep his vow of loyalty to the lord, and would not reveal the whereabouts of this enchanted place. He wondered if, once he had left it, he would ever find it again. Did he want to? Conflicting emotions overwhelmed him.

Before entering the castle he had cold-bloodedly taken what woman he wanted, admittedly extracting himself gracefully afterwards, in true romantic manner but without a thought for the consequences or future of the female he had defiled. *They enjoyed it as much as he did, didn't they?* Now, even as he made his preparations to leave, part of him wanted to stay, to learn more about Isabella, to develop their relationship. For a fleeting moment, he wondered if he could stay in a bizarre ménage-a-trois with this woman and her husband, both of whom had enchanted him. It was a strange feeling that made his stomach lurch, as if it were full of bad wine. It was more like the feeling he would have before a great battle, not knowing whether he would be alive the next day or not.

As he changed clothes, discarding the elaborate robes of ceremony, he wondered at the way in which he was analysing feelings as if they were items of physical pain. He was torn by memories of his earlier life, where he chose what to do, did it, and never analysed whether he had done right or not. Now he was only too aware that this place confused him, made him think of consequences where he had never done so before.

He *had* to leave.

But not before he had solved the question of who had written the poem of Gawain. He had come too far, and the clues in this castle were so many that he was certain the poem had been written in this place. Somehow, he intended to find out today, even if it meant him looking in every room in the castle. And then he would go. He had to end this quest, not for his master, Gaunt, or for the bounty he had been promised, but to satisfy himself.

He searched through one of the bags and found what he was looking for. A pair of embroidered hose with padding down the seams, upon which were gold embroidered stitching in a rich pattern. Given to him by one of his favourite wenches at Court, and, despite the elaborate patterning, practical and warm too. He had added a chosen weapon for her to hide inside the padding. He now unravelled the stitching which was soon a confusion of braid on the floor and the padding fell, detached from the stockings. He undid the package and drew out of it something which clattered to the floor. He picked it up and handled it, as if weighing its usefulness. It was an Italian stiletto with a thin rapier-like blade and a peculiar right-angled handle from which were hanging loose threads of thin well-tooled leather. With these, he tied the weapon to his left wrist, using knots he had been taught. By the time he had finished nobody would know he had a lethal dagger and special tool hidden in his sleeve. He pulled his padded jerkin over the shirt.

He was dressing as if preparing for battle or a long ride. He carefully placed cloak, panniers and weaponry in an orderly pile on the floor.

As he worked, he suddenly felt drowsy and realised that the wine, which he had tried not to touch, was having its usual narcotic effect on him. He had had to drink his lord's health and other toasts so it was not possible to avoid drinking altogether. But he had also consumed much water as well as wine, even though it tasted slightly rancid. He knew that, even if he slept soundly, he would wake at dawn. Staggering to the bed, he pulled the coverlets around him, thinking it would not do for any night caller to see he was fully dressed. He was sure his Lady would not be able to visit at night and fully intended to be out of this chamber before she came again. He felt himself drifting into blackness.

* * * * * *

He woke suddenly next morning as he knew he would, refreshed with his mind racing. There was a grey-black sky outside, with no moon but, for the first time, he heard the strange birdsong of winter which showed that dawn was approaching. It was still too early for lords and ladies to be awake. Even so, he knew he might encounter early risers like bakers or stokers of the great fires for cooking. After his preparations of the night before it was only seconds before he was ready.

Today he would find out, either by asking directly or by stealth, who wrote the poem *Gawain and the Green Knight*. First, he would investigate the layout of the castle to ensure a means of escape if he was not allowed to leave voluntarily.

He tried the door. It was unlocked and swung open soundlessly and he guessed that his lady had probably oiled it with tallow to ensure her morning visits were as quiet as possible.

Looking out into the corridor, he saw no one in the dim light from a dying flare. He shut the door behind him and moved along the corridor. Each turn of this inner walkway was lit by a similar flame, the tallow smelling rancid in the cold night air. All was quiet and he guessed that even the servants were still slumbering.

He followed the path Isabella had shown him the day before. He moved silently. Then he heard something. He froze. Someone was moving slowly behind him but the noise of slapping footsteps reassured him; this was not a person who had been instructed to follow him, he was sure, otherwise they would be much quieter. He looked back but could see no one. He moved on, rapidly, along the corridor and scuttled behind the tapestried hanging, hiding the door into the library. He stood quite still and waited. The steps became louder, passed his room and then stopped. Priedeux heard a scraping, a heavy breathing, another scraping and the steps continued away from where he was standing, moved along the corridor, and stopped again. He heard the same scraping noise again. Then the slap-slap footsteps faded away. Priedeux carefully peeped from the curtains to find that the flares had been extinguished in the corridor. so that it was now pitch black. Priedeux let out a sigh of relief; it had been the lighterman, staunching the dying embers of the flares in the corridors which would soon be lit by the dim daylight from the narrow windows. Relief soon turned to action. He would have to work fast before the lackey returned this way. Would the library need the same treatment? He doubted it; no one would leave an unattended flare in a room full of precious books.

He turned and faced the heavy door into the library. He paused, but there was no further sound so he turned the handle. The door opened easily, it was not locked, and he slid inside. It was not lit but the high up windows let in the eerie light of the first light of day. Priedeux did not stop to linger among the books but strode quickly to the opposite door which led into the next corridor.

This was still lit by flares and he hurried through, fearing the lackey would be on his rounds here soon. He reached the winding staircase and took the steps two at a time to the bottom, where the door into the courtyard had been locked. He remembered the bunch of keys from which Isabella had extracted the key to this door. He cursed himself. He should have, somehow, tried to obtain the keys from her.

He tried it and sure enough it was locked. He pulled at the knots on the stiletto on his arm and it came away into his right hand. Priedeux bent down and carefully probed the lock with the thin blade, listening as he jiggled the implement from one side to the other, pushing it in further or pulling it towards him. A series of tiny clicking noises reassured him. Then he stood up and tried the door. It gave. Before he prised it fully open, he tied the stiletto back in its hiding place on his left forearm.

He put his ear to the door but there were no sounds to alarm him. Except for the lighterman, he was sure the castle servants still slept. The only spot where action might be taking place would be the kitchens and they were on the other side of the courtyard. And if the ovens were heated and the first batch of bread being made, he would be warned by the yeasty hot smell. He opened the door and stepped out into the cold grey of dawn and sniffed. There was no welcoming odour to whet Priedeux's early morning appetite. He was right; no servants about yet.

Even so, he would not risk taking the shortest route across the courtyard but slid along the walls, partly to hide from any early watchers but also to avoid the noise of his boots crunching on icy night snow. Beneath the parapets, the snow was damp mush.

He reached the stables and whispered gently to his horse, who rose from sleep to whinny gently at him. As he stroked its mane, he heard soft noises behind him. Someone was approaching the stables. Had he been followed? He threw himself into the hay at the back of the stall, and waited. In the dim gloom of the entrance, a hooded figure entered, its shape accentuated by a covered lamp that it carried. Only one person, who could be easily overcome if he discovered Priedeux. As he waited, the figure walked on past Gringolay's stall, without stopping, its shadow from the lamp now showing large. Priedeux rolled to the edge of the stall and carefully raised himself, peering over to watch the flickering light move to the back of the stable. The light silhouetted the figure onto the roof as a giant cowled triangle as it moved towards a stall containing a pony. Priedeux guessed at a small man, heavily robed and covered. His shape reminded Priedeux of the mysterious figure who would disappear at his approach. Was this who he had been looking for? Should he confront the person now or would they raise a hue and cry? He decided to watch and wait. He watched as his early morning companion saddled the pony, dealing with the tack in a quick, efficient manner, as if he were an accomplished horseman. There was no stealth about the action. Eventually all was done and the pony was led out of its stall. Priedeux ducked as the person led the animal through the stables. He decided to follow if the person left the castle. He waited until pony and rider were out of the stables and then ran to the entrance. He watched as the rider moved, with his steed, which, Priedeux realised now, had pads over its hooves to deaden the sound, to the side door of the drawbridge. A stone in the thick wall was pressed and the door opened.

The hooded stranger pressed another stone, Priedeux marking him well as he did it, and a narrow bridge, wide enough for a single person, descended slowly over the moat on well oiled chains. As it rolled down, the hooded rider mounted the pony in an ungainly manner, and walked the pony silently out of the castle. As Priedeux watched, the drawbridge seemed to close of its own accord.

Priedeux tingled with anticipation. Surely this was the monkish poet who was the creator of the work he knew so well, a work that was so evocative it could incite this area to full rebellion against the true king. Had he been warned by Lord de Coucy to make good his flight? Priedeux tried to recall all their conversations and began to wonder if he had given himself away. He was sure he had not but his arrival might have been enough to alert de Coucy. It all fitted. De Coucy, with his cat and mouse ways, must have guessed that Priedeux had been sent to seek out the seditious writer. Although Priedeux had made promises of loyalty to de Coucy, how could he be sure of Priedeux? And even if Priedeux was faithful to him, he couldn't be sure that such loyalty would stretch to others in the castle. If de Coucy had any honour, he would not want one of his servants, who had served him well by writing the poem for him, to be put in any danger. So, thought Priedeux, the easiest solution would be to tell the writer to disappear from the castle for a while. Priedeux convinced himself that the figure he had seen was the writer, and he had written the tract for de Coucy. So he had advised the writer to leave under cover like this, assuming that Priedeux would be in deep slumber, after the drugged wine of the night before.

He checked that the courtyard was still clear. It was becoming lighter and soon anyone peering out of the window when they woke, could see him. He turned to attend to Gringolay and, after fitting his tackle, followed the lead of the previous horseman, and, tearing some rags he found in a corner, and stuffing them with straw, he wrapped the horse's hooves in them. Then he followed the first rider to the gate. It was now a crisp, cold dawn, the sky rapidly blueing via soft lemon and apricot, from grey. It would be a bright day, he could almost smell it. He fingered the wall and found the stone, as it wobbled slightly under his touch. He pressed it, using the flat of his hand like he had seen the first rider do. At first it did not work, so he tried pressing different parts of the stone. Perhaps he had made a mistake and this was not the correct one. He tried others but they did not have the same feel as the first stone, although he could see no difference. He continued to press the first stone as Gringolay started to fidget, and suddenly it moved and the gate opened. He mounted Gringolay and found the second stone easily, pressed this in the way he had observed and the single drawbridge swung noiselessly down. Priedeux made a mental note that, if he ever had time, he would inspect the mechanism of this silent opening for with chains and pulleys he believed it was almost impossible for such a device to be so quiet.

He led the horse across and again was pleased that it did not flinch at such a strange path. Once over the bridge, and as Gringolay's back hooves stepped onto the hard iced earth, Priedeux turned to see the single plank being pulled back into its position in the wall of the castle. Again he was impressed by the mechanism and wished he had time, to investigate the workings of the drawbridge. Instead, realising he must hurry, for the first rider had a good few minutes' advance on him, he spurred Gringolay on. He was not unduly worried about following, having stalked other foes in the past, and if this one was a mere poet, he would not be able to evade Priedeux.

He grinned, for he reckoned the person whom he was to follow was an innocent, if he really was the poet. Priedeux thought all writers or musicians must be naive to use their imaginations in such ways, and sit in a room scribbling away all day. Surely their blood must freeze in their marrow if they did not exercise, practise fighting or riding. His prejudices were confirmed for there, before him, was a clearly marked trail. For a moment, Priedeux wondered if it was a trap, but he reasoned that the poet, for he would think of his quarry as that now, had no idea he had been seen and was now being followed. Anyway, Priedeux did not know how to get back into the castle without an outcry, so he would have to go on now, and take his chances.

If the opportunity arose, he would kill his prey, and collect his reward from Gaunt, without betraying the rules of the oath of fealty he had sworn to de Coucy. Now that the poet had left the castle he could kill him outside, without betraying his oath. If he were called to account he could argue that he thought the man was a stalker, an enemy of himself and de Coucy, without betraying his real intention. He did not think he would have to make such explanations, for he would soon be far away from this place. As soon as he had finished this job, he would head south, back to the Court. As he plodded along, he caught glimpses of the poet but he kept just out of sight of him.

The track the poet used led into the woods, the opposite way from which Priedeux had approached the castle, which seemed to him to have been days ago. Could it really have been only three days? He could no longer see the poet, who was hidden by the thickening woodland, but from the way the marks were spaced out, he guessed that his quarry was taking it at a light trot. Surely he must know the woods well, for a good horseman would not wager his neck by taking a knock from a strange branch whilst going fast through such terrain. Priedeux would not risk his horse and relied on the tracks. It was a cloudless day and the sun filtered through skeletal branches giving him all the light he needed. It was not likely to snow today so the trail would not be obliterated. Even better, the sun had melted the snow slightly so that the padded hoof marks were even more defined.

The track led deeper into a forest of tall oaks, where there was no shade and no snow had fallen through the overhanging branches. The ground here was of mud. Priedeux became ever more alert, aware as he was that the trail could be leading him straight into an ambush. He fingered the stiletto and the knots, checking the ease with which the weapon was released into his hand. He unwrapped his sword from his cloak and pulled the cloak over his shoulders to stop the dripping snow from penetrating his clothes, but also to hide the weapons.

The sun was well up now and shone almost horizontally through the trees, making them seem long and taller than they were, more menacing as well. It illuminated the trail a good way in front of him but he could not see the rider ahead. The wood seemed to dip and rise, with valleys and clearings, where the snow deepened and the path he was following became deeper where the small pony had had to pull its padded legs clear of drifts.

Then the wood changed and it became thick with evergreens, hollies and stunted pines. Priedeux realised he was climbing, and the snow was becoming thinner now as if a strong wind had cleaned the higher mounds and sent drifts of it down into the valleys where it had settled. The air became clear with the clean fragrance of the pines wafting to him. The trees, being evergreen, also held narrow bands of icy snow on each branch, so that it created a curtained thickness around him, blocking out the rays of sun. He went on, but the snow petered out and the ground became harder, with stones and large granite boulders pushing up. He lost the trail of hooves. Even so, there were still clues. Where the first rider had gone, there were branches where the snow had been dislodged, and small powdery mounds on the ground showed Priedeux the way to follow.

Suddenly the trees ended, as if human hands had cut a swathe in them. He was in a ravine. It might have been because the thin winter sun was blocked by the tall rocks either side but he felt a shiver of anticipation. There were some trees which slanted down from high above him, their hold on the earth precarious, but at man height all he could see were granite boulders, marbled with orange and white stripes, as if the place had been torn asunder and he was standing in the very heart of a mountain. There were great pitted roots showing and mossy banks where the snow had not penetrated. Jagged rocks seemed to hem him in so that there was only one way he could go. The air was thinner here, and despite being very fit, Priedeux felt his breath labouring. As he came clear of one larger than man-sized outcrop, the wind whistled around him with a violence he had rarely felt, as if the world wanted to attack him, forcing him and the horse to take breath before pushing forward. He dismounted and started to lead Gringolay forward slowly, checking each sparse branch for evidence that someone had recently passed, for evidence of his quarry. He walked forward soundlessly. At least the whistling wind would hide any noises he and his horse might make. Except for the wind, there was no movement, no birds singing, no wild creature foraging, and even Priedeux, hard bitten as he was, began to feel the isolation of the place as a menace.

Suddenly, he could hear the rush of water, as if it fell violently over hard granite. It sounded like thunder. Or a giant playing with a huge anvil and hammer. As he entered another channel through rocks, the noise was silenced. He moved on and suddenly the sound of the water thundered again.

He kept going, until he saw before him a mossy clearing of rocky promontories, with a centre point all emerald created by a thick carpet of moss. On the farther side was the waterfall that was the origin of the thunderous sounds, a great gushing of steam, rainbowed in its centre at the sun touched it.

Yes, this was the shrine for the Green Man. The place described so well in the poem.

Then he saw the hooded and robed figure, sitting on the mound of moss, interspersed with patches of rough grass, the pony waiting quietly at the edge of the place. As he entered, a rush of warm air assailed him and he took a deep breath, noting the heady aroma of some kind of summery perfume

227

that could not have come from anything growing at this high altitude. Here, it seemed, was a haven of warmth amongst the coldness of it surroundings. There was no snow, only dark greenness. There was no rushing wind, just a pall of still air. The human seemed to be part of the stillness. The figure was sitting away from Priedeux, watching the rushing stream, chin in elbow, elbow on knee, as if day-dreaming.

Priedeux slid off Gringolay, certain that, with the roar of the waterfall, the figure would never hear him approaching. He pulled his sword from his scabbard and the stiletto from its position so that he had both weapons ready, and walked forward until he was almost on the person. This time, he would not kill in cold blood. His curiosity was aroused. He needed to speak to this person who had led him on, led him through this quest, with the poem and recently, with the games in the castle they had both left, as if teasing. Priedeux realised that he had grown to love the story of the poem, reading and re-reading it through the months he had travelled. He knew he had come far and could not end this journey with a quick kill and a running away. This person deserved more than an assassin's stabbing. It was as if Priedeux knew him as a friend. He positioned himself on top of the mound, his prey below him, the cowled head and foreshortened body before him and then he cried:

'Who are you? What will you do here?'

The figure jumped, and turned, dislodging the hood of the cloak, and looked up at him. As the hood fell back, it revealed startled dark eyes in a soft female face, circled by dark hair that fell over those soft curves of shoulders and tight curvature of breasts.

'Isabella!'

Chapter Eighteen: The poet revealed

'Deal me my destiny and do it out of hand,
for I shall stand your stroke, not starting at all.'

'Isabella, what do you do here?' He repeated her name as if it
was a mantra, his voice echoing in the enclosed space. He
realised he'd spoken loudly not only because of the shock of
seeing her but to be heard above the roar and thunder of the
water.

   She had stepped back. She stared at him with her head
held high. He could see that he had not really startled her.
She knew she had been followed. He stepped closer, trying to
move down to her level but she gestured him away and stood
regally before him. He waited, saying nothing. He realised
she was in charge and he stood still, hoping that all would be
revealed soon enough. She looked particularly beautiful, the
ride having put some dark bloom into her cheeks and her eyes
glowed.   The moss on the ground and the dark trees
surrounding this arbour gave her face and hair a greenish look.

   'I hope I am to get an explanation' He said, to break the
silence between them.

   She smiled. He wanted to take her in his arms but her
bearing forbade him and he knew he would have to be led by
her. She had a dignity which made him respect her, as he had
never respected a woman before. In one way she reminded
him so much of fighting men he had lived with in the past.
Despite her femininity, and lithe seductive body, she looked at
him now with the straight look a man would give.

   'So you managed to follow? How did you..?'   The

questions were more an introduction to conversation, he felt. He answered the second question first. 'I was in the stable, watching, so I saw how you got out.'

She nodded. Still she did not explain. He felt he needed to make an excuse for following her.

'I thought you were that shadowy monk figure I keep seeing in the castle, I thought I'd follow.'

'Monk? Oh, yes, Aylwin the idiot, he is harmless but very shy. But why would you want to follow him?'

He decided to tell the truth, for it had stood him in good stead on this quest.

'I need to speak to the poet who wrote *Gawain and the Green Knight.*'

She visibly started and stepped back from him. He continued, 'my quest led me to your castle and certain events have made me believe that he was living there, or at least he is under the patronage of your lord.' He thought he detected a knowing smile cross her face. He went on, now starting to walk from side to side as if it helped him tell her his story. 'When I saw you leaving I suspected it might be that monk, and I thought he might be the writer I sought. I believe him to be a bookish man, a hunting man, a knowledgeable man, but more than that I cannot say.' He quoted Chaucer word for word, as it had been drummed into him.

She was now grinning. 'Ah, well, Aylwin will not be your man then.' She paused and then asked: 'But why do you need to meet with the writer of that poem?'

'Do you know it?'

She nodded: 'Very well, almost...' She stopped and repeated her question: 'Why do you need...?'

He interrupted her. 'I cannot say, as it may endanger you. I would ask you another question. Are you privy to your lord's council meetings? Does he meet with his knights to make war plans and conspiracies?'

She looked puzzled. She shook her head. 'Only to plan

hunting expeditions or games for the feasts. He has had his fill of conspiracies, courts, and battles. He explained that to you last night, and it is true. As I told you, he no longer wishes to travel, not even on pilgrimage. I am the one who keeps contact with the outside world, or tries to.' She stopped.

He detected again the wistfulness in her voice when she had spoken of travelling before. He realised that Isabella was a great woman, an individual who would risk much to travel the world. He had met women before who used the excuse of a pilgrimage to Jerusalem, Rome or Assisi or other holy places such as Canterbury to satisfy their wanderlust.

'Aah, I wish to God what you say is true; that your husband does not plot. Then what is the purpose of the poem?'

She came to him then and a gentle hand was placed on his forearm in a gesture that had become familiar to him. She said, in her low tones. 'Please, tell me, what is the import of the poem for you? I know it well, perhaps I can help?'

He looked down at her and knew he had to trust her; otherwise his whole life now would be a wasteland. He realised that he truly loved this woman in a way that he had never loved anyone before, not even his mother.

'I have been sent to kill the man who wrote it.'

She stepped back in utter dismay and he caught her before she fell over a tree-root. Why was she so aghast?

'It was not written by your husband? A favoured clerk?'

She looked away then, and he saw her take a deep breath. When she looked up at him, her face was resolved and calm. 'Tell me why you have to kill the writer.'

'My master believes it is written to incite rebellion among loyal subjects.'

She looked so surprised that he thought she could not possibly know anything about the author. Her mobile features changed and a slight smile tickled her lips as before.

'The language, you understand.' He continued. 'The

description of the two courts, the second castle being so much more attractive, the clemency of the Green Knight. When you told me that your lord had adopted the colours of the Green Knight, I felt it was an omen. I knew I had come to the right place.'

He was talking to her back now for she had walked away from him, towards her horse and he became alert, wondering if she would try to mount and ride away. But she stood, head bowed, in a gesture that showed she was thinking deeply. There was a long silence and he again became conscious of the rushing of the water like so many courtiers shuffling and whispering in the background. He waited, for the very air seemed to be pregnant with secrets it would soon reveal just as the grey clouds that were now gathering, would soon drop their next fall of snow.

Then she turned and faced him. Her arms were folded below her breasts and she stood her bearing regal. Then, in her low, vibrant voice she said clearly. 'Then you must kill *me*. Go ahead, I know the sword is ready, you must make it clean and quick.'

For a moment the import of what she said did not sink in. All he saw was a dignified, brave, beautiful woman speaking nonsense.

Then he said in total shock. '*You!* You wrote *Gawain and the Green Knight*? But...'

She finished the sentence for him. 'It is impossible. Impossible that a woman could write such a thing?'

He did not answer or go on. He put his head to one side and contemplated her. She returned his gaze steadily, calmly, with a resolve he had not seen in their bedroom meetings. It was as if the morning's ride had given her a feeling of self-worth that she had hidden within the castle. He thought of all they had spoken about, the books she had read, her admission that she could speak and learn new languages quickly. She had revealed all with a shy femininity; now she was bold. But there was something that niggled at him. The hunting, and the horse-riding. She had said she could not ride a horse. He had seen her do so today. So she had lied to him. Was all the rest a lie? Was she hiding someone else? If so, who?

'Tell me, you said you came here with your husband, in a wagon, for you had not been taught to ride.' It was as if the unrelated question relaxed her.

She smiled at him. 'I told you the nuns had not taught me. My husband insisted I learn, for he would have me follow the hunt. He said it was necessary for exercise. This morning I needed to think and felt the need to ride. I could feel, last night, your restlessness and I felt sad, knowing that I might lose you soon. And I have heard rumours, from outside.' She spread her arms then, as if she would embrace the whole dell. 'This is my favourite place, a holy, peaceful shrine where only I come. In summer the rocks are baked hot, and there are celandines and forget-me-not and other summer flowers to brighten it. Even now, it is warm.'

She reached out to him as if to welcome him to her special place. 'Yes, I usually go with my lord when he goes hunting when we do not have guests. You intrigued me with your talk of the court and the Green Man. It was easy to persuade my lord that I should stay behind and entertain you. I wanted to find out if the poem had achieved its end. I sent copies out to certain people and I thought you might be the messenger.'

'Messenger?'

She approached him where he stood near the mound, and pressed on his arm to invite him to sit. He spread his cloak and they sat on it together. Gawain felt no cold penetrate from the rock beneath and realised Isabella was right; this place had a warmth of its own, even in the depths of winter.

'Messenger?' He repeated. 'For what reason?'

'The poem I wrote is a pastiche of all those love poems that have been written - but it has one purpose. You will recall I told you my mother's shield contained a pentangle and she was given to my father in marriage by one John of Gaunt. That is all I know of her and that she was highly born and I have always wondered about her. Her and her family.'

She looked up at him wistfully. 'I want to know her lineage,' she said simply, and went on. 'The idea came to me that if her kin read of such a perfect five-sided knight, they would want to know who had written it, would recognise the clues and would come and seek me. They would follow the ride of Gawain, all the clues, like you did, and eventually find me. I sent out copies with riders and told them to take them where they would. They left some time ago to the five corners of the world but I fear that they have gone so far that they have fallen off the edge. Nothing have I heard, except when you arrived. I thought you may have been sent to find me, but you gave no sign, even when I confided in you, and then... ' She shook her head. 'I am truly sad if great men read the poem wrongly.'

He pulled her to face him and saw the concern in her face. He suddenly remembered Gaunt and Chaucer and the sinister meeting they had had in Gaunt's chamber when he had been sent out on this quest. Should he tell her that his master was none other than the man who had given away her mother in marriage? Or that he was the one who had sent him to kill the man who had written the poem? Instead of incitement to riot, one of Gaunt's protégées had produced a child who wanted acknowledgement from her unknown relations.

The irony of it made gurgles in his stomach and he smiled at her but it turned into a laugh and then great uncontrollable laughter erupted out of him. She too, after watching a second, caught the infectious giggling and started laughing as well. She gasped, at one point. 'Wha-at, what am I laughing at?'

Through gulps, Priedeux explained. 'Chaucer.was right, except for one thing! He told me to look for an educated *man*. *A man* who knows his Latin and his Greek. A hunting *man!* A *man* with many books. A *man* who loves materials, the touch of them. A *man* who knows what good food is...' He was still laughing, and at every accentuation of the word 'man' Isabella laughed as well. They both held their bodies bent and fell against each other in a macabre hysteria of giggling.

Slowly their giggles died away. They clung to one another, partly for support as the laughter tore at their bodies, but partly for the need of each other. Isabella grew serious.

'You have to kill me. That is your mission. How could you return to your master without doing the deed?'

'I have to kill the poet. The poet is believed to be a man. I cannot kill you, my lady. I have learnt to do many things in my life, through necessity and otherwise, but I will not do this deed.'

'But you must, for you will need to return to your King, otherwise surely he will send others and others. And I will be discovered one day. And so will my lord and I would not wish that. He has been good to me and, although I love him not, I care for him and will always stay with him.'

She pulled herself away then, and walked to the edge of the water. The spray caught her on the face and she lifted a hand as if to wipe it. When she turned and faced him, her face *was* wet but it all seemed to be around her eyes.

Priedeux suddenly saw and understood. This woman loved him; their intimacy stretched far beyond just the physical, even though they had known each other for only a short while. And he knew he loved her, as he had never loved anyone before. A great sadness filled him too. He knew she would never go with him, even if he asked her to.

She interrupted his thoughts. She spoke loudly, so she could be heard above the rushing fall. 'There is another thing you must know. I have heard stories from the outside. Troops are on alert, there are movements of soldiers around the country. There are rumours of a great argument between two lords, settled by a sword fight, that have made great factions at your court. You *must* go and be part of it.'

As she was speaking she came near to him again, her hand on his sleeve, her moist eyes beseeching. Priedeux nodded, taking the small hand in his. He too realised that he could not take this person with him if he left and he knew he had to go soon.

'I am loath to leave you Lady, for you have taught me what love is, through your beauty and kindness and your body. I will always love you.'

Her eyes shone as she heard this. 'Priedeux, I could see the love in you when you walked into our hall and into my heart at that moment. You would hide it with a great armour of cynicism but I know it will always be there. And I will stay here and keep it in my heart forever.'

He wrapped her in his cloak and they made love, gently and for a long time, so that, when they had finished, the sun was moving towards the evening. Afterwards he stroked her hair, her face, her body as if he was a blind man and he was recording every part of her. Eventually he stood, and murmured, 'I will away, my Lady, and I promise to protect you and de Coucy as far as I am able.'

Then without looking back, he strode across the dell, mounted Gringolay, turned the horse's head and rode out, not knowing which way he would go.

Chapter Nineteen: Interlude

'Now Gawain goes riding on Gringolet
in lonely lands, his life saved by grace'.

After a while Priedeux noticed the sun's path and realised he was riding north-east but he let Gringolay take him. He did not care, there was such an ache in his heart that nothing would expunge it except hardship, hunger and hard riding.

As he rode, Isabella's face, her body, the very essence of her, seemed to be constantly with him. He kept touching his forearm where her soft hand had rested in that sympathetic way, as if the spot was permanently indented with the shape of her fingers. He felt a strange almost disembodied lust as he remembered her sinuous, perfectly-shaped body, her loving movements. As he rode, he saw strange hanging mosses in the trees and it reminded him of her long tresses as he had last seen them, darkly, lushly mahogany with green tints from the moss beneath her head. Her voice echoed in his ears. 'I wrote it, the poem. *Gawain and the Green Knight* is mine.' The consequences of what she had said made him smile.

But there was also a feeling of failure. Failure at not completing the job he had been given by Gaunt. Failure at giving in to emotions that he had hidden for years, or that he never knew he had. He was a *fighting* man in Heaven's name, and he despised those who let their emotions rule their actions. He should have killed her, she was a temptress, a witch, to have such power over him. Even as he thought this, he knew it was not true, and touched that part of his arm again where he could remember those delicate fingers resting, oh so gently that it was like a wraith's touch.

When he heard water he thought of her bathing or sitting in the ravine, waiting for him to return. He forgot the freeze of winter and saw her in a summer shaded arbour, all green and lush, her soft body gently bloomed by the sun.

When the wind blew he thought she whispered to him.

A deep peat-pool would be to him her dark Mediterranean eyes. When he pulled his cloak around him he felt her arms encircling him.

When he ate it seemed dust in his mouth compared to the morsels that she had fed him; the wine turned to acrid ale.

And all beds were hard and lonely after the luxury of lying with her.

As he rode on, further and further from her, he often thought to turn back and ask if he could stay with her and her lord. Something stopped him and he knew what it was. He was afraid he would never find that castle again. He was afraid she would haughtily refuse him. He was unsure how he would react to seeing her. Would he still feel that magic, that awe of her? Or would he see her as another lay, another experience, as he had always felt towards women?

His sense of loss overwhelmed him and a part of him was surprised at the strength of the emotion. It was as if he was physically bereft of all he had ever felt before meeting his lady.

He rode for many days with the conflicting emotions wafting through him, caring not what would happen to him until he came to flat plains of marsh. He knew he should dismount and lead the animal. He knew there would be places where pools of muddy sucking water could claim both of them. He did not care, but let Gringolay take him, trusting now in the horse's sure footedness.

'For you, my good horse, have not been addled by human love, as I have, and 'tis a very strange thing for such as I to be mixed up with.'

One day, many moons later, as he rode along, dusk fell and then there were mysterious lights that danced and flickered around him. If it was summer he would have said they were glow-worms, but even though he had been riding for some months he knew it could not be summer. It was as if Gringolay wanted to follow the lights, and the man let him. He was sweat-hot and then cold and he realised that marsh fever had gripped him. His hold on the reins loosened and his head slumped. The horse slowed and eventually stopped, and started grazing on the rough marsh grass.

After a while Priedeux was gripped by a violent shivering which convulsed his body. The horse interpreted this as being spurred on and, like the well trained animal it was, lifted its head and started to trot. Although they rode through marsh, there were hidden stones and large tufts of the reeds. Priedeux tried to control the animal but the fever had made him weak and his feeble attempts at reining in the creature came to nothing. It was not long before the horse stumbled and its cargo of man, drifting into a semi-coma, slipped off and fell onto soft spongy grass. As he landed, a pool of water rose with the weight of him and the cold wetness hit Priedeux as if he had been slammed by a mallet. He lost consciousness and something inside him was pleased for he began to suspect his sanity.

When he woke it was as if all the dancing lights that had been leading him onwards, had combined together. He was dazzled by them, so, at first, he could not see where he was. Slowly, his eyes started to focus. He tried to move but his whole body ached and he groaned. He seemed to be on a rough pallet and as he stretched out he touched the wall close beside him, and it gave, and he realised he was in some sort of tent. There was a figure outlined in a corner who now moved to bend over him, aroused no doubt by his groaning.

'Aah, you awake, at last.' The voice was soft and came from a small, well bred face surrounded by blonde hair.

Priedeux, confused and feverish still, wondered if this was an apparition. Before him were the features of the girl to whom he had given the talisman aeons ago. He was sure it was she, the swineherd, whom he had left in the Wirral in another lifetime, or so it seemed to him. She bathed his forehead with some cool sweet-smelling herb and he tried to smile but he could feel his eyes closing again. As he sunk into unconsciousness he heard someone else say, 'let him sleep, he needs sleep.' He recognised a male voice, again strangely familiar before he sank into unconsciousness again.

The next time he woke, he did not open his eyes, but listened. There were muffled sounds all around him, of men moving, a scraping noise which reminded him of squires cleaning weapons before a battle, the slap of leather on leather, the clopping of hooves or of wooden clogs clapping on stone. All strangely familiar but as if from another dimension. Someone whispered and he was sure there were people nearby but he could feel the presence was benign.

He felt comfortably warm. He could smell sweet herbs and, faintly, potage; vegetables, meat, a mixture brewing in some cauldron nearby. This was not a place for the great spit and roasting pig or cow. It was a temporary encampment, then, where utensils and weapons could be one and packed up quickly, tents folded, and the company moved on, he guessed. And no evidence they had ever been in the place. He felt very much at home, as if he were in one of the temporary campsites before a battle, in one of the City States on the mainland. In his lazy, dreaming way, he seemed to go back to his childhood and imagined that, at any moment, Sir John Hawkwood would stride in and rebuke him for lying in so long. Then uneasiness set in, and something uncomfortable intervened. He tried to recall what had brought him to this place, tried to recall where he was, but all he could remember was feeling hot, then cold, and feverish. Nothing before the dancing lights of the marsh and trying to keep to his saddle. Had he been through some battle which had been so horrific he had expunged it from his memory? A part of him was almost pleased he could not remember. He knew there was something he would rather forget, as if it was a gangrenous limb that he knew he had had to have cut off. He continued to lie, eyes closed, letting all the sensations penetrate, keeping his breathing steady. Then he heard what he could only interpret as a female laughing, and, within the laughter, whispering his name. 'Priedeux, pretend, Priedeux, pretend, awake now, all is over.'

He opened his eyes, and something inside him felt vaguely disappointed. He decided to investigate that feeling later but for the time being he would deal with what he could see now. Sitting at his side, as if she had full authority over him, was indeed the blonde girl to whom he had given the seal of the wandering lord. She held a wooden bowl which was steaming and smelt strongly of chicken and vegetables. He realised he was extremely hungry.

'Aye, I've been watching you since morn and knew you would arise from the deep soon. Come, if you can, sit up. We will make a meal of this.'

He tried to rise, but was as weak as a nun who only prayed and never left her convent. The girl, despite her small stature and age, put her arm around his shoulders and helped him up, placing a bolster behind him. She started to feed him with a large wooden ladle.

As she held this to his lips, after blowing on it, she explained. 'We found you lying, your foot still in the stirrup and sure your horse is like a good servant for he stood still and just kept nosing you until we dislodged you. How long you had lain in the mists of the swamp was difficult to say but surely you have been to the gates of hell. It has been many days and many medicines which have brought you back.'

'Where am I? My horse, Gringolay, safe?'

'Safe, both of you, the horse well rubbed down and fed. You are with my Lord Owen, who had to disappear from

Wales before he was due to be killed.'

Priedeux shook his head. She spoke as if he should know Lord Owen.

She explained. 'The man whose seal you gave me. I found him and am now in his company. We are in the marshes of Lincolnshire, safe from prying eyes for the time being until we are assured of our destiny. Lord Owen was indeed of my kind and we now repay you for that wisdom of yours.'

As she spoke, the man she spoke of, opened the flap at the end of the tent and came in, with a 'How does he do?'

The girl looked up. 'As you can see, ravenous and conscious. But he is still tired.'

'Aye, we will have him with us some time before he is fit for the court again!'

'The court?' Priedeux managed to ask. 'How do you know of such things?'

'We have our spies. Lepers and outcasts usually. They are not noticed as they gather information and most people ignore them as they travel the breadth of the country.'

Priedeux, as if the words affected him, did feel tired now, and could not cope with more. He fell back, turning his head away from the proffered ladle. The girl looked up at the lord, who nodded, and they left him as his eyelids flickered and he drifted into a healthy sleep.

His robust health and strength meant he grew better each day. He had suffered fevers before and knew to take the recovery slowly but within a few days he could walk and they showed him Gringolay. The horse looked chubby with lack of exercise, but whinnied a greeting, and, it seemed to Priedeux, one of relief, as Priedeux fussed and stroked him.

'Soon we will be on our way again, my brave and noble steed.'

As Priedeux recovered from his illness, he also recovered his recall of the lady and the knight but now it was suffused as in a dream and the pain was less. He realised the disappointment on first waking was because he had hoped it would be his Lady Isabella who was sitting on his bed. Now he knew the reason for his disappointment, he could deal with it. He knew what he had to do and as soon as he could mount and stay in the saddle for half a day, he approached the Lord Owen.

'I must be on my way, for I endanger many by being away from court longer.'

'I know it,' said that wise man. 'I have repaid the kindness you did for me and mine at the ford and the girl likewise. We would wish you to tarry with us but we know your destiny and that of the court.'

Priedeux obviously looked quizzical. The man shrugged and smiled. He did not elaborate but added. 'Surely the girl you sent me has been a great asset to me, even when I despaired of the life of myself and my people. She is a great seer and has foretold that my descendants will be Kings of England, under the name of Tudor, but not yet and we have to wait the appointed time. I tell you this so that you will understand that you have not sojourned with common sort, despite our current nomad way of living, but I know you will not reveal such stories to those who pay your way. You have played your part in our destiny, although you do not know it. Go in peace, and prosperity.'

Priedeux left them with his saddlebags stuffed with food and headed south. The air was still chill with the remains of winter, although there were wild narcissi peeping through grasses along the wayside. The winter snow was thawing, although on the slopes that faced north there were still great swathes of white to be seen. The road itself was not so muddy as it could have been although there were deep icy ruts that he took care to avoid. He found the great north road and followed it south, knowing he would not pass Wilcomstou and being grateful for that. A feeling of regret about his family flowed over him but another part of him did not want to know what had happened to them. Best not to dwell on it, he was thinking as he rode into London Town through Moorgate in good spirits.

He passed through the crowded streets, finding the noise and bustle intrusive and jangling after his experiences. He knew he was still not perfectly well. Moving on out of the walled city he headed north west and soon crossed fields, bare now of the usual grazing sheep and cattle, towards Gaunt's lodgings outside the City walls, at Ely Palace. There, he was surprised to find the place closed, so he hammered on the Porter's lodge.

The gate was not opened immediately and he wondered at this. He looked up at the casemented windows, all firmly closed. He noticed that there were no banners flying, and it dawned on him that there was none of the usual clamour of daily life in a busy place. No smoke filtered from the chimneys, no smell of the herbs used to keep the floors and beds clean and flea-free, wafted from the building. He hammered again.

This time there was some reaction. The small side porter's gate was slowly opened. A face peered out, familiar to the traveller, who grinned at him.

'Priedeux, is that you?'

'Wallers, my old friend. How are you, how is it with everyone here?'

'Shush, not so loud. I'll open up, but we are a sorry bunch that is left.' He disappeared and a few moments later the gate was drawn to one side and Wallers emerged and took the reins of Gringolay. He almost pulled the horse in and quickly barred the gate again. As they entered the yard, which was empty, Wallers cocked his head to one side as if listening. Priedeux dismounted and waited. Something was amiss but he would not ask, expecting Wallers to speak first. Instead, the old servant turned to his visitor and studied him. Priedeux ignored his stares and surveyed the space, empty of ostlers and butchers and bustling minions. He was about to say something when Wallers gestured him into his cubby hole at the side of the gate.

'Have you ridden far? You look as if you slept in a good bed last night.'

Priedeux smiled and shrugged. 'I'll not tell of my ride, until you tell me where his Lordship is, and when I can see him.'

'You mean Gaunt, John of Gaunt?'

Wallers asked it as if incredulous, and Priedeux began to wonder if either Wallers or he had lost their senses.

'Of course, I mean Gaunt! Come, man, I'll not be playing Yuletide games now.'

'You'll not know then?'

'Know what? Wallers, out with it.'

'Aye, you cannot know. Gaunt is at Leicester, dangerously ill they say, and the clouds do gather around the throne. Men have been done to death, others to exile.'

He moved nearer to Priedeux then, looking up at him. He whispered: 'It is as if the end of the world is coming...the end of the century draws nigh and soothsayers are muttering.'

'Wallers! I never knew you were so superstitious.'

But the old servant went on. 'And it is like we are all waiting for the death knell and then... more men will die, I know it.'

Priedeux was becoming impatient and shook the man.

'Tell me - what men? How? No! That can wait, I must see Gaunt, to tell him I have completed my mission. Leicester you say?' He turned back to his horse, and said, 'sorry Wallers, open up, I can't wait for the full story - I must to Leicester.'

Wallers was still muttering as he unbarred the exit. As Priedeux rode away, he wondered what fortune, good or ill, might lie ahead.

Chapter Twenty: The end of the quest

They all asked him about his expedition,
and he truthfully told them of his tribulations...'

He rode the horse hard and reached Leicester the next day, at dusk. What he had seen along the way, disturbed him. Smoking hovels, crofts destroyed and lame animals wandering free in winter. As he approached one village there was a cry and a woman, struggling to hold onto her brood ran screaming into the scrub. At a crossroads, there was a man hanging, rotting in the noose. It reminded Priedeux of the civil wars he had seen on the continent, neighbour revenging himself on neighbour for old feuds. War giving an excuse to settle old scores. What Wallers had said began to seem prophetic rather than the mutterings of a slavering man in his dotage.

Eventually, the road led him across the River Soar with Gaunt's Castle, newly built of shining sandstone, on his right. Priedeux had ridden for some miles along the shore of the river, trying to find a crossing, but all he found was marsh and bogland, left over from the winter. He knew Leicester had been built at a fording point on this river and carried on until he found the official bridge. He would go to the town first, to enquire if there was any news. With the intention of finding an inn, and up to date news, he rode past the castle. He desperately wanted to find out what was going on. He knew Gaunt could be unforgiving; especially if he was suffering from old wounds, and Priedeux did not want to approach his master until he knew he was in a reasonable mood. He also wanted to find out if his lord's visit was official, if the townspeople knew what was going on. If it wasn't, how would he explain his unexpected arrival; something else for him to think about. The scenes he had witnessed as he travelled up north made him unusually wary.

This feeling was accentuated when he entered the gate into the town. He felt as if he was being watched, but no one challenged him.

The narrow streets were strangely quiet, the shops already shuttered, even though it was not yet the time they would normally close. There were not even the usual apprentices gossiping at the doors after their day's work was done, or blocking the way as they walked three across, on their way to the alehouse. When he asked at the first inn, the Blue Boar, why there was such a silence he was greeted with shrugs and monosyllabic grunts. He realised they did not take kindly to strangers. As he left, one of the locals sidled out of a side entrance and ambled up to him as he was about to mount Gringolay and said, in a dialect Priedeux could only just understand:

'He be in his chapel.' The man pointed further on, towards the castle walls and a high thin spire which stood out against the darkening sky.

'And good may it do you, stranger.' Priedeux did not bother to pursue the point but reined Gringolay in that direction, only to find the assembled drinkers standing at the door of the inn, grinning at him. He left quickly, perturbed and eager to be with the court he knew and understood, tired now of roaming.

He decided, as he had not been able to find out anything in the town, that he would take the horse to his lord's castle. At least there he could claim food for himself, and fodder for Gringolay. He rode through the turret gateway. Nobody challenged him. He found the stables in a corner of the courtyard, which was deserted. Tethering Gringolay himself,, he found some hay and left it for the horse. That would have to do until he could return.

He left the stables and, led by the sight of the tall spire which had been pointed out to him, he headed that way. He found the door to the church and waited, reluctant as always to enter. Slowing a short distance from it, he hoped to waylay his Lord Gaunt as he left the service. His boots echoed strangely on the cobbles of the courtyard, which was devoid of the normal groups of hangers on, pie-sellers or women plucking chickens ready for an evening meal. The silence, broken only by his foot-falls, was making the hair on the back of his neck prickle.

Ignoring the feeling, he concentrated on his quest, intent now on finding Gaunt and reporting to him. Although Gaunt was as pious as any other courtly gentlemen, it was a strange time for him to be in church. Priedeux assumed that his lord had recovered from the illness Wallers had spoken of and, as a safeguard into heaven, was saying mass as a thanksgiving for his life. He surveyed the chapel before him. Built about three hundred years ago, Priedeux guessed, with unusual zig-zag stone carvings around the entrance. It contrasted strangely with the newness of the castle. He waited. It was quite dark now and he was sure that any service would be over. What was going on? The only way to find out was to go in. He pushed open the heavy door and entered.

The slow chanting of hidden monks told him that a solemn mass was being sung. He moved into the nave slowly, anchoring his sword so it did not clank against stone pillars. The air was thick with the blue smoke and intense sickly savour of incense. He could see no one; the nave was empty and unlit. He could not work out from where the monks' voices emanated. Stepping carefully so as not to make to much noise, he moved down the gloomy nave into the choir, making for the place from where the singing came. He saw no-one so he passed through the rood screen ignoring the strictures of priests who claimed that no lay person should enter the chapel behind and headed for the north wall. There, he found a window-like aperture and, when he peered through it, he was surprised to see another chapel, a mirror image of the one he was in. Instead of the plain carvings of the chapel he stood in, the other one was decorated with ornate, colourful paintings on the walls and pillars. There were rich peaches, yellows and blues used to depict saints. Where he stood, there was no seating but the other had pews nearest the choir. Here the cross on the rood screen was dull and even in this light Priedeux could see it did not match with the magnificence of the golden crucifix in that other chapel. He realised he was in the parochial part of a double church, and the chanting of the mass was a private affair in his lord's chapel, where only his retinue would be allowed in.

Priedeux stole out of the place and walked round the tower and found a grander entrance on the north side of the church. The great wooden door was set into a stone arch, carved with exotic animals. He turned the iron ring set into the centre of the door, and it moved silently and he went in. He entered a chapel of lights, so different from the lesser church on the other side of the wall. Here the incense was so strong that he felt his nose tickle, but resisted the sneeze that threatened. The chanting of the monks echoed into the wooden beams of the roof so high above, and in the curves of the deep windows. He moved down the nave to the crossing and stood before the rood screen, realising that the monks were on the other side, hidden from him by the tracery pattern.

He put his face close to the rood screen and peered through. He would not enter, while it was occupied by the monks. They would be horrified if he did. Giant candles lit the scene. In the centre, there was a great sarcophagus, too grand to be anything other than that of a nobleman, giant flares illuminating the banners hanging from sconces in the pillars and thickly carved statuary emblazoned on the side of it. The banners seemed to sway slightly in the heat from the flares. He watched as the monks, eyes closed, chanted their familiar plainsong, standing in rows in the choir stalls, the rise and lilt of their voices resonating around that part of the chapel even more than when he had first entered. Priedeux was so moved he found himself kneeling. He slowly understood the pattern of the words, and realised this was a requiem mass. He looked around and could see no other mourners and thought this could only be a private affair between the monks and a dead benefactor, he having paid heavily for the privilege of prayers for his soul. He must have been very rich, thought Priedeux.

He watched and waited. There was no sign of Gaunt and he began to wonder what to do next. Eventually the monks slowly moved out of their places and, heads bowed and still chanting, they left the place, disappearing through a side exit, the slow slap of their sandalled feet beating time to their song as they went. Priedeux waited, and then, convinced he was alone, strode into the choir, his feet padding to a different rhythm, on the stone floor. No lay person would normally be allowed into the choir but Priedeux didn't care for such restrictions. He had to know who the dead person was.

As he reached the sarcophagus, the stench of rotting human flesh overcame the strong smell of the incense, old herbs and other aromatics. The coffin was lidless and, as he bent over it, and looked inside, Priedeux, for all his toughness, turned away towards the sedilia, sat down and retched.

Despite the advanced decomposition he recognised John of Gaunt.

His master, his hair and beard carefully combed and dressed in the finery of an official ceremony at court, was dead. And from the smell he'd been dead for some time.

Now the grins of the locals made sense.

Priedeux sat for a time, trying to think. The shock of seeing the body left him numb. After a while, he returned to the sight, fascinated now that his initial shock had abated, and looked down at the decomposing body, no longer possessing the dignity and aura of the living man. The chain of Lancaster rested on the collapsed breast and a thin crown was fixed onto the head. Ermine-edged robes were carefully positioned across the angular frame. But the smell belied all the artifices of grandeur. Priedeux guessed he had lain there for some days, if not weeks. Even though it was late winter, it was not so cold as to stop the natural putrefaction of a long-dead body. At least the chill had kept away the flies. As he gazed it was as if the features turned into a ghastly grin, but Priedeux kept his ground, refusing to run in horror. He knew that shadows caused by flickering flares could play tricks especially in an evocative place like this church. He looked up at the candles and realised there was a draught of some sort in this holy place. As he stared again at that face, once so stern, now so devoid of strength and character, Priedeux heard a slight sound, a swishing of cloth behind him. He did not unsheath his sword ready for fight. In this place, at this hour, with the dead form before him, he could not believe he would fall foul of an assassin's attack. He assumed it would be the monk chosen to sit with the dead throughout the night.

He turned slowly and looked into the gloom but at first saw no-one.

'Who's there?' he called, his voice sounding so loud in the empty chapel that it almost made him jump. Suddenly, as if separating from one of the outer pillars, a cloaked figure came forward.

'Priedeux, 'tis you, returned at last. How do you like the sight of your master?'

'Chaucer. What do you here?' Priedeux turned away. 'And this? Why this?'

The old poet moved forward and leant over to look at the body of his kinsman.

"Tis not a pretty sight. It was his last wish, written in his Will. None would dare disobey. He stated that he should be left lying in state at the place where he should die for forty days and forty nights, no doubt thinking that might save him from Purgatory.' Chaucer spoke ironically.

'How long has he been here?'

'Oh, the time is nearly done, and then we move to London where the burial will take place. It will not be a good journey. You have heard of the troubles at court?'

Priedeux was silent, and Chaucer continued. 'You know nothing? There is already unrest throughout the country and soon it will erupt into full scale war between Richard and the nobles. Let me tell you over wine. Come with me, or do you wish to spend the night with your old master?'

Priedeux shook his head and Chaucer turned away and led him down the nave to the great Norman door. They walked across the courtyard into the castle, and Chaucer led him into a spacious room. Nobody else seemed to be about, no servants or other nobles. Priedeux felt as if he was stepping back into a time in which he did not belong. There was the blazing fire, there was Gaunt's great chair, and the hangings, brought from London, and set up so that the room was so similar to the one in which Priedeux had had that fateful interview that he felt time slipping from him. Chaucer sat down near the fire, ignoring the great chair. He raked over the logs, creating sparks, which lit up the room, before turning to his guest. He leant back as he had done before, in that first meeting so many months ago, as if he would not be seen but would observe, so that his face was hidden from Priedeux.

There was a pause. Then he spoke. 'I am sorry you missed your master. How did your mission go? You can tell me.'

Priedeux hedged. 'First, why civil unrest?'

'The King banished Bolingbroke, Gaunt's son and his cousin, and my nephew, and, as soon as Gaunt was cold, he requisitioned all his lands. Bolingbroke has returned with an army behind him, angry at the King's audacity. He comes to fight for his birthright and his lands now that his father is dead.'

Priedeux said nothing. Chaucer sighed and continued. 'I am here by default looking after my wife's sister's affairs. It is a sad day when cousins quarrel, especially when they are kings and dukes. It is not good for the realm. It would seem that the end of the world will come with the end of the century. I am glad I am an old man and will shortly follow my Lord Gaunt.' He spoke sadly but then repeated, his voice quiet but full of authority. 'Tell me of your quest.'

Priedeux hesitated a moment, but then decided.

From his jerkin he pulled a bag of silver and threw it on the table where it landed near Chaucer.

'Sir, I have failed. I have ridden hard and long, but heard or saw nothing of your peculiar man who wrote the poem you made me read.' He paused and repeated. 'I have not been able to find the man who was the poet. I heard of no rumours of rebellion in the west; all was peaceful when I left. The only trouble I had was with the king's men. I therefore return the silver.'

Chaucer did not touch the pouch. He replied softly: 'How can all be peaceful when the King tries to return from Ireland with a host and Bolingbroke is raising troops and all the lords are gathering in their factions? How can you not have noticed?'

'I know nothing of this. I have been ill, my Lord, these many weeks past.'

Chaucer said nothing and it seemed as if the silence would stretch into infinity. Still he sat with his face shaded and Priedeux had no way of judging his thoughts. Eventually he spoke. 'Tell me about your journeys. Where you found yourself, the way you went. And returned.'

There was a quiet menace in his tone. It was obvious that he did not believe Priedeux knew nothing about the political situation. Priedeux sat down as well, to show he was equal to this man. He rubbed his hands before the fire, and then began. He described his journey, and his meeting with the Stanleys. Chaucer nodded and muttered. 'Aye, I have heard of them; they are not so far away as to have escaped the notice of my brother-in-law's spies, but we thought them harmless to the King and his schemes. They are but greedy robber barons with no political sense.'

Priedeux waited but Chaucer said no more so he began to describe his return trip eastwards, omitting the part that took him to the high rocky places where he had come across de Coucy's castle. He told of his illness and his sojourn with what he described as illiterate travellers. He explained about his marsh fever and the care he had received from those travellers who, once they had seen he was well, had sent him on his way before he had had a chance to find out who they were. He suspected that if he concentrated on these points he would be able to explain his long absence. He was also sure that, with their mobile canvas houses and the way they had moved from the Wirral to Lincolnshire, his friends would have abandoned the place in the flatlands and moved on again, so he was not betraying their trust. He told his story like a soldier, coldly, as if reporting manoeuvres, or the result of a spying mission. He completed his tale with his arrival in Leicester and the reaction he had obtained from the locals, which caused him to make his way directly to his lord's castle. He stopped abruptly.

When he had finished, there was another long silence from his companion, the only noise being from the fire as the logs snapped and crackled. Priedeux watched as azure smoke rose from the crevices of a branch. Chaucer was so silent, that he was forced to look at him to see what he was at. He was leaning forward, and now Priedeux could see the intelligent face. It had a tinge of kindness in it as if he understood men and was studying Priedeux closely.

254

Then he started to clap, as he had done on that first meeting.

'A good military report. And all useless, all too late. You do not fill in the detail either.'

Priedeux ignored the last statement, realising its potential. He queried. 'Too late?'

Chaucer nodded, and went on. 'There is rebellion now throughout the land, and particularly in that very region. My kinsman's children are heeding the rallying cry of their oppressed peoples and even now are returning to take up the call against the King. As I say, it is a sad day when cousins fall out.' He paused and added. 'You helped to make this war, you know.'

Priedeux was astonished. He had not been at court and now he was being accused of making a war.

'Helped? Me? I have not even identified the writer of what Gaunt called a seditious piece of writing. How could I have done anything to start these troubles?'

'Indeed no, you have not found the poet. But you certainly made the men of Chester suspicious. They could not work out whether you were the King's man or not. Then you managed to convince them that the King himself was plotting against them, how I do not know, and they have abandoned the King now. The Cheshire bowmen have slunk back home, removing their loyalty badges of white harts and the King no longer has an army.'

'Why, where is the King?' Priedeux asked.

Chaucer looked at him sharply then. 'You have not heard even that, in your travels?'

Priedeux shook his head. 'Tell me, I need to know!'

'The King is stranded in Ireland, and none of the lords will go to his aid now. At one time he believed he had help from a renegade Welshman called Owen but even he has disappeared. All he has are mercenaries who will run when they see he has no gold or a crown.'

255

As he spoke, Chaucer slowly moved to where the bag of silver lay. He picked it up and tossed it back to Priedeux who caught it. He was about to throw it back again when Chaucer said sharply. 'Take it, take it as your pension.' He turned away, but then looked over his shoulder and added. 'You are no longer of use to your dead master or his kin, and I too am disappointed in your stories. I suggest you lose yourself in the marshes again.'

As he was about to leave the room, Priedeux sprang forward to stop him.

'Wait, there are some things I would ask.'

Chaucer stopped, his head on one side, his little pointed beard jutting out, looking down at his arm where it was held by Priedeux. 'Well?'

'I was followed, by a hangman. Was he sent by Gaunt?'

'A hangman? Oh, I heard a rumour about some insignificant officer being murdered. Was that you?'

'He was stalking me; it was me or him.'

'Yes, the horse was found. Still with the hangman's gold in the panniers. So, you do not steal what is not yours.'

Priedeux showed his annoyance: 'Of course not.'

'What else do you want to know?' Chaucer leant forward as if *he* would learn from Priedeux's questions. Priedeux hesitated. What could he lose now, except to solve the outstanding riddles of his quest.

'The seal. I was told it was not genuine, but they let me go, the Chester men. I am sure it was inspected by others, and no-one said anything. Was it the King's seal?'

Chaucer smiled then. 'Aah, you may as well know. It was done for your protection, I assure you.' He paused. 'No, it was not genuine. But the Chester men were warned to let one pass who had a pass that was not a pass - that was the riddle they were given and they believed it. We knew, Gaunt and I, that, if you met those who were not the King's men they would kill you as soon as they saw the seal was genuine. So, by spreading the rumour in that part of the world, that you travelled illegally, we tried to protect you. Gaunt always looked after his own, you should know that.'

As he spoke, he moved round Priedeux, reached the door and seemed to glide through it. Priedeux watched him as he left. After a long while, he got up and weighed the bag of silver. Then he too left the room, marched through the courtyard, out of the gateway and was soon lost in the back streets of Leicester.

HONI SOIT QUI MAL Y PENCE

Historical note

The events described regarding Richard II are factual; Gaunt and Chaucer are of course real people. I have used the church and memorial at Bunbury. If you follow the descriptions in Gawain and the Green Knight, as I did, you will travel along the northern Welsh coast, back again and into the Wirral – after that, it becomes a little difficult to follow so the Castle of de Coucy will never be found. Apart from this all the characters are fictional.

All the quotes at the top of the chapters come from various versions of Gawain and the Green Knight, which is a medieval poem that was written shortly before the events described in the novel. It is true that the author's identity is not known but it is generally believed, because of the dialect in which it is written, that it derived from the west Midlands area. I suspect no experts would say it was written by a woman but it does have a wonderful way of describing fabrics and interiors whilst the hunting scenes seem to me to come from a textbook.

Priedeux will be seen in later mystoricals.

Coming Soon from Goldenford

Jay Margrave – *Luther's Ambassadors*

Meet Priedeux – reformed character and friend of Anne Boleyn

Anne Boleyn has one overriding ambition: to reform the Catholic Church. The only way she can achieve her aim is to marry a powerful man and use her wiles to influence him to make the changes she wants. This man, of course, is Henry VIII. The mysterious Priedeux acts as mentor, messenger and sometime critic. When Anne's schemes are going awry he is there to fight her battles; when her life is threatened, he saves her; when she needs a confidante, he is there at her side. But for how long can he survive the political battles of the Court without himself becoming a target for powerful men?

Also Available from Goldenford

Irene Black – *The Moon's Complexion*

Bangalore, India 1991.   Ashok Rao, a young doctor, has returned home from England to choose a bride.

But who is the intriguing Englishwoman who seeks him out? Why is she afraid and what is the secret that binds them together?

The lives of two strangers are turned upside down when they meet and the past comes to haunt them. The Moon's Complexion is a tale of love across cultural boundaries. It is also a breath-taking adventure tale played out in the mystical lands of Southern India and Sri Lanka and in the icy countryside of winter England.

'I challenge anyone to put this book down…utterly irresistible'
Sophia Furber, editor, London Student Newspaper

'Wonderfully written love story set in Southern India…a captivating read'
Ottakers' Bookshop, Guildford

Jacquelynn Luben – *A Bottle of Plonk*

It's 1989 – a time when Liebfraumilch, Black Forest gateau and avocado bathrooms are all the rage, and nobody uses mobile phones.

When Julie Stanton moves in with Richard Webb one Saturday night in May, she doesn't expect their romantic evening together to end with her walking out of the flat clutching the bottle of wine with which they were to toast their new relationship.

But then Julie and the wine part company, and the bottle takes the reader on a journey through a series of life situations revealing love, laughter and conflict.

'Luben proves herself to be a sensitive and pithy new novelist.'
Sophia Furber, editor, London Student Newspaper

Esmé Ashford – *On the Edge*

Tramps with bad feet, a sheep rustler, a busker invited to dinner; a weird monster who devours a nasty husband and a child who learns from a visit to the fun fair; limericks and blank verse; it is all here.

Anne Brooke – *Pink Champagne and Apple Juice*

Angie Howard has one ambition - to escape from her home in the idyllic Essex countryside and set up her own café in London. Once there, she seeks out her long-lost Uncle John, whose lifestyle is not at all what she expected.

Before she can achieve her goal, she has to juggle the needs of a glamorous French waiter, a grouchy German chef and her exuberant, transvestite Uncle John.

What's more, if she manages to keep the lid on all that, what will she do about the other hidden secrets of her family?

'an amusing, fast-paced novel, full of action and comedy'

Marsha Rowe, co-founder of Spare Rib

info@goldenford.co.uk
www.goldenford.co.uk